MARTHA ASHLEIGH

Shadows in the Past

AN INSPIRING STORY OF
FAITH, FORGIVENESS, AND REDEMPTION

Enjoy!
Have fun seeing
the similarities
between
the
islands —
Best wishes — Marty Ashleigh

TATE PUBLISHING
AND ENTERPRISES, LLC

Shadows in the Past

Published by Tate Publishing & Enterprises, LLC
127 E. Trade Center Terrace | Mustang, Oklahoma 73064 USA
1.888.361.9473 | www.tatepublishing.com

Tate Publishing is committed to excellence in the publishing industry. The company reflects the philosophy established by the founders, based on Psalm 68:11,
"The Lord gave the word and great was the company of those who published it."

Cover design by Rodrigo Adolfo
Interior design by Jake Muelle

Published in the United States of America

ISBN: 978-1-62295-944-0
1. True Crime / General
13.03.13

Dedication

For Dave, who always laughs at the right time.

Acknowledgments

The blessings of life:

A good mate, a good family, good friends, and a good dog

At times it's true
The world nearly runs out of love
but promptly wraps loneliness
in enough hurt
to sell it across the counter
lavishly
Hurt, then, is cheap,
love dear,
No bargains here.

—Most Rev. Sylvester D. Ryan,
"A Canaanite Hunger" (1969)

Prologue

1938–1949

"You're saying he made this in his garage?" Jack Curtis walked slowly around the magnificent table, trailing his hand across the rich warm surface. He stepped back, folded his arms across his chest, and then shook his head in wonder. "And he designed and made it by himself?"

"Yes. It's astounding," Jack's wife answered. "He came to measure the dining room three weeks ago. After he finished measuring, he just sat in the room for about thirty minutes. Then this morning, he knocks on the door and brings this into the house!"

Jane Curtis watched her husband as he evaluated the new addition to their elegant San Francisco Victorian. The table was perfectly proportioned, and its components were joined with the utmost care. Jacob, the young carpenter from Oakland, had selected thick slabs of black walnut wood to use in creating the table. He had fashioned the hardwood into a graceful yet functional work of art.

It was becoming more evident with each completed project that young Jacob Engstrom was a remarkable craftsman. Given the right materials and tools, he could build anything. His garage was his workshop. In that small space Jacob built custom furniture for the growing number of wealthy residents in San Francisco. Each piece he designed and delivered generated more requests for his talent. Jacob was proud of his work, but he knew he could not maintain such a schedule indefinitely. He saw this part of his life as a down payment for what he really wanted to do.

Jacob and his wife Sofia were saving as much as they could, given the economy of the times. Sofia was a resourceful woman who supervised the neighborhood cooperative garden, managed the soup kitchen at Our Lady of Miracles Church, and helped new arrivals from war-torn countries in Europe assimilate into the melting pot of East Bay society. In the evenings, the couple took long walks around Lake Merritt in downtown Oakland and talked about their dream for the future. With each passing month, they felt more confident that their shared dream would become reality.

The dream was simple. The young couple wanted to own a farm. Each had grown up in a rural setting—one in Minnesota, the other in Poland—and together they sought to provide the same kinds of experiences for their future children. They had saved almost enough to buy a small plot of land in the fertile San Joaquin Valley in central California. Now during their walks, they discussed how much extra money they would need so that they could build a home and a barn.

A few months passed, and although they hadn't planned children so soon, they were ecstatic to learn that Sofia was pregnant. The baby was due around Easter. Jacob started to work longer hours in his garage. Their savings grew faster than ever, and they believed that it might be time to start looking at potential properties. But everything changed one Sunday in December when Japanese pilots destroyed a good portion of the US Navy's Pacific fleet. The horrible war that had been raging around the world finally gripped the United States, and young American couples found their dreams fade to nothing as the young men went off to fight, and the young women waited at home in fear.

Like most able-bodied American men throughout the country, Jacob scrambled to enlist. His skill and reputation as a master builder provided him an opportunity to join the United States Navy Construction Battalion (CB). His Seabee unit was assigned to various Pacific Island locations where they built surveillance outposts, living quarters, communication stations, and other outbuildings. It was not long before the men recognized Jacob's superior skills in project design and construction. Jacob simply saw himself as a man with a wife and a baby on the way, and he was worried. Without knowing how long the war would last, how could he be sure that Sofia and the baby would have enough to support them while he was on active duty?

The solution to his dilemma presented itself within a week of his arrival to what would be his final wartime assignment. It was late November 1944 when Jacob and his division arrived at the northernmost tip of the entire North Pacific sector: the Aleutian Islands in the Territory of Alaska. During the days he helped build a series of permanent communication outposts in strategic locations along the island chain.

But on the cold, arctic nights Jacob saw the mess hall become a poker hall as soon as the tables were cleared. The games lasted until there were no more bets to be made. For the first few weeks, Jacob watched the other men play. He observed the behavior of the winners and losers. He looked for subtle changes in the faces and body language of the men who were betting. After he saw how the game worked and how the players behaved, he started to play. He was cautious at first, but he soon discovered that it was easy for him to get a read on the other men. More often than not, Jacob sensed what each man held in his hand. He didn't know why it was so, but Jacob found that he had an uncanny ability to win at poker.

One spring night in 1945, Jacob's good fortune at cards changed the course of his life. The bets all night were particularly big and daring. The men knew the war was ending, and they would soon be going home. The evening poker games became more frantic as the weeks passed by. Everyone seemed to be searching for that one big win before leaving. This particular evening was ending with a showdown between Jacob the carpenter and Rudy the welder. Both held what most would claim was an unbeatable hand, and each was willing to bet everything to win.

On the final bet, Jacob put down his last bit of cash—one hundred dollars. Almost as an afterthought, he threw in his

Kodiak bearskin rug. The decibel level of the room increased almost immediately as the spectators passed the word about the bearskin rug. Everyone in the unit had seen the rug, and most of them secretly coveted it. Jacob kept it on top of his cot, spread smoothly over his blankets like a big furry bedspread.

He won it in a poker game two months before from a Canadian trader who lived six months each year on Kodiak Island. The rug, over eight feet from neck to tail, was topped by a massive head permanently frozen in a toothy snarl. Jacob assured Rudy that it was priceless, but he was willing to sweeten the pot with it to demonstrate how serious he was about this final bet of the evening.

Rudy, who had tossed in nearly all he had on the previous raise, was frantic. Checking every pocket, he could only scrape together forty dollars in small bills. Adding in his lucky silver dollar gave him a total of forty-one dollars. He couldn't even match the money from Jacob's raise, let alone the value of the bear. But Rudy could not let the hand go. He knew he had a winner, and he really wanted that bearskin rug! He sat for a moment, put his forehead on the table, and covered his head with his arms. As he sat up slowly, it was clear he had made a decision.

He admitted that he owned something of value if only Jacob would find it in his heart to accept it. Rudy claimed to be the owner of a large parcel of California property. The land was undeveloped, but it had a variety of features: a year-round freshwater source, large expanses of meadowland and foothills, a mountain, hundreds of trees, a beach, and a private ocean cove. It was oceanfront property all right, but it was on some island off the coast of California. Rudy admitted to Jacob that the island was remote and undeveloped, but land is land. Jacob agreed to accept a signed note as long as Jerry and Ken would stand as witnesses.

The betting was finished, the deal was struck, and the suspense grew. The two gamblers sat motionless as the observers crowded around. Soon there were Seabees buzzing four deep around the makeshift poker table. Finally, Rudy, with a grin and a flourish, placed his hand face-up on the table. Four kings stared up at the crowd. The navy men whooped and whistled. Jacob just shook his head in disbelief. Waiting until the group settled down, Jacob spread his cards out face-down on the table in front of him for all to see.

Then he reached out and proceeded to turn them up one at a time: ace of hearts, ace of clubs, ace of diamonds, jack of spades, and when he finally turned over the prettiest card in the deck, the ace of spades, nobody made a sound. Then the silence was broken by a single high-pitched wail. It was Rudy. He stood, turned, and walked out of the mess hall without saying a word. The hall erupted with noisy shouts and guffaws.

Rudy made good on his promise. Soon Jacob, wife Sofia, and four-year-old Freddie were camping out on their new property on Santa Teresa Island, one of the channel islands off the coast of Southern California. With every cent he had and with generous loans from his father and uncle, Jacob built the Eagle Cove Lodge. The doors opened to welcome the first guests in 1947. Although it took another four years for Jacob to complete the project, the lodge was a great success from the very first year of operation.

The combination of beautiful natural surroundings, comfortable rooms, excellent food and service, and plenty of activities available to lodge guests made the Eagle Cove Lodge and Family Farm a popular destination for those who lived on the West Coast. Crossing the channel by boat to vacation on an island added an exotic element that continued to attract visitors year after year.

Chapter One

Santa Teresa Island, 2011

It was past midnight, and John was still awake. His body was bone tired, and he hadn't slept for almost twenty hours, yet sleep escaped him. For the third time he scrunched his pillow into a crescent to support his neck. His new bed was comfortable enough, and the light breeze that flowed through the window screen was fresh and clean, letting the salt-tinged sea air in to mingle with a subtle trace residue of lemonwood soap.

The light from the full moon streamed through the windows to create a random pattern of shadows on the floor. His old down quilt with its familiar texture and smell cradled him in a comfortable cocoon. Everything seemed perfect for a good night of sleep, but there he was, alert, eyes open wide, and mind going a mile a minute.

John had never experienced insomnia. For a long while, he simply tried to clear his mind as he lay quietly in bed. It wasn't long before he realized it was impossible to wipe away the variety of disconnected ideas that were swirling in and out of his consciousness. He tried to organize the images in his mind into some cohesive order, but his thoughts kept dissolving into a fuzzy, unfocused mess. Turning over abruptly, he stared toward the window. The breeze felt good on his face. He sighed, closed his eyes, and wished for sleep. He considered counting sheep but wasn't too sure how to go about it. Was he supposed to imagine a big flock jumping over a fence one at a time?

Still alert after several minutes of organizing sheep, he attempted to recite in his mind all the states and their capitals. He kept a loose tally with his fingers as he immediately identified thirty-five. John continued at a slower pace, finally stopping at forty-seven. By now he was completely awake and a little angry.

He knew these cold in fifth grade. What was the capital of Vermont? And was the Tennessee capital Knoxville or Nashville? Was it Tallahassee or Tampa for Florida, or was Tallahassee in Tennessee? Which three states did he leave out altogether? A wave of restlessness crested and flooded over John, drowning the last of his resolve to seek sleep. With a sigh, he threw the quilt back. In one motion, he pivoted his legs around, put his feet flat on the floor, and stood up next to the bed.

John, at seventeen, had just passed the six-foot mark. Until recently, he was all arms and legs, but during the past year he had gained nearly twenty pounds, mostly muscle on his arms and upper torso. He stretched across a pile of boxes to reach the switch on the wall. John squinted and blinked in the sudden glare of the overhead light. The big house was very quiet. Through the open window, John could hear the faint sound of halyards and shrouds slapping against the masts of the sailboats anchored in the cove below—the song of boats at rest. He knew that if he could be out there right now in a boat rocking gently on the water, he'd be sleeping like a baby.

He checked the time on his cell phone—3:20 a.m. After pulling on a pair of baggy old shorts over his boxers, he found the T-shirt he had worn yesterday and slipped it over his head. He grabbed his sweatshirt, stepped into a comfortable old pair of Reef flip-flops, and entered the dark hallway. He was temporarily disoriented.

Which way was the kitchen? He turned right and walked carefully with one arm stretched out in front of him. Reaching a right turn in the hall, he suddenly knew exactly where he was. A small light illuminated the wide step that led to the family den. This cozy room and the family bedrooms were reserved exclusively for the lodge keeper's family. The rest of the rooms in the lodge were open to guests.

"Don't be surprised when you find a lodge guest raiding the fridge in the kitchen in the middle of the night," Grandpa Fred said yesterday. "We encourage them all to make themselves at home here, and they do. You can just bet they do." The kitchen lay between the family den and the big lodge dining room. An ancient but serviceable square table dominated the alcove created by a large bay window on the east side of the kitchen. Although guests were served a hearty breakfast daily in the big lodge dining room, it was not uncommon to find an early rising guest eating cereal and fruit at the kitchen table. Grandpa said that after a month or two, the family would get used to having guests show up just about anywhere in the house at all hours of the day or night.

This is our home now, John thought. He walked quietly through the service porch behind the kitchen. The porch served as laundry room, linen storage, and pantry. John had to walk around tall stacks of boxes and books that blocked the wide glass door leading to the herb garden outside. He continued through the dining room and stepped into the main parlor, a spacious room with a high-beamed ceiling and a massive fireplace built from the distinctive island stone mined from the island quarry.

In John's estimation, this was the best room in the house. The vintage grand piano, the only real treasure his family brought to the island, had finally arrived yesterday. John thought it looked right at home nestled in the far corner of the room. The dim yellow light from the front porch fixture streamed through the large bank of windows beside the piano, creating an inviting circle of warmth around the instrument. John was drawn toward the piano and soon found himself sitting on the bench and staring at the keys. He was tempted to play, but it was too early. He had been away from the instrument during the whole tedious move, and he just now realized how much he had missed it. Applying no pressure, he brushed his hand lightly across the ivory keys. The creamy white surfaces seemed warm to the touch, almost alive.

Unconsciously, John's hands began to trace the first few measures of his newest piece, a Rachmaninoff prelude. He had played other works by the Russian-American, but this piece was special. The subtle and understated beauty of the various melodies and countermelodies wove a sensual tapestry of sound that had already burrowed into John's psyche. Although he had worked on it for only a couple of weeks, he could feel how the piece was beginning to take possession of him. It was not the most difficult piece he had ever studied, nor was it one of the composer's most familiar works, but it had an elusive quality that intrigued him, and John felt confident that he could interpret the work as it had originally been conceived.

His mother's CD collection had multiple recordings of the preludes by various pianists. A few weeks ago when he first decided to learn the Prelude in E-flat Major, he listened to several renditions of it. He was amazed at how the exact same piece could be interpreted in so many ways. Later that night, John had written a long entry on his blog about how hard it must be for a composer to rely on another person to recreate each musical composition. Sure, the notes and markings on the score told the performer about pitch, meter, and rhythm in absolute terms, but every other aspect of the music was relative: tempo, flexibility, volume, voicing, articulation, phrasing, and the more subtle considerations of breath, space, and nuance were all the responsibility of the performer.

John acknowledged that it was the nature of the art form that a composer must abdicate complete control. As a serious music student, John knew that his role in the re-creation of a piece of music made him a sort of artistic collaborator with the composer. With the mastery of each new work, John felt obligated to reflect the intentions of the composer. John poured over every source of information on the score and in the various annotated descriptions of the music he studied. As he learned and performed a new piece, John tried to know the work through the eyes, ears, and intellect of the composer.

Then as time passed, the work would become a product of his own artistic inclinations as well. When he posted these observations on his blog, John received dozens of online responses. Since starting his blog last summer, he had a growing cadre of interesting readers, many of whom sent regular feedback and opinions of their own. He was pleased to find other musicians who also seemed to care deeply about their craft.

Closing his eyes, he imagined the sound of this newest challenge. It was a hauntingly beautiful work. When he first heard it played on a John Browning CD, John wrote the word *melancholy* on the insert, and then he attached a sticky tab on the plastic case that simply said "Learn Op.23, No.6." Now as he sat in front of the keys, he could hear each note clearly in his head. Without a sound other than that which he carried in his mind, his left hand began to form the opening melodic line as it meandered gracefully through two octaves in the rich tenor and alto registers of the piano. John could feel the music begin to control him.

His right hand entered, shaping the slow octave melody that would draw the focus from the left hand then finally emerge as the primary theme. John's hands and arms were relaxed. His body moved gently in response to the glorious music that filled his imagination. Though he touched the keys so delicately that the hammers remained still and the strings stayed silent, John could imagine every note and the harmonies they created. Finally, he reached a point in the piece where he could not continue without the score in front of him. A few fumbles caused him to lose the inner connection with the music. Dropping his hands to his sides, he sat quietly for a moment, stood, and stretched.

No longer concerned about losing sleep he turned and walked over toward the nearest set of french doors that opened onto the veranda. He slipped out quietly and wandered down to the farthest edge of the porch. The moon was well on its way toward the western horizon, but it still cast an eerie light on the world below. Not only could John see the boats in the cove from here, but he also had a clear view of the twinkling lights on the mainland coast far across the thirty-mile channel. He pivoted one of the roomy old Adirondack chairs toward the right so that it faced east. He sat and stared at the horizon.

Somewhere from that general direction, the new day would begin. John tried to guess the exact spot on the horizon where the sun would burst forth to start its daily journey across the sky. As yet, there was no visible sign of any change in the night darkness. The stars were visible but obscured somewhat by the bright moon. John leaned back in the chair, a bit surprised that there was no moisture on the canvas cushion; then he remembered how Grandpa Fred had said September was the warmest and driest month of the year here on the island.

He thought for a moment. Today was Saturday. He and his family had left their home in the Sierra Nevada foothill town of Sierra Glen early Tuesday morning, exactly five days ago. Only five days. It was clear to John that those days had altered his future dramatically and irrevocably. Was it only a week ago on Saturday night that he had gathered with his friends at Jamie's, his next-door neighbor in Sierra Glen?

A dozen young people met there in the Harland's basement, mostly classmates and neighbors John had known his whole life. John thought back to the farewell party, a night already fading behind a scrim of nostalgia. He felt a little guilty about the promises he had made to stay in touch. Truthfully, he probably wouldn't write any letters. Maybe he'd post a note or two on his Facebook wall, or maybe he'd text Jamie. But so far, he hadn't written once, nor had Jamie.

John liked his old friends, and they all seemed to like him, but he did not feel especially connected to anyone. The friendships he had were not a result of shared interests and shared dreams. Ever since he had moved from Sierra Glen, John had been trying to decide why it didn't bother him to move at the start of his senior year from the only home he had ever known. Yesterday, it occurred to him that he felt no regrets for leaving because he had nobody in his life so far who would qualify as a close friend.

Up to this point, the relationships he had with others seemed to be based on proximity and convenience. Nobody he ever met knew anything more than the most cursory facts about his life. He was sure that nobody from his whole hometown had ever visited his website or read his blog. The fact was that he felt closer to his Internet acquaintances than most of the people he knew in person.

Because sleep was impossible John considered exploring some more of the big house. Since their arrival Wednesday afternoon he and his sisters only had time to check through the family wing of the sprawling building. John had spent a couple of hours last night cleaning out several decades' worth of old papers, newsprint, photos, and miscellaneous stuff from the built-in cupboards and drawers that filled one side of his new room. Years before, his grandfather had sacrificed the walk-in closet that had originally been attached to his bedroom in order to build a small bathroom. Now the bedroom had plenty of built-in storage but only a tiny closet for hanging clothes. John didn't mind at all since he had a great view of the cove and the northeastern sky.

His thirteen-year-old twin sisters, Emma and Lucy, chose a large room across the hall to share. They had always shared a room and could not imagine living apart. Their new room had a huge closet and private bathroom attached. His parents had a small suite of rooms that included a bathroom, an alcove for their bed, and a small sitting room complete with comfortable chairs, a wall of books, a desk, and a fireplace. Across a narrow breezeway was a small three-room suite where John's grandparents, Fred and Mariel Engstrom, had lived since 1972. Finally, the spacious room and bath next to John was occupied by his great-grandfather, Jacob Engstrom.

Jacob, the designer and builder of Eagle Cove Lodge, was ninety-three. Since his stroke last year, it was clear that Grandpa

Fred and Nana Mariel needed help managing Eagle Cove. They wrote to their child, Christina, and asked if she and her family would like to come help run the lodge. After all, it would belong to them someday. This would be a fine opportunity to learn about the lodge. More vital was the fact that this would be a chance for Daniel and Christina to be with Jacob for the time he had left.

As founder of the lodge, Jacob possessed the knowledge of lodge history and traditions. Jacob was the soul of their future inheritance. After two months of deliberation, Daniel and Christina Garrett finally chose to join the family business. They sold their house and most of their belongings and then they packed all their remaining possessions and moved to the island with their three teenagers. Since several lodge guests would be arriving in just a few days, the whole family was working hard to get things in order. The homeschooling would have to wait for at least one week.

Chapter Two

John, completely awake now, felt a sudden surge of energy that was impossible to contain. Abruptly he rose from the chair, and instead of turning back into the house, he hurried down the porch stairs. Somehow, he was being drawn toward the shoreline. The moon had dropped lower in the sky, but it still provided plenty of light for John as he followed the path down to the water. He crossed the sloping lawn and reached the bluff. The walkway that led from the lawn down to the beach had been built from natural rock and paving stones by his great-grandfather, Jacob, decades before.

The wide steps, with deep treads and shallow risers, were irregular and followed the natural contour of the bluff itself. It was only a drop of about eight vertical feet from the lawn's end to the rocky edge of the beach. John crossed the rocks and sandy beach until he reached the water. Here on the lee side of the island there was no surf, only the steady tidal movement and occasional wind surge. John walked on the wet sand along the ocean's edge. He heard a whining sound behind him and turned to see his dog, Rocky, up on the lawn. John whistled softly, and Rocky bounded down the embankment to the beach. John could see the black lab's tail rotating in happy circles as he ran across the sand. John waited until Rocky reached him. Leaning down, John scratched the old dog's ears.

"Hey, boy! How did you get out of the yard? I thought Dad had it pretty secure." John thought he and his father would have to add some additional fencing to keep Rocky safely inside the herb garden fence. All of a sudden, Rocky stopped wiggling and stretched his nose up into the air, assuming the pose of a pointer. He began to whine under his breath, then he relaxed and sat down. John turned and looked back down the shoreline. He saw the silhouette of a figure approaching him along the beach. Whoever it was waved to John in a friendly manner. John automatically waved back. As they drew closer to one another, John saw that it was a girl.

She was tall and slender, and her hair was pulled back and clipped into a ponytail. Little wisps of hair had escaped the clip and blew softly around her face. She wore clothes almost identical to his, but somehow she looked neat and clean. Suddenly John felt self-conscious. His boxers hung below his shorts, and his T-shirt was filthy. With hair uncombed and the taste of last night's onions in his mouth, John did not want to meet anyone, especially a very pretty girl, but it was too late.

They both stopped walking when they were about four feet from each other. She smiled at him. It was a brilliant smile that lit up her face. John usually felt awkward meeting new people, but there was a winsome quality about this girl that made him feel comfortable and at ease. Her smile intrigued him. He found himself nodding to her in a natural way, just as he might greet an old friend.

"Hi," she said, continuing to smile at him. "You must belong to the lodge family. We heard there was a new group of you coming in to help run the big lodge. We all wondered when you'd finally get here. The whole West End has been watching for you." Her voice had a cheerful quality that appealed to John. When she told him her name and asked what his name was, he was eager to answer so she would begin speaking again.

"I'm John. I couldn't sleep, so here I am walking on the beach in the middle of the night. It's good to meet you, Casey. What are you doing out here?"

"Well, I couldn't sleep either. I think maybe a bright moon affects people in an odd way, especially people our age. Don't you think so?" Before John could respond, she said, "Say, let's keep walking down to that point." She pointed to the outcropping of rocks about four hundred yards down the coastline. She turned and stepped over beside him; they walked in comfortable silence until suddenly she trotted ahead and picked up one of the flat rocks that were so plentiful along the shoreline. She turned toward the water and tossed the rock neatly so that it skipped four times on the calm surface of the cove.

"Hey, that was good," John said as he looked for a rock to throw. The first he picked up wasn't quite flat enough. Casey, who was helping him search through the beach pebbles, stood up and hurried over to John.

"Look! It's a sand dollar!" She held out the flat round shell for John to see. "I didn't think you could find these around here. Isn't it beautiful?" They stared at the delicate design on the top of the unusual shell. "If you find one, it means you'll have good luck as long as you hold it close and keep it dry. In Spanish it's called a sea sweet or a *dulce del mar.*" Casey pressed the shell into John's hand. "Take it. I have one already."

John took the shell and slipped it into the pocket of his shorts. No more than a few seconds later he found the perfect skipping rock. Picking it up he smiled at Casey then turned to toss it. Rocky saw John's arm go back. With a bark he bounded into the water in pursuit of the rock. After the second skip, the rock disappeared. Rocky swam in a wide circle before he emerged from the salty water. He ran back toward John then immediately shook off the excess water, drenching the two teenagers.

"Wait, Rocky, stop!" John said, grabbing the dog's collar. "I'm so sorry, Casey. I should have caught him sooner. Are you wet?" Both of them laughed out loud at the absurdity of the question. They used their sleeves to wipe the water off their faces.

"I'm fine, it's okay. I'm just glad there isn't much wind tonight. We'd freeze! Come on. Let's keep walking."

She smiled again then turned and began walking with long strides. John fell in step beside her, matching his steps with hers.

"Well, how do you like the island so far?" she asked. "Are you all moved in yet?"

"We just got here on Wednesday afternoon. We've been busy unloading our stuff and finding a place to put everything. I think it's going to be impossible. My mom tried to get rid of a lot of furniture back home when we were packing to move, but we still filled a big truck with our stuff. Then we had to take it all to the barge. Dad and I went with Grandpa Fred in our flatboat to pick up everything at the barge landing down at East End. It took two trips and all day Thursday before we got all our junk up to the lodge. A lot of things are still sitting out on the veranda."

John paused to catch his breath. He realized he was dominating the conversation. "It's a good thing that Grandpa decided not to book any guests into the lodge this week while we are getting settled. I guess he knew what a mess it would be for a while." John laughed and added, "It's more than a mess. The place looks like a bomb exploded in it. The only room that's even halfway presentable is the main parlor. Oh, and our piano arrived yesterday. It looks great in that room."

"Who plays the piano?" As she spoke, she turned toward him, continuing to walk backward as she looked into his face. She stumbled slightly, and he reached to catch her hands before she fell. They stood, hands clasped tightly for a moment, until she caught her balance. Then another moment passed. John could feel the sensual attractiveness of this unusual girl. Embarrassed, he dropped his hands to his sides as he turned quickly. He took a step around her and kept walking.

"I play," he said; he tried to keep his voice even, although his heart was pounding in his ears. "I've been playing the piano since I was four. My mom plays too. She taught me until I was thirteen. Then I had another teacher for a few years. But Mom and my grandmother are going to keep teaching me here on the island. In fact, Dad and Mom and Nana Mariel are going to be teaching us, my sisters and me, all the other subjects too. We're going to be homeschooled. I'm just starting my senior year."

She trotted for a couple of steps to catch up with him then fell into stride beside him once again. "I wish I knew how to play an instrument," she said wistfully. "It must be wonderful to be able to make music whenever you feel like it."

"Well, you can't play the piano whenever you want because it's kind of loud. I wanted to play a little while ago, but I'll have to wait until nine in the morning. That's the rule my family made for me because I used to sit and play anytime I wanted, day or night. I guess it was kind of annoying!"

"I bet your mom was never annoyed when you played." Changing the subject, she said, "Say, do you like to sail? I love to! Maybe we can go out sometime in one of the lodge sailboats. Your family has a few really nice boats for day sailing. What do you think?"

"Well, I've done some crewing for my dad in a Snipe, but I'm not very good on the tiller. I've mostly sailed on lakes. But my grandpa taught me how to sail here in the cove last summer. I could handle most of the smaller boats. If you want, I suppose we can take a lodge boat out. My dad might not let me, though. He probably thinks I'd wreck the boat."

"I'm sure he doesn't think that at all. Why would you say that?" The smile seemed to fade from her voice, and John worried that he spoiled something between them. He wanted to just say he was joking, but he wasn't exactly kidding. His father never seemed very happy with anything John did. Even when John brought home straight As, got fives on the AP tests he had taken so far, then aced the SATs, his father just told him there was more to life than studying.

It seemed to John that he could never do anything to please his father. The week before they left their old home, John was responsible for trimming and cleaning up the front yard. John was working when his father arrived home. His father sat in the car watching John for a few moments. Then he got out of the car and slammed the door in anger. John could feel the heat from his father's wrath, although he could not figure out what had triggered it. John remembered exactly what his father had said to him. No, that wasn't quite right. John could remember what his father had yelled across the yard to him. Just thinking about that day made John feel sick to his stomach.

"Aren't you finished with that yet?" Dad was standing next to his car in the driveway. "How in hell can you take a simple chore and turn it into a big production? Just trim the long branches off and rake it all up. Is that so hard?" His father took long strides across the yard as he was yelling. When he reached John, he grabbed the clippers from John's hands and turned to the bushes. *Snip! Snip!* In no time, he had butchered two large green juniper plants.

"Now finish up!" With that, his father stomped into the house. He slammed the door behind him, leaving John to finish the chore. The rest of the bushes in the yard looked trimmed and tidy, but they were graceful and natural looking. John had been careful to trim each plant so that the end result was attractive and well-balanced. Except for two junipers, he had achieved the right effect. John was startled when Casey tapped him gently on the shoulder. John realized he hadn't yet answered her.

"I'm sorry. I was just thinking about something." He looked over at her. She looked confused over his abrupt change in mood. Her expression was sympathetic and open. There was something that was compelling him to be honest with the girl, even if he ended up disappointing her. Her eyes were asking him to share something of himself with her. And he did. He told her how the past two years had been so hard at home. He told her how his father treated him. John certainly did not want sympathy. He just wanted someone to know what he was feeling. She listened well. When he finished talking, he was relieved to see her warm smile once again. She offered no advice, nor did she offer up her opinion about his family. Casey simply thanked him for sharing his thoughts with her.

After a few minutes of comfortable silence they reached an old rowboat that had been pulled far up onto the beach. They circled it then leaned against it. Rocky made his own dog circles then plopped down on the soft sand between their feet and slept. John thought back about whatever he and Casey were saying about sailing, and then he made a quick decision.

"Well, I'll probably be able to take a boat out on Tuesday. How would that work for you?" He looked at her expectantly.

"Sure. How about if I meet you on the beach by the lodge boat shed at noon?" She turned toward him once again. They were only a foot apart from one another. John stared at her, studying the contours of her face. She really did look familiar to him, but he could not recollect where he might have met her before. She smiled again then turned her head directly toward the east and pointed.

"Look, you can see a tiny bit of glow on the horizon. That's where the sun will come up." She continued to watch intently. He acknowledged her statement with a barely audible "Hmm" as he continued to study her face, now in profile. Time seemed to relax its relentless grip on the world around them. He wasn't sure how long he had been staring at her, but he wasn't self-conscious at all. He was not even surprised when his thoughts wandered into his memory banks and emerged with an echo of the prelude he had been playing silently at the piano before he came outside. When was that, a lifetime ago? Here he was, on the beach in the early morning hours, staring at a girl he met only minutes before, and yet … What was it?

He tried to grasp the fleeting thought that was tickling his mind. As he stared at her, his ideas began to take shape. Just as he had absorbed the Rachmaninoff prelude aurally into his mind during the past few weeks, he now saw a visual equivalent of the music right here beside him, at this moment, not more than a few inches away. There! In the girl's manner and warmth was a reflection of the rich poignant melody—the melody that spoke to him with urgency, the melody that overshadowed all of the other music that he knew, demanding his full attention. It was the very melody he felt in his heart and heard in his mind at this moment. This girl was a human rendering of the melody, and he sensed the melody would forevermore trigger a visual image of her. John accepted that she and the music were integrated now in his mind into one artistic statement: a musical portrait.

What am I doing? he thought to himself. *This is unreal. Who is this girl, and why am I thinking these thoughts?* He stood silently. He wanted to explain his feelings, but how could he possibly make her understand how she had acquired a new facet to her being, thanks to him? He would sound like a psychopath if he told her how he sensed the essence of beautiful music around her, a distinctive leitmotif perceived just as clearly and real as a subtle dusting of scented talc. Whoa! Where did that come from? He thought he'd better get his drama-queen tendencies under control right away. He had made a mistake a few months ago where he tried to tell Jamie how important music was in his life.

Jamie had laughed at first, but when he realized John was serious, Jamie seemed puzzled and uncomfortable, and he quickly changed the subject. John was glad because he did not want to have to explain anything. Shouldn't there be someone who just understood automatically? The way he felt about music was one aspect of his true inner self. He had never once let anyone know how music affected him. Oh, he had talked with his Internet friends about the aesthetic response and how or why certain compositional devices may trigger it, but the discussions had been clinical, stuck in third person.

He held back admitting anything about his own responses and feelings. Nor had he ever shared with another soul how he perceived the world around him, how he searched to find patterns and connections in the events of his life, how he wanted to know reasons for everything, including life itself. He wanted to understand death, suffering, love, peace, music, and poetry.

Finally, he longed to find someone, just one person, who could see him and appreciate him for who he was. Was he a misfit? Perhaps. A disappointment? Probably. Maybe he was just a poor guy who was born in the wrong century, into the wrong family, in the wrong hemisphere, maybe on the wrong planet.

He shook his head slightly to clear all these thoughts that were spinning freely and dangerously close to the surface. If there was anything that bothered him more about himself than his drama-queen tendencies, it was his frequent mind trips into heavy-duty introspective self-indulgence. It was a good thing that nobody could read his mind. He took a few breaths and consciously relaxed the tension in his shoulders and arms. When he spoke, he was surprised to hear that his voice sounded normal.

"About the sailing, I guess that sounds fine. But where do you live? Is your place nearby?" John willed himself to stay in the present and keep away from the mind excursions that he seemed to be drawn into. He did not want this enchanted encounter with Casey to end. He had to know more about her.

"Well, I'm from the Sorenson Sea Camp. It's down the coast toward Mirabella just three coves away. But you probably knew that. Have you been warned off of the camp yet? I've heard it all, you know. The bad blood between the families goes way back. It seems there is a feud or war or something like that. I'm not sure if anyone can explain what it's all about, but I think it started with Jacob Engstrom and Peter Sorenson when they were building the two places, you know, the lodge and the sea camp. Then some other things, not very good things, happened and made the problems worse."

She paused for a moment, then said thoughtfully, "It might be best not to mention anything to anyone about me for a little while. For now, it just seems easier to avoid any conflict. Your great-grandfather Jacob might be really mad if he knew we were talking together." Her voice faded for a moment, then she continued, "But I'll see you on Tuesday at the beach, okay? Hey,

I guess we better get home now before anyone misses us!" She smiled and reached over to touch his shoulder with her fingertips. "I'll see you around."

"Yeah." John stood and watched her walk around the rocky outcropping and disappear into the shadows of the fading night.

Chapter Three

The sun was streaming in though his window. John rolled over onto his back. Where was he? It took a few seconds to clear the strands of disjointed dreams that were tangled in his head. Yawning, he realized he was in his new room at the Eagle Cove Lodge. He closed his eyes and tried to remember his walk on the beach last night and how he met Casey. How did she look as she first walked toward him on the beach? The whole encounter seemed to have an elusive quality that made him begin to doubt whether or not it really happened at all. He had never been so at ease with anyone in real life, let alone a stranger who happened to be a beautiful girl.

Right, a beautiful girl just happens to walk down the beach in the middle of the night, and we talk, and she likes me. John's thoughts were filled with doubt and self-deprecation. *Yeah right, and by the way, she looks like my music sounds. That is so lame!* John felt foolish. What a cruel joke his mind had played on him; of course it was all just a fantasy. Burrowing his head under the pillow, John tried to reenter a dream state so that he could visualize Casey again; but her image in his memory was like a pastel drawing left outside overnight, where the damp night air gradually dissolves the soft edges into pale streaks of nothingness. John could not recall how she looked, but he still had a clear grasp of how she made him feel. He had never been so open and honest with another person.

Thoroughly frustrated, he felt unable to stay in bed any longer. He stretched once more then got up and headed straight for the bathroom. His cell phone was on the tile counter. He picked it up and checked the time—10:00 a.m.! How could it be so late? John hurried through his bathroom rituals then dressed in clean clothes that he pulled from a tall stack on his dresser. Slipping into his flip-flops, he picked up his wet towel and his dirty clothes from yesterday, and he carried them toward the big hamper out on the service porch. In the kitchen, he found no evidence of breakfast. Everything was neat and tidy. John scrounged around and found the Cheerios, a banana, and an almost empty carton of milk. After eating quickly, he put the dish and spoon in the dishwasher and was about to return to his room when he heard someone in the lodge dining room. It was his mother's voice, but she was speaking Spanish.

She must be working on her language program, John thought. His mother had been exposed to Spanish when she was a child here at the lodge, but decades of disuse had all but erased her ability to speak and understand the language. When they decided to come to the island, she purchased a language program for her computer and worked at it each day. John was surprised at how well she was able to communicate with the Spanish-speaking employees already. He listened for a few moments. She had earphones on, so John could only hear her responses.

"La niña come el dulce. El niño come el dulce. Todos los niños comen los dulces," her voice floated clearly through the open door.

Dulce? Suddenly, John rushed to the service porch, moved quickly toward the hamper, lifted the lid, and grabbed his dirty shorts from yesterday. He felt in the pocket. There, he felt something! He hadn't been dreaming after all. As he pulled his hand from the pocket, his initial excitement imploded into a black hole of disappointment. He did not hold the sand dollar, the lucky token, the *dulce del mar* that Casey had pressed into his palm in the early hours of this very day. There in his palm was only a flat beach pebble with rounded edges.

John held the smooth rock in his hand and thought it felt perfect for skipping across the water. Had he thrown the sand dollar by mistake? He could not have made such a careless mistake. No, the night had been a dream, a very realistic and elaborate creation of his mind. There was no Casey. The rock he held was just some old rock he picked up somewhere, probably yesterday at the beach. For a moment he was consumed by a terrible sense of longing for what he had lost, but when he saw his mother enter the service porch and approach him with a smile, he shook off the last remnants of sadness and put the whole encounter out of his thoughts.

"Good morning, Johnny. I thought I heard someone in here. You slept late today," she said as she gave him a hug and a quick kiss on the cheek. "I think your father is expecting you out in the barn. Was it your day to collect eggs?" John groaned then turned toward the door. He waved to his mother and dashed through the herb garden. He knew morning chores were finished. As usual, his father would be disappointed that John had not done his part.

As if I can help it when I oversleep. So I'm sorry, Dad, I didn't mean to get up so late, but I met the girl of my dreams, but then it turned out to be a dream of a girl … a figment of whatever, but she seemed so real. She even had a theme song, would you like me to hum a few bars? John kept a running one-sided conversation going in his mind as he stepped through the garden gate and turned up the gravel path toward the barn. He could hear his sisters laughing somewhere over near the chicken coop. Rocky barked once, and then he was silent.

John reached the barn and entered through the huge wooden sliding doors under the hayloft. He heard voices coming from the tack room in the far corner of the barn past the stalls. It sounded like his father and Grandpa Fred were there talking. John walked toward the voices. As he passed one stall, Cherry put her head out and nickered. John stopped to pat her on the neck. She nosed him playfully and nibbled at his shirt.

"You know me too well." He spoke quietly to the young mare as he pulled a sugar cube out of his pocket. She nuzzled it off of his outstretched hand, tickling him with her whiskers. John turned when he heard his father's voice from the tack room.

"I just hope living here will shape him up. He's bright enough, probably too bright. And certainly he seems to have genuine talent, at least Christina and Mariel agree on that. But he isn't interested in sports, he's never gone out on a date, even though he has had plenty of girls call him, mostly to get help with homework. I'm not sure he has any friends that he cares about. He just doesn't exactly fit in anywhere, even in the family." John heard his father sigh. "He usually chooses to avoid social situations, and he seems to prefer living his life inside his head. It drives me crazy to hold a conversation with him when he's mulling things over in his brain."

"You know, Daniel, John seems just fine to Mariel and me." John was pleased to hear his Grandpa Fred speak in his defense. He listened as his grandfather continued. "He's respectful and nice to us and to his sisters. He does show a rare talent in music. He's quiet, but he and I have had some pretty lively discussions about politics and the environment. I wouldn't worry. Let the island take care of him for a while. The daily responsibilities here at the lodge with the animals and grounds will help him grow up. Give him a chance."

"You sound a lot like your daughter," Daniel continued. "But look at this morning. He slept in late, even though we all have morning chores. He was supposed to feed the chickens and collect eggs this morning, but his sisters covered for him while he slept. Plus, we all have to be ready to take the boat into town for church today. I don't even know if he's awake."

"Well, I just think of how he was a big help in getting the furniture from the barge landing on Thursday, and you said yourself he doesn't do many physical activities. He's probably exhausted. And as far as his chores today, it's still a novelty for the girls to take care of the chickens. Don't worry too much. John will get in the routine of things soon enough." Grandpa Fred spoke in a convincing tone. "You'll see."

"Well, I hope so," Daniel said without much confidence. "I hope you're right."

John quickly retraced his steps so that he was closer to the sliding doors. He moved one noisily and then he walked directly to Cherry's stall, clucking with his tongue.

"Here, Cherry, good girl! That's a good horse," John said, using a loud voice as he pretended that he had just now entered the barn. He stroked the mare's neck affectionately for a few moments. Cherry was confused because John had forgotten the sugar this time. She made a noise in her throat and tossed her head impatiently.

John's father Daniel and Grandpa Fred came from the tack room and walked toward John. John turned when he heard them. He acted surprised to see them there.

"G'morning Dad, Grandpa," John said. "I was just giving Cherry a sugar cube from the bowl in the kitchen. I hope that's okay. She kind of expects it from me. I guess I shouldn't have given her any on that first day."

His grandfather answered, "It's fine if it's just one lump, but try to avoid giving it to her two days in a row." He smiled. "It seems she's training you pretty good, huh?"

"I guess. Say, Dad, I'm sorry I overslept this morning. I had a hard time getting settled last night. I think it was after five when I finally fell asleep. I didn't wake up until ten!" John looked at his father and tried to read his reaction before he continued. "I'll go take care of the chickens now. What time do we need to leave for church?"

"The girls took care of the chickens and eggs. Maybe you need to get to bed at a regular time. It was very late when you finally left the den." Daniel looked stern as he talked. "We need to leave no later than eleven thirty this morning if we plan to get there in time for twelve thirty Mass." He looked at his watch. "Oh! It's later than I thought. We need to leave in about ten minutes. Please go tell your sisters. I think they're still by the chickens."

"Yes, sir," John said to acknowledge that he heard his father. What else could he say? John rushed over to the coop and found the girls leaning against the corral talking. The basket of eggs was on the ground beside them. He called out to them.

"Dad said we're going to leave for church in just a few minutes. Are you ready? Do you want me to put the eggs away? Hey, thanks for collecting them this morning. I owe you one. I guess I overslept."

"It's okay," Emma, the noisy twin, answered. "It's fun to get the eggs. But you can put them in the cooler." She looked over at her sister. "Come on, we better go to the bathroom before we have to get in that boat! I thought I was going to wet my pants the last time we rode in it."

The girls giggled as they rushed to the house. John picked up the egg basket and followed his sisters partway back to the lodge. He cut through the herb garden then entered the service porch where he put the whole basket in the cooler. He'd have to wait until after church to clean them and pack them in egg trays.

He hurried through the house toward his room to find his tennis shoes and a pair of socks. It took him a few minutes to find his left shoe, but finally he was ready to go. Just as he stepped out onto the veranda, he caught a glimpse of his grandmother and mother descending the rocky steps to the shore. He rushed to catch up with them.

"Mom, Nana! Wait!" In just a moment, they were all standing together at the bottom of the steps. They turned left and followed the walkway toward the lodge pier. Five large lodge vessels were secured in slips extending off the pier. There was a powerful ski boat, a large fishing rig, a smaller open-style boat with an outboard engine, the flatboat, and the passenger transport affectionately named the *LaZBoat*. The graceful *Wind Star*, a wide-beamed old sailing ketch that was used for evening cocktail voyages and overnights, was moored out in the cove along with several other boats. The others, mostly sailboats, belonged to various islanders who lived in one of the small settlements up and down the island coast.

Eagle Cove was a large natural harbor, well suited for protecting boats during most kinds of storms. Papa Jacob had always extended a warm welcome to the lodge neighbors. Each mooring was assessed a small yearly fee to help defray the cost of maintaining the moorings and the dinghy dock. Another eighty yards past the pier was the lodge boat shed. Several small sailboats, kayaks, surfboards, bungee boards, and inner tubes were stored in trailers and on neat racks in the shed.

The twins and John sat in the bow of the *LaZBoat*. Christina and her mother, Mariel, sat in a row near the center with Mariel's father-in-law, Jacob Engstrom. Directly behind them were the lodge cooks, José and Marina Escobar, with their toddlers, Alicia and Abel. Both children wore life vests over their church clothes. Sitting beside the Escobars were Roberto Avila and Hector Diaz, employees of the lodge and devout churchgoers.

In the next row toward the stern was the bridge, boasting a captain's bench wide enough for two people. The wheel and bench were protected by a wide fiberglass awning and a tall windshield. John's father and Grandpa Fred sat on the captain's bench and talked quietly until everyone was aboard. After reminding everyone to stay seated, Grandpa Fred started the engine.

"All set?" Grandpa Fred looked around at his passengers and he said, "Okay, here we go." With that, he steered the bulky boat away from the pier, out of the cove, and then down the coast toward Mirabella. The small town was situated just a few miles short of East End. Mirabella was the only incorporated section of land on the island. The Santa Teresa Catholic Church was at the center of town, about a ten-minute walk from the harbor. Normally, the family attended Mass at 8:00 a.m. because Sunday brunch at the lodge was slated to start at 10:30 a.m.

"You know, I hope you are all enjoying the peace and quiet this week," Nana Mariel shouted up at the three teenagers, causing them to smile back at her. She realized how silly it must sound to scream "peace and quiet" while they were bouncing along in the incredibly noisy *LaZBoat*. "Oh, you know what I mean. When we have lodge guests, they seem to show up everywhere, even going to church with us. You just wait. Next Sunday, there will be at least one guest riding in this boat with us at seven in the morning. Just wait and see!"

Grandpa Fred steered the boat along the coastline. He pointed out various places of interest to the Garrett family as they passed by. Suddenly, Papa Jacob sat up straight as he pointed toward the land and shouted, "Say, there's Misty Falls! And look there! See that thing? It's up on that bluff, next to Misty Falls. It's that old sea camp fire ring." He was pointing toward the summit of a gentle hill high on a cliff overlooking the ocean.

One section near the top of the hill had been crudely leveled to create a spot for the fire ring. Large logs were arranged in concentric circles around a wide open area. In the very center was a fire ring built with granite rocks. The whole structure was in a general state of disrepair, overgrown with bushes and vines, and littered with rocks and leaves.

"It's a mess, isn't it? That hill is part of our property. There was a wide grove of island cherry trees there. It was a beautiful spot, so quiet and secluded. But then one day, Peter Sorenson took a few hired hands and cleared a big patch of the trees and shrubs off the side of the hill, leveled the ground, then piled rocks and logs around to make a campfire ring." Papa Jacob was scowling as he continued to talk. "He ruined some of my best land! His property line is almost a hundred yards down the hill on the other side, but he just came up and destroyed my property!

"Well, when I heard that awful noise they called singing one night, I took a couple of my crew out to investigate, and that's when we saw the mess he made of my hill! I sued him the very next day. I had to hire the surveyor to come out and measure. Sure enough, Peter had made a mistake, but there wasn't much to be done to fix it. You can't just rebuild a hill and put the trees back. Then he offered to buy the land, and I think that's what he had in mind from the beginning. I think he wanted his campfire on the hill overlooking the water, so he just built it there!" Papa Jacob was shaking with anger.

He gasped for a moment then continued, "Well, I'll tell you, there was no chance he would get that land. We sure didn't want to listen to a bunch of campers singing and carrying on every night. They built another campfire ring down near their beach at the sea camp. When they're really loud, we still hear them. Can't imagine them right up here on our hill, no, I can't even imagine that." Papa Jacob grew quiet, and before long, he was leaning on Mariel's shoulder. He was fast asleep.

John stared at the hill as they passed by. He was surprised at the outburst from Papa Jacob. He could feel the anger in Papa Jacob's voice. Each word had a sharp edge, honed with a whetstone of hate. Recently, John had heard that same recriminating tone in the voice of his father. John was troubled when the hateful words spewed from his father, sometimes lashing out toward his mother and sisters, but most frequently directed toward John himself. Could his father hold on to that anger for decades as Papa Jacob seemed to be doing? As they chugged past the fire ring, John tried to think of more pleasant things. Curious about something Papa Jacob had mentioned, he turned to Grandpa Fred for more information.

"Grandpa, what exactly is Misty Falls? I can see the cloudy mist coming off that cliff, but what's causing it? Does the ocean surge have enough power to splash all the way up there?" Just as he was watching the mist on the cliff top, the late-morning sun caught the glistening moist air, creating a subtle rainbow that shimmered briefly then disappeared.

Emma saw the rainbow and shouted out to the whole boat, "Hey, did you see that? That was so cool!" She was pointing to Misty Falls as she started to stand up. Her sister grabbed her and pulled her into the seat, but not before the whole family and other passengers felt the boat wobble for a few moments.

"Best to stay seated while we're in this old tub. Hate to go swimming in my church clothes!" Grandpa Fred smiled at Emma. Then he added, "The rainbows are pretty, aren't they? They appear most every morning and late afternoon, whenever the sun is low enough in the sky and shining bright enough to catch the water prisms."

John wondered at first if he had just imagined the rainbow, but after Grandpa Fred's explanation, John stared over the stern of the boat back toward the misty cliff where he caught glimpses of several more rainbows.

"It is quite a remarkable sight, isn't it?" Fred said. "Up on that hill is one of the natural springs that we've found on our property. This one flows from near the summit of that hill behind the fire ring down to the cliff." Fred pointed to the hill that was rapidly fading from their sight as they chugged toward Mirabella. "That water source isn't strong enough to create a creek or even a trickle, but there is enough moisture to form a slick under the wild meadow grass. When the flow reaches the cliff, it just dissipates into the air."

"Is it fresh water?" John didn't think a spring could exist so close to the ocean.

"Well," Fred said, "this particular spring is a little brackish, but I think it's caused by the very light pressure that is driving it upward. We have a nice freshwater reservoir underground on our part of the island, and most of the springs that emerge from it have a healthy flow. The rate of flow on this one is very slow, and there seems to be some ocean seepage from underground. It's one of the springs that we don't rely on for our water supply."

After Mass, John stood in the church courtyard with Papa Jacob. The summer flowers were still blooming all around the magnificent fountain that bubbled in the middle of the yard. Papa Jacob had just finished explaining how he and Father

Andrew had built that fountain in 1953 and how Father Andrew had passed away just a few years later. The 1958 parish council voted to name the splendid structure *Father's Fountain* to honor the memory of their beloved priest. Papa Jacob's chin quivered as he spoke.

John put his arm around the old man's shoulders and was surprised to feel how thin his great-grandpa had become. It was clear to John that someday soon, Papa Jacob would be joining his old friend in heaven, but the thought did not really sadden John. He had heard Papa Jacob talk at length about how he missed his wife, Sofia, and how he was ready to join her in heaven as soon as God decided it was time.

John helped support Papa Jacob as he hobbled over to the bench beside the fountain. Jacob sat down carefully, and John sat down beside him. Papa Jacob was still the figurehead lodge keeper, but since his stroke last year he could not do much to help in the day-to-day running of the lodge. Grandpa Fred had explained to John that Jacob greeted guests and answered questions about the island, but the hard physical work was now in the hands of the rest of the family. As John sat quietly next to his great-grandfather, the old man cleared his throat and began to speak.

"You know, Johnny," Jacob's voice was so soft that John had to lean in close to hear, "for the past few months, I've been so worried. What would become of our beautiful lodge? Who really cared about all that we have accomplished at Eagle Cove? But now, since Christina and all of you have returned, I don't worry at all anymore. I see you young people, and I just know that there will be at least one of you who will share the vision. Now I believe there will always be family here who is committed to keeping the lodge traditions alive in the future. Life can be good here on the island. I know the lodge will prove to be a good provider." Jacob turned toward the fountain.

John privately thought that he and his sisters would enjoy the next few years on the island, but it seemed a very remote choice for any of the three to take over the lodge in the future. He thought how he would be graduating from high school and going away somewhere to college next fall; he really wasn't sure if he would ever return to live on the island after that.

But John cared about Papa Jacob's feelings, so he would say nothing to destroy the hope that Jacob had just expressed for the well-being of the lodge. This had been the first conversation of consequence that John remembered having with Jacob. Over the years, John had always tried to avoid Papa Jacob during the obligatory summer visit to the island. Jacob was often angry over some small thing, and his patience was short.

Thank God for Grandpa Fred and Nana Mariel, thought John. His grandparents had acted in tandem to keep Jacob's wrath from spilling over onto the visiting family members. Finally, Jacob told John he wanted to sit there alone for a little while so he could think about Sofia and Andrew.

As John turned away, he saw Grandpa Fred and Nana Mariel across the courtyard. They waved him over and then proceeded to introduce him to many of their friends. Christina, balancing a full cup of coffee in one hand and a scone in the other, approached John. Melted butter mixed with warm honey was dripping down her arm. John hurried over to the snack table and grabbed a handful of napkins.

"Thanks, John," Christina took the napkins and attempted to wipe away the sticky goo. "This scone is delicious, but I'm making a mess!" One of Mariel's friends hurried into the parish hall kitchen and returned with a few dampened paper towels. In the meantime, Fred had wandered over to the snack table for a scone of his own. He licked his fingers after each bite.

"This looked too good to pass up," Fred said as he swabbed his chin with a napkin. Which of you lovely ladies made this incredible edible?" Fred smiled at the group around him. John watched the friendly group as they laughed and chatted together. He was surprised to admit that he was actually enjoying himself. He noticed that Emma and Lucy were in the midst of a group of young teenagers near the refreshment table. They were all laughing and sneaking extra cookies off the tray whenever the hostess wasn't looking. His mother, who had also been observing the girls, looked over at John and rolled her eyes in mock disapproval of her daughters. Then she turned to Mariel and spoke softly.

"We should think about getting back soon. We still have lots of work to do getting the stuff off of the veranda and inside someplace. There must be a place to store it all." She sighed. "It makes me tired to just think about going through all that junk again. Now I wish we had just left it all in Sierra Glen." John thought that his mother seemed younger and somehow vulnerable in the presence of her parents.

"There's plenty of time." Mariel tried to alleviate her daughter's worries. "We have a group of guests arriving on Thursday afternoon and another group coming in on Friday, so that gives us four days to get everything in order. Fred and I thought you could use the extra room behind ours to store all your things that don't fit in easily somewhere in the lodge. That way, you can tackle the job of sorting it all out without having the pressure of time hanging over you."

She smiled at Christina and John, and then she added, "But it is a good idea to get home. We can get quite a bit done before supper this evening, and then we'll do a little planning for the rest of the week. Sometime today, I'd like to hear you play, John. You can use your piano or mine. Mine is newly tuned, but yours is not too bad after the move. It's up to you. After your piano has had a chance to get acclimated to its new home here on the island, we'll be sure to tune and voice it."

"How long does it take before we can tune it?" John was anxious to play his own piano. Nana's Steinway was a great instrument, but John was familiar with the old Mason & Hamlin. It had been his steadfast friend for over thirteen years. Nana had made it clear that he would have to do most of his practicing on her piano since his was smack in the middle of guest territory. Certainly, the guests did not come to the lodge to hear endless scales, arpeggios, and passagework. On the other hand, Grandpa Fred had announced that the guests would be delighted to hear John play occasionally. Soon, John would learn about lodge "on time" and "downtime" for guests. Then he could plan his own playing time on his piano during downtime, when the guests were pursuing activities outside the lodge building.

"We should probably wait at least two or three weeks," Mariel said. "If there are any major problems in the next few days, I can make some minor adjustments, but generally it's best to wait and do the entire instrument at once." John knew that in addition to being a fine pianist and music scholar, his grandmother was also quite capable of tuning, voicing, and repairing most problems on a piano.

Christina walked over to get the twins. Going back toward the fountain, John found Papa Jacob leaning over on the arm of the bench. He was dozing quietly. John woke him gently and helped him walk toward the group that was gathering for the trip back to the lodge. It was a quiet group, except for the girls. They were filled with chatter about their good fortune. It seems the island had plenty to offer after all. They had discovered there was a bumper crop of teens on the island, and lots of them were good-looking boys.

Chapter Four

Tuesday morning at breakfast, John sat next to Grandpa Fred at the big square table. They were eating Canadian bacon and french toast, all prepared and served by his grandmother, Mariel.

"Nana, is there any more bacon? And oh, how about the french toast?" John was already eating his second helping. He had scooped fresh-chopped peaches on top, and it was delicious. He made room on his plate for the extra bacon and french toast that Nana carried over on a spatula.

"Thanks," he mumbled, mouth full of food. He turned to face his grandfather. "Grandpa, is it okay if I try sailing one of the boats today? I'd like to go out around noon if that's all right with you."

"Sure, Johnny. It's going to be a pretty calm day, so this would be a good time to practice everything you learned last summer. Just be sure to wear your life vest, and stay inside the buoys." He wiped his mouth with his napkin and then he blew his nose noisily into the napkin.

"Fred! Can't you do that away from the table? Honestly! Who blows their nose at the breakfast table, and into a nice cloth napkin?" Mariel's words sounded stern, but John and Grandpa Fred just laughed. John noticed the glances that passed between his grandparents, and he was heartened by the obvious affection they held for one another. John could remember not too many years ago how his own parents had that same kind of easy, loving relationship. Now he only saw it once in a while. Most of the time during the past couple of years, there was a tension that belied the conversation of the moment. Even Lucy and Emma were disturbed by the constant simmering anger and resentment that had taken up residence in their house. Lately, John felt relieved when one parent or the other had business away from the house for a few hours. He and his sisters had learned to avoid saying anything that might spark an argument. As it was, his parents seemed to be angry with each other all of the time, even though they rarely said cross words out loud.

Well, our family seems happier here at the lodge, John thought to himself. His mom and Nana seemed to be great friends. John had heard all the mother-daughter jokes, but he never saw the clichés acted out within his own family. Even his father, who was usually filled with a tense energy and a lightning-fast fuse, seemed happier here. His father got along with Grandpa Fred really well; there was a feeling of mutual respect and affection between them that was encouraging.

Both Papa Jacob and Grandpa Fred were pleased with the new arrangements, and they said so several times during each day. Both of them praised the skills that Daniel brought to the lodge. A skilled carpenter by hobby and a fine accountant by profession, Daniel was welcomed and appreciated from his very first day on the island. And since John's mother had spent so much time at the lodge when she was young, she knew how things were done. John was surprised to learn how many different skills his mother had. She was so relaxed and sure of herself around all of the animals—chickens, cows, pigs, goats, and horses. When she was nearby, even the grouchy old mule acted like a big, friendly dog.

Apparently, everyone in the family recognized how well his mother and the animals got along. Sunday evening at supper, Grandpa Fred had stood up at the table and tapped his spoon on his glass. He glanced around the room and waited for a response. There was still a buzz of conversation, so he clinked the glass a little harder then cleared his throat loudly.

"Excuse me, but I feel the need to make an announcement."

He stopped talking and looked around at everyone. Nana had laughed quietly and rolled her eyes in an exaggerated way. When Grandpa saw her, he shook his finger at her and smiled. The whole table sat in anticipation.

Grandpa cleared his throat again and continued. "I'm not sure anyone else has noticed, but the animals are in a state of euphoria because they have noticed something very important. They have all realized that the Queen of the Animals has returned, and I am pleased to say she is sitting here among us. Long live the queen!"

Everyone looked around, wondering what Grandpa could mean. But Nana Mariel laughed and went over to stand behind her daughter's chair.

"Come on, dear, stand up and be recognized." Mariel gave her daughter a little nudge. John watched as his mother blushed and laughed. Finally, Christina stood, took a big breath, and straightening her shoulders, assuming a regal air. Nana Mariel placed an old Burger King crown on Christina's head. The newly crowned monarch waved to her subjects around the table in the style of Queen Elizabeth in a motorcade. Everyone clapped and cheered. Then Christina held up her hands and signaled for silence.

"We, that is the royal *we*, are pleased to be here in our motherland with our subjects, both human and nonhuman. We would remind all who are present at this table have a duty to learn the name of each animal who lives in our midst. You will need to know the proper name of each as well as the given name. It is our, that is the royal *our*, goal to educate the guests about our animal friends. For example, Cherry the horse is more than that. She is a Morgan mare, five years old, her color is called roan, and she is a very capable and reliable member of our community. She is sure-footed and obedient. Each of the twelve saddle horses at Eagle Cove has a similar story worth knowing.

"The royal *we* is happy to say that you will all participate in Animals 1A on Wednesday morning, an important class led by the royal *we*, that is, me. This will be an overview class for all residents. Please meet your queen, that is the royal *us, me* at 9:00 a.m. sharp in the barn. And please come in clothing appropriate for mounting a horse or a mule. Thank you! We now grant good wishes to all!" She waved once more then sat.

Her family gave her a standing ovation. John thought to himself that the playful interchanges and ongoing silliness that were so much a part of his early childhood seemed to be surfacing again, and he was glad.

John finished his breakfast, excused himself, then carried his plates over to the sink, rinsed them, and put them in the dishwasher. Yesterday, Nana Mariel had actually held a dishwashing class with the whole family sitting in the kitchen observing. He could hear her words clearly in his mind.

"We have two dishwashing machines here in the kitchen. The big one is for lodge use. The small one is for family use. Now, rule number one is this: we never leave a dish, glass, spoon, or anything else on the table or counter or in the sink. Since there will be guests with us practically every day, we maintain a very neat and clean environment throughout the whole lodge."

She smiled as she talked, and she was very organized as she continued to explain how to load the dishwasher, where everything was stored, and where to find cleaning supplies. In just a few minutes, John and the others seemed to feel comfortable with the rules and the procedures. She answered a few questions, then she dismissed them. His father had grumbled a little about how it felt like having to go to school, but Nana had just teased him gently.

"Yes, Daniel, this is Dishwashing 1A, and you will receive your grade after one week. I'll be watching." She smiled as she gave him a quick pat on the shoulder. John was pleased to see the beginning of a smile form on his father's lips. He thought once again that maybe it was a good idea after all to have moved to the island.

Chapter Five

Tuesday was shaping up to be a very warm day with a light steady breeze coming in diagonally from offshore. At breakfast, John had promised Grandpa Fred that he would wear his life vest. He also agreed to stay within the lodge buoys that were set at the reef about a half mile from the shore. Passing through the kitchen and overhearing the end of the conversation, John's father had tried to intervene, saying John was not ready to take any boat out without an adult.

Grandpa Fred gently disagreed. He reminded Daniel how well John had handled the boats last summer; he also noted that it was a perfect day for practicing, warm and calm with a light steady breeze. Daniel had merely shrugged his shoulders and sighed. Then as he left the kitchen, he turned and reminded John to be careful with the boat.

John entered the boat shed and glanced around at the variety of crafts. Because he wanted to stay with just one sail, he rejected the Hobie 16 and the Snipe and the Rhodes. He'd wait for a few weeks before he attempted anything with a mainsail and a jib. He turned and saw the racks holding three each of Lasers and Sabots. A self-bailer would be best in the cove, so he eliminated the little Sabots from consideration. Looking back at the Lasers, his mind suddenly filled with images of a bright blue Laser skimming across Sierra Glen Lake, leading the fleet of colorful Lasers across the finish line.

A trophy would join the dozens of ribbons and trophies that already adorned the other half of John's old bedroom in Sierra Glen. As John stared at the racks of boats, he realized that he hadn't seen the blue boat for almost two years. He thought maybe he would ask Mom about it sometime. He wouldn't ask Dad, that's for sure. Although he could not say why, John had no interest in sailing on any of the Lasers. When he turned to the other side of the boat shed and saw the bright green Finn, he smiled. This was it. He remembered when his Grandpa Fred let him take out this very same boat on the final day of their visit last summer. According to Grandpa Fred, the fifteen-foot-long Finn was the best small classic racing dinghy ever made—a speed machine.

Grandpa showed John how to rig it, and then he patiently reviewed the basics of sailing, including how to right the boat in case it capsized. Grandpa was a gentle but firm teacher last summer, and after three afternoons working up to it, John felt reasonably confident in his ability to handle the trim little boat. He remembered the freedom and power he felt all at once as he went skimming back and forth across the cove. Last year he was barely heavy enough to keep the boat from capsizing, but this year he thought his extra weight would be perfect. A wave of excitement and anticipation washed over him.

John maneuvered the small trailer holding the Finn out of the boat shed and directed it down toward the water. There was a moment when he thought about Casey. He would not be doing this if she hadn't suggested it.

Well, yippee, subconscious! he thought. *Couldn't just plant the idea of sailing in my head. So why did you invent Casey then erase her from my life? Not very thoughtful of you!* John looked down the beach in hopes that she might be real and show up after all, but there was no sign of her. At the edge of the water, he slid the boat off the trailer and onto the wet sand of the launching area. Here, all the rocks and pebbles had been removed from the beach, and a layer of fine sand had been added to protect the boat bottom from getting scratched when someone launched the boat into the water or sailed back to the shore.

As he rigged the boat, he felt a second wave of excitement tinged with a speck of fear. When everything was in place, he double-checked to be certain he had rigged it correctly. Then he slid the fully rigged boat off the trailer and set it next to the water with the bow facing into the wind. After he pulled the trailer up into the trailer storage area, he had a sudden fleeting thought about Casey, wishing she was more than a figment of his imagination. Then he chastised himself for getting undone over a dream. With a sigh, he tossed his flip-flops onto the dry sand and pushed the boat into the water.

Grasping the gunwales, he placed one knee on the boat and used his other foot to give a mighty shove off the shore. As the boat glided out, he slipped into place, grasping the tiller and the mainsheet. His kinesthetic sense recognized the subtle pull of the sail as the breeze began to fill it, and he responded by adjusting the tiller and mainsheet. All that he learned from Grandpa Fred was clear in his mind, but he was heartened to see how well he had internalized the necessary physical responses to the changing wind and sea. He reveled in the combination of freedom and control, the essence of sailing solo. He laughed out loud. What a rush! He tacked back and forth until he was beyond the moored boats. There was still a good quarter mile before he was close to the buoys.

This section of the ocean was his alone, and he practiced beating hard into the wind, then falling off the wind through a beam reach and into a broad reach. He found that the little currents in the water lifted him slightly on starboard tack, but on port he had to work hard to keep his line. After nearly an hour out, John decided that it was time to try a controlled jibe. He purposely waited until he was closer to shore where the wind was lighter. John remembered Grandpa Fred telling him that a jibe was just a different way of turning the boat around.

Instead of passing the bow through the wind as in a tack, the bow moves away from the wind. John felt secure in tacking because it hardly required any adjustment to the sail. He just had to shift his weight up to the high side as the boat came about. It had taken him only a few minutes to regain the feel of tacking. He figured it was like riding a bike or roller skating; once you have mastered the skill, you never really forget. Now he felt he could do those maneuvers without thinking at all. It was beginning to seem as natural and automatic as breathing. He felt a little nervous about trying the jibe. Last year, Grandpa directed him to adjust the boom quickly during the jibe and then loosen the mainsheet to allow the sail to fill. John thought he could do it, but he'd have to concentrate during the whole procedure. Remembering how Grandpa decided to demonstrate an unplanned jibe still made John laugh. Just before they capsized and landed in the water, Grandpa had yelled just one word, "Duck!"

After four successful jibes, John was feeling more confident. He decided to try some other maneuvers that he had seen the Laser guys do up on the lake. He tried turning a tight 360 degrees in each direction. It was tricky because it involved combining tacks and jibes and quick weight shifts and sail trimming. Because he trusted his own understanding and ability and because he had faith in the capabilities of his boat, John felt relaxed and in control. After sailing out toward the buoys once again and tacking and jibing on a zigzag course parallel to shore, John realized he was starving. He jibed, then he glided on a broad reach all the way to the shore.

He steered clear of the moored boats and headed right up to the launch area. He turned into the wind just before he reached the shallows. Flipping up his rudder as he raised the centerboard, John quickly slipped out into the knee-deep water and directed the boat up onto the beach. As he furled the sail around the mast, he looked up to the beach where he had thrown his flip-flops. There he saw his father and Grandpa Fred sitting in beach chairs with an empty chair and picnic basket between them. John hurried over to see them.

" Hi, Dad, hi, Grandpa, how long have you been sitting there?" John was hoping they had a chance to see him do his 360s.

"We've been watching you for nearly an hour," Grandpa Fred said. "Mariel brought this basket down to us about a half hour ago. She sat with us a little while. All three of us enjoyed watching you,

Johnny. You must have had a great sailing instructor." Grandpa laughed and said, "Remember, 'Duck'?"

John smiled and nodded.

"John, you handle that boat very well," Daniel said. "But are you big enough to sail it in heavier winds? That's a lot of sail on it. You most likely won't be able to control it in stronger weather."

"I think it'll be okay. I was a lot lighter last year, and I could handle it in medium wind then. I felt really good today. I was even wishing the wind would pick up so I could go faster and really hike out."

John was surprised when his father offered a compliment, but he wondered why Dad was compelled then to say something to undermine his progress. Who knows if he will be able to sail it solo in heavy winds? But why question it? John thought that it would have been nice for his father to just stop talking after telling him that he handled the boat well.

Fred was looking through the picnic basket. He found sandwiches and sliced apples. There were some cookies and a bag of potato chips. Mariel had packed some bottles of juice and a couple of wine coolers in a cold pack.

"Mariel said she didn't have much to choose from. We have to do a big shopping for the groups that are arriving starting on the day after tomorrow." Fred looked at John and Daniel and added, "But hey, it looks damn good to me. Here, have a sandwich. "The three ate and drank and relaxed on the warm beach. Mariel had made tuna salad with chopped pickles and mayonnaise.

Fred looked up and asked the others if either of them knew the difference between mayonnaise and snot. When neither could claim to know, Fred said, "Oh, oh! I'm not going to let you make the sandwiches tomorrow!"

"Hey, what do you call a fish with no eyes?" John asked, and when the others could not answer he said, "A fsh." John made an explosive sound of consonants with his mouth.

Then Daniel added one of his own. "You know, Jacob told me he saw an eye doctor on one of those Alaskan islands, but I think it was just an optical Aleutian."

Soon, Fred was rolling out one silly joke after another as John and Daniel groaned and smiled. Before long, all the food was gone, and the sun was dropping behind the lodge. They put the boat away, gathered their picnic trash, and headed back. As they walked in comfortable silence, John knew they had all absorbed more today than the simple warmth of the sun and sand.

Chapter Six

After sailing, John returned to his room in the lodge. He showered, then he dressed in comfortable shorts and a polo shirt. He had worked on the piano with Nana Mariel for over an hour on Sunday afternoon, and he was anxious to spend some serious time with his music before dinner so he could apply what she had suggested. He was surprised how much he had enjoyed his lesson with her. She explained things clearly and corrected him gently, but she was relentless until she was sure he was doing his best in response to her coaching.

Back in Sierra Glen, his mother had been his piano teacher for all but two of the past twelve years. John was gifted and motivated to do well, and he made fine progress under Christina's tutelage, but his lessons were sporadic. Somehow, other activities and responsibilities interrupted their time together. Christina thought John needed formal weekly lessons. She arranged an audition time with Dr. Ames, a highly regarded professor in the music department at Sierra Glen University.

Dr. Ames recognized that John was talented and agreed to teach him. John progressed well and he enjoyed Dr. Ames, but he actually missed the flexibility of his haphazard lessons with his mom. After two years of study in the university prep studio program, John finally asked his mother if he could have her teach him again. After all, Christina's own mother had been her piano teacher from before kindergarten until Christina left the island to study music at USC.

John had learned at least one or two pieces by Mozart every year since his second year of piano. His mother helped him, but since lessons were not on a regular schedule, he became proficient in learning a new piece on his own. Christina was always there to assist when he got stuck with some technical problem, but most of the time he learned the music by himself. But when Nana introduced a piece for study, she had something important to say about every measure. John felt he had learned a semester's worth of information from Nana in just one lesson.

He grabbed his music and his notebook and wandered into the main parlor. He was pleased he would be able to use his own piano today. Sitting on the bench, he thought about how Nana had set the tone for their lessons together. She knew so much, but she gave him credit for having valid ideas and opinions as well.

She gave him the least flexibility in matters of technique. He knew from past experience when he was learning a new piece, he was sloppy with his fingering and inconsistent in his approach to passagework. Nana noticed his initial disregard for these important elements of good performance. She took almost an hour sitting next to John on the bench while she helped him with hand position, alternative fingering that fit his hand, finger crossings, and finally, she showed him how to attack and release the notes in a phrase. She explained how he could practice some of her suggestions by making little exercises out of the various phrases in his piece.

But John was most pleased about how she collaborated with him on matters of style and interpretation. With a renewed respect for his grandmother's skills and accomplishments, he started to see her as a real person, independent of her roles as a grandmother, mother, wife, and even as lodge hostess. He never thought before about how it would be for a serious musician to live in a remote location, far from other serious musicians. The nearest groups of professional musicians were across the channel. Didn't Nana miss playing chamber music? Were there other musicians on the island? But at his lesson, before he had a chance to ask her about herself, she opened the Mozart sonata album and started to talk.

"You have already studied several of these sonatas. After looking over your past and current literature, I've decided that Mozart's K. 310 would be challenging both musically and technically. I know you've heard it performed by your teacher at Sierra Glen back when you were a sophomore because I went to that recital with you. Do you remember? I recall how you went on and on about the first movement, so I know you'll enjoy studying it. This sonata in A Minor is an exciting piece, John, and it is one of the few piano works that Mozart wrote in a minor key."

Mariel turned to face John. "I consider this sonata to be one of his most profound works. It requires maturity and patience." She stopped talking, then she looked directly into his face and offered a challenge to him. "John, are you willing to spend the time and energy it's going to take to master this work?"

John thought for a moment, then he barely nodded, unsure whether or not the question had been rhetorical.

Nana smiled and said, "Good! Now, let's look over the basic structure of all three movements, especially in regard to key center, meter, and tempo. Then we'll talk about ways to approach learning the first movement. I am so pleased you will be playing this wonderful piece. It's going to be fun for me to see you grow with it."

John could hear her words in his head as he started his practicing. He tried to follow each of her suggestions as he worked for nearly two hours. He was unaware of the passage of time until his mother came to retrieve him for dinner. She told him it would be ready in about ten minutes. As soon as he stood up, he realized how exhausted he felt after spending the afternoon sailing and the last couple of hours at the piano. Also, he was famished!

He stretched his arms over his head then bent forward from the waist and pivoted from side to side. His mother watched him as he tried to work the tension from his body. She stepped toward him and guided him back to the bench. He sat down once again, and Christina began to knead his shoulders and upper back with a firm rolling motion. John closed his eyes and sighed with contentment.

As she massaged the tension from his neck and arms, she spoke quietly. "You know, Johnny, I was listening to your practicing just now. It brought back so many memories to me of my own studies. I did not realize at the time what a remarkable teacher Mom was. It wasn't until I went away to college that I saw how much I knew and how much I was capable of doing compared to the other students. Living here on the island, I was isolated. It turned out that Mom gave me a strong grounding, and she encouraged me to play literature that challenged me and helped me grow as a musician. I was never limited by thoughts about what was appropriate for me to study. I read chamber scores, orchestral reductions, jazz charts, pop lead sheets, hymns, little pieces, big pieces, modern, Baroque, Romantic, you name it."

She stopped moving her hands for a moment. "When I heard you play those little passages of your new piece and then listened to you making up little technical exercises, just like Nana told you, well I had a flash of déjà vu." She smiled wistfully, part of her still in the midst of a memory from her own youth on the island.

"I'm glad we came here, Mom. So far, it's been better than I expected, and I like Nana Mariel and Grandpa Fred a lot. I even feel like I'm getting to know, or I guess I mean I'm starting to understand, Papa Jacob. I've been wondering about some things, though."

John stood up and fell in step beside his mother as they headed toward the kitchen. He hesitated before speaking. It was as if he needed to practice in his mind how to approach his questions. Finally, he just blurted out, "What do you know about the Sorenson Sea Camp? Have you ever been there?"

John was curious to find out more about the history between the two families.

"Oh, sure, I went there a few times when I was a kid. Your Uncle Matt and I snuck down to the camp to go to a few parties, and a couple of times we went down to a big Harvest Festival square dance they used to put on every year, and maybe they still do, I don't know." Christina smiled at the memory. "Of course, we could never tell Grandpa, I mean your Papa Jacob, about it. He would have grounded us for life."

"But why? Was it because of that fire ring on the hill?"

"Well, yes. That was the beginning I guess." Christina looked thoughtful. "But it was much more than that. There were some unpleasant things, things that might not seem that bad to you now in light of different standards nowadays, but it all caused quite a scandal then. Then the unthinkable happened."

Christina stopped talking for a few moments, then shook her head slightly as if to clear an unpleasant memory. Soon she continued, "As a result, my grandpa hated everything about the whole Sorenson family and their camp too, so we all stayed pretty much away from it."

"Did they have any kids, you know, that you met on the school bus, or maybe you knew at school in Mirabella?" John wanted to know more, but he sensed that his mother wasn't entirely comfortable talking about the subject.

"Well, there was Abby who was a year younger than me, and then there was Keith who was the same age as Matt. They were Peter Sorenson's grandchildren. Their father was Peter Senior's first child, Eric. He was really a nice man, but we only knew him from when we snuck down to the camp and when we went to the school varsity games. The Peterson kids, Carolyn and Jeff, moved to the sea camp sometime during elementary school. They were a little younger than Matt, maybe by two years or so. Their mom was Janet, who was Eric's sister, Peter Senior's third child."

Christina stopped for a moment to organize her thoughts. "You know, I haven't thought about any of these people for years. I think Janet had married and left the island right out of high school. She returned to the island with her kids after she got divorced. Janet stayed on at the sea camp for years helping to run the operation. For all I know, she's still there. You could ask your Nana Mariel. Anyhow, Keith and Matt were good friends from the first time they met on the bus in first grade. They both played in the elementary school band, and when they got older, they both played on almost every school sports team together."

Christina smiled briefly, then added, "Even though he was two years younger than I was, Keith had a giant crush on me."

Christina smiled as she searched back through time. John watched her carefully. Not for the first time since their family had arrived on the island, John noticed how much happier she looked and, yes, even younger and prettier than she had seemed back in Sierra Glen.

"What happened to Keith? Is he still here on the island?"

"Oh, I don't think so. He left for Berkeley after he graduated from high school, and your uncle Matt also went up north to college at Santa Clara. I think they stayed in touch for a little while. Matt and I wrote back and forth pretty regularly. Real letters, snail mail, believe it or not, no Internet. The first year or so, he mentioned Keith, but I think they lost track of each other by the time Matt left for seminary. I heard that Keith went back to the Midwest to med school, but I don't know what happened after that." Christina stopped talking, then added almost as an afterthought, "I wonder if Matt knows anything more about Keith?"

"Can't you just call down to the sea camp and ask how to reach him?" John thought that would be the most direct way to satisfy her curiosity and, now that he knew of Keith, to satisfy his own curiosity as well.

"Oh no, I couldn't do that. Not with Grandpa feeling the way he does about the Sorensons." She stopped walking. "Maybe I'll give Matt a call sometime and ask if he knew what happened to Keith." She smiled at John and abruptly changed the subject. "Say, I've been thinking about your school classes here at home, the ones we'll start on Monday morning. I think with breakfast, then house duties and farm chores, it would be realistic to plan for 10:00 a.m."

Clearly, she was done talking about the Sorenson family. "Well, think about how you would like to arrange the day, and we can work out a more detailed plan later in the week." Suddenly, her stomach growled, causing them both to laugh. "I must be hungry. I'm glad it's time to eat now."

"Same here, I'm starved." John could feel his stomach rumbling too.

"You know, Johnny, I almost hate to admit it now, but I am so glad to be free of cooking three meals each day forever. Now I can cook for fun." Looping her arm through John's, she said, "It's like our new life here on the island is really beginning. Our first lodge guests arrive the day after tomorrow. I hope we're ready!"

On Wednesday John and the twins finished their early morning chores quickly. They gathered at the kitchen table for a big breakfast, and by nine sharp, the whole family had arrived in the barn. Christina was ready for them. She had a two-page list for each of them that summarized all of the animals that lived on the farm. All the animals had names, except the chickens. When John asked why, Christina just said it was hard to cook and eat an animal that had an individual identity. She spent most of the time with the horses because they were the animals that the guests came into contact with most often.

Jacob wanted every family member to feel comfortable saddling, grooming, feeding, and riding all the horses. He also required everyone to know how to muck out a stall. Emma and Lucy had spent most of their first week with the horses, and they were very accomplished with all the tasks their mother showed them. John felt fine about saddling and riding. It took him some time to master the currycomb. He didn't feel very safe around the hindquarters of the horses. After horses, they met Marilou the cow, Sandra Dee the fat ewe, Grace the goat, Rosemarie the hog, and Cisco the barn cat. Finally, Christina introduced them to Milton the mule.

Milt was a clown who loved to be the center of attention. He was the smartest of all the animals. Unfortunately, he preferred women to men, and he could be quite stubborn. The twins, however, could convince Milton to do anything. They had decorated a straw hat for Milt, which he wore willingly. Daniel and John both thought it looked silly, but when Daniel laughed and pointed at the silly yellow flower attached to the brim, Milton turned his backside toward Daniel and nudged him into the corner of an empty stall. With a grunt, Milton sat down in front of Daniel, trapping him in the stall. It took the twins and Christina several minutes to convince Milton that he should get up now and leave Daniel alone.

After the animal class, John helped his father and Grandpa Fred carry the remaining boxes and odd pieces of furniture from the veranda and service porch into the small room behind Fred and Mariel's suite of rooms.

"I didn't know we had so much stuff," Daniel said. "We should have left more of it behind, but we got rid of so much of our furniture back home, we thought we were packing light when we finally moved."

"Don't worry about it. Some of the pieces that you brought look great in the lodge, especially the game table. Oh, and the piano, of course," Grandpa Fred said. "That armoire that we put in the honeymoon guest suite is perfect, and we're happy to have the extra chests of drawers in the bunk rooms."

"What about all these books?" John looked at the boxes stacked in the small room. "There must be twenty boxes here. I can't believe we brought all of these. We gave away at least this many before we came. Should we give them to a library or something?"

"Well, I've been thinking we might build some nice shelves for the two interior walls in the clubroom and make it like a study or library." Fred was thinking out loud. "You know, walls of bookshelves filled with well-loved books always look good, and plenty of our guests spend hours reading. Why not have a big supply of books right here at the lodge? What do you think, Daniel, could we make shelves from that stack of milled lumber that we have in the tack room? It's been there forever, and it would be nice if we could use that space for the new saddles."

"We should design them to look like vintage floor-to-ceiling library shelves," Daniel said, already planning how to approach the building project. "That wood is just right for a project like that. I wondered why you had it there. Was it left over from something? It's cherry, isn't it? Or is it mahogany?"

"It's mahogany. Dad had planned to build some storage shelves for one of the family bedrooms, but then after the plane crash, he just put everything aside and never really got back to it. I worried a lot about Dad during that time. He just sat on the veranda or in his room and stared at nothing. It seemed that losing his daughter and then losing his granddaughter, each in such a tragic and unexpected way, almost ruined Dad. But then one morning, he got up early and got the big dolly from the barn. He brought it over here and transported all that wood from the family wing over to the tack room."

Fred stopped talking for a moment. His voice was husky when he added, "Dad never talked about the crash or the project that he had scrapped. I really think during that period was the first time I ever thought my dad was getting old. Before that, I just thought he and Mom would live on here at the lodge forever." Fred smiled and added, "That's probably how you are going to feel about me someday, but for now, Mariel and I both plan to live here at the lodge for plenty of years. Hell, we might even grow old someday, but don't count on it."

John was eager to ask about the plane crash and the girls that Grandpa Fred had mentioned, but those seemed to be sensitive topics for his grandfather, and by the time John had a question formed in his mind to ask, Fred and Daniel were talking about something else. He figured that he would just have to get some information from Nana Mariel later.

After lunch, John was responsible for washing the veranda down and cleaning the veranda furniture so it would all be ready for the new guests. A few days before, his mother had worked in the potting shed, preparing three large planters for the veranda. She started with some big geranium volunteers she found growing along the trail leading into the hills. She included some smaller leafy plants and added a few impatiens for more color.

John and Hector lifted the heavy pots up onto the veranda and moved them from place to place until Christina finally decided everything was perfect. She thanked Hector in Spanish, and he responded at length in rapid Spanish. They both laughed as Hector waved and walked toward the barn. John watched the whole encounter with interest. He thought once more how he had never appreciated how much his mother knew or how much she could do.

"What did he say, Mom?" John was curious.

"Well, after I thanked him for helping with the planters, he just said how glad he was that we were moving these flowerpots around instead of the big potted palms." Christina laughed as she added, "You know, I think that's why he hurried off." She turned and stared at the big trees that graced the veranda. "These palms might look nice if we moved them a few feet toward the right, or maybe the middle one toward the left. What do you think, Johnny?"

"I think the palms look fine the way they are, but if you really want to try moving them, well, we might be able to push them over a few feet." John stared at the mature trees, unsure if he and his mom had the strength to slide the big palms even one inch. He was beginning to think Hector had the right idea when he rushed off. Christina smiled at John.

"Oh, sweetie, I was just teasing. Everything looks great. Thanks so much for all your help. I couldn't have done this by myself." As Christina gathered her gardening tools, she added, "You're a good sport, Johnny. Thanks again. Now, you might want to use this time for some piano. I know you're anxious to work on your music."

John smiled and waved to his mother as he retreated into the house to practice.

Chapter Seven

Nana Mariel had explained that tomorrow afternoon, the first twelve visitors were arriving, then on Friday morning there were fourteen members of one family arriving for their annual September vacation weekend at the lodge. John knew that this afternoon was the last time he could use his piano for concentrated practice. After all, it was sitting in the busiest public room in the house. Initially, John had asked if their piano could be placed in the family wing, but his father had refused to even consider it. John agreed that it looked good in the main parlor, but it was not simply a piece of furniture. It was his instrument, and it was not portable like a violin or a sax. As John took his place on the bench and stared at the familiar keyboard, he sighed in resignation.

Well, old friend, he thought, *beginning tomorrow, everything changes. I'm going to miss you.* Then he put aside all peripheral ideas and worries as he worked on his new Mozart and his Rachmaninoff. When he needed to take a break from the intensity of studying new pieces, he played other pieces that were securely within his performance repertoire. Starting with a Bach prelude and fugue, he followed with a Brahms intermezzo, a Chopin valse, a slow sonata movement by Beethoven, a set of pieces by Muczynski, and finally he played the last movement of Ginastera's first sonata.

When he finished, he was exhausted. Little streams of sweat ran down his forehead from his hairline. His back felt damp, and he was so thirsty he nearly ran to the kitchen for water. He grabbed one of the reusable water bottles that the lodge kept for hikers and filled it from the filtered water spout. After guzzling half of the bottle, he refilled it, screwed the top on securely, and stepped through the service porch door. He waved at Nana Mariel, who was busy working in the herb garden.

"John, I loved your music," she said. "I was listening through the window. What a treat to hear you play so many styles, and play them so well. We'll figure out a lesson schedule soon so we can begin next week." John approached the row where she was tying up tendrils of something that looked like pea pods.

"That sounds fine, Nana. I'm really hot and kind of stiff from sitting on the bench for so long just now. I'm going to take a walk up toward that old fire ring on the hill. I thought the sea breeze off the ocean would feel good. Is there any path with shade that you would recommend? What's the best way to get there?"

"It will take you about a half hour to get there, maybe a little less." Mariel smiled as she added, "I guess it wouldn't be a hike according to your experiences living in the Sierras. Think of it as a walk in the park. Just follow the bluff path that starts at the lawn before you head down the stone bluff stairs to the beach. Turn right—that would be toward Mirabella—and just follow the path.

"It's a lovely walk, cool and scenic. You might see some deer. Be sure not to get too close to the young ones, though I suppose most are half-grown by this time of year, and the mothers are not so protective. Also, there are many quail that live in the underbrush that grows on the high side of the trail. There is no running water up there, but I see you are carrying your water bottle. Good. There is a small spring up on the hill above the fire ring, but it feeds into an underground creek. It never really surfaces at all, but it does create a dangerous mud slick."

Mariel laughed. "Perhaps I'm giving you way more information than you asked for, but, Johnny, do remember to stay outside the little rock walls that enclose the runoff. It can be very slippery between the walls."

John smiled and nodded. He was used to Nana Mariel giving detailed instructions. He figured that was just the way she always was and always would be. He was about to turn toward the trail when his grandmother continued speaking. "Do you have your cell phone? There is spotty reception along the bluff path, but you'll be able to call without any problem once you get to the top of the hill. Let us know if you are going to be later than six. Is it about four now?"

John checked the time on his phone display. "It's a few minutes before four now. I won't be past five thirty or six at the very latest. Thanks, I'll see you at dinner."

John headed out the gate and crossed the lawn. Sure enough, just before he got to the first step that led to the beach, there was a gravel path heading to the right. It meandered irregularly toward the high hill where John remembered seeing the old fire ring. The path veered inland slightly as the terrain became steeper. There were still wildflowers everywhere, and the trees and shrubs were covered with old blossoms and pods. John knew this would be a spectacular walk during the springtime when the earth gave its best effort to paint the land with color.

John heard some rustling in the thick underbrush that grew on the inland side of the trail. It did not sound like a large animal, but he hugged the other side of the widening trail nevertheless. Suddenly, there was a rush of sound, and at least a hundred quail ran out in a massive group that moved like a swirling eddy in a swollen creek. Then as if controlled by one mind, several of the larger ones that led the group took to the sky.

The remaining birds darted back into the safety of the underbrush, taking care to keep the smallest and youngest safely in the center. The wings of the flying birds made a swishing sound as they launched themselves into the air. John knew that quail, like most other wild creatures, instinctively do whatever is necessary to protect their young. He wondered if all of the more complex animals shared the same level of protective feelings.

In the case of humans, he thought most people would do just about anything to protect their own children. The interesting question might be if adults would gladly give up their own lives in order to protect the children of strangers. John had read that elephants will protect the young of their herd, and wolves will do the same for their young pack members. It had to do with survival of the species. As John walked up a gentle incline toward the center of the fire ring, his mind was still mulling over the dilemma that would surely arise when a person's will to keep living comes into conflict with a person's need to guarantee the continuation of the human race.

John felt his calves start to burn as the trail got steeper. Stopping for a moment to breathe, his thoughts returned to the present. As he walked, he passed by several island cherry trees that were thriving in the moist ocean air and warm September sun. But within the next few steps up the trail, the trees gave way to several dozen rotted stumps, most of which had collapsed into themselves. The stumps and root had rotted sufficiently for the wood to turn into loose organic mulch.

Over the years, the prevailing winds and the gentle rains, the wild creatures of the island, the various birds, both endemic and migrating, all contributed to the assimilation of the mulch into the rich soil on the hill. The resultant fertile loam had lodged into several of the spaces formed by the campfire structure. All around were beautiful ferns and flowering plants growing wildly beside, on top, and between the large logs that had been fashioned decades before into multiple rings of seating around the fire pit. Beyond the fire ring was another thick growth of ferns, some as tall as trees.

Two beautifully rendered parallel stone walls meandered from near the top of the rise all the way to the ledge of the cliff—at least that's what John thought from what he could see already. He decided to follow the swampy trace up the hill to the very top. He thought this must be the spring that Grandpa Fred had told him about, the one that created Misty Falls. It was a longer hike that John anticipated, and he was out of breath when he reached the summit. He found that up here, the stone walls were barely a foot high.

Then suddenly, the walls tapered into a single wall that rose only a few inches from the ground. After about ten feet, the wall merged into a small stack of smooth wet stones. John realized that this was the origin of the underground spring. Jacob must have formed the rock pile and rock walls to keep the ground over the spring's path from getting permanently scarred when hikers fell on the slippery surface.

There was so much moisture leaching out from the soil surrounding the stack of rocks and the walls that John could feel it condensing on his arms and neck. Water dribbled down his body, and water dripped from his forehead into his eyes. Wiping his eyes clear with his T-shirt, John turned and looked down the damp path between the walls. Unable to see very much, he followed it back down a little ways until he could see the end of the path as it dropped over the cliff far below. It became clear to him that Jacob must have built the walls to keep people and animals from falling and sliding over the cliff. That cliff was the very place where Papa Jacob had shouted out, "Misty Falls."

The walls enclosing the water slick averaged about six feet apart near the top of the hill, but as John followed the path of the water down toward the ledge of the cliff, the walls fluted apart to nearly twelve feet. The walls became a little thicker and taller, generally more substantial, as they progressed down the hill. John could see how smart this design was that allowed for optimum safety, yet did not detract from the natural beauty of the land. John knew what his mother meant when she said that Papa Jacob had the eye of an artist as well as the skill of a master craftsman. The ocean water below the cliff was striated into brilliant variations of blue. John marveled at the unexpected beauty that surrounded him. What a waste that nobody had enjoyed this spot for over six decades.

John looked for a place to sit. He found a flattened log lodged under a broken log that had fallen across it. The two logs formed a natural backrest that was surprisingly comfortable. He took a long drink of water from his bottle, then he pulled his feet up onto the log and leaned back. The sun was warm and soothing, and the breeze brought the light fragrance of ocean shore up from the beach to mix with the scent of the various plants growing all around him. He felt like he had discovered a secret garden.

He was tempted to close his eyes for a few moments, but he could project the outcome of that decision—his family would have to send a search party, he'd mess up dinner, his father would be disappointed, his Papa Jacob would feel betrayed because of the tainted history of this place, his sisters would probably laugh, but worst of all, his mother would cry. No, he wasn't going to take a chance on being home late tonight. Instead, he looked up at the puffy white clouds that floated overhead. He noticed a plane, probably a 747, that was on a high approach pattern headed for Los Angeles International. He figured it was coming in from across the Pacific, maybe from China or even Australia.

His mind was spinning around from subject to subject again when he heard an odd sound. It was a breathy sort of musical tone that started and ended abruptly, then repeated several times. John thought it might be some bird, or it could be a young wild goat. John stood up and walked toward the sound. He walked through the center of the fire ring, and as he emerged from the other side, he saw a sight that amazed him.

There leaning against a log and facing out toward the ocean was Casey. She held an instrument of some kind, and she was trying hard to make a sound that resembled music on it. John was surprised to see her here. After all, he had all but decided that she was a product of his dreams. How then could she be here right in front of him? *Maybe I'm dreaming again,* he thought, *Or maybe not!*

"Hi, Casey, I thought I heard something over here." John started to say more, but at the sound of his voice, she jumped up, turned toward him, and spoke quickly.

"Oh! You startled me!" She started to laugh. "You mean you thought you heard something that sounds like music? Please say yes!"

"Well, kind of, maybe," John answered truthfully. "Actually, I thought it might be a baby goat who was lost and calling for its mother."

"Thanks a lot. I guess that's better than saying I sound like a sick cow. That's what everyone said back at the sea camp. That's why I'm up here. Nobody ever comes here."

"So what are you doing with the recorder?" John pointed to the instrument she had in her hands. "I thought you didn't play an instrument."

"Does that mean you think I play this? Thanks again. Nobody else thinks there is any hope for me. I'm really not sure exactly how to play this. We had a set of different sizes of these at the camp, but nobody knows how to use them since the music counselor moved off the island. Most of them are plastic, but two others are wood like this one. I'm trying to learn from a little paper that explains the fingering and stuff. I just can't figure out what to do with the blowing air part."

She smiled ruefully. "Plus, I don't know anything about the notes, so I can't understand much of the instructions anyway."

"Let me show you how to control the air passage." "John held out his hand, gesturing for the instrument." She wiped it off on her shirt and handed it over.

"I kind of slobbered on it. It seems to accumulate spit. Oh, that sounds gross!" She sounded a little self-conscious.

"Oh, don't worry about that. This is nothing compared to a brass instrument. They drip spit all the time. Anyway, when you blow into this, hold it really lightly in your lips, no teeth, then you say a silent 'dew dew' with your tongue. It's just like you are saying the word *dew*, but without your vocal chords getting involved. Listen." John held the little instrument in position, formed a note with his fingers, and blew into the mouthpiece. A sweet tone wafted out over the ocean. He changed his fingering and blew again. Another higher note sounded and drifted on the wind.

"Wow! Can you play a song?" Casey was amazed that the simple wooden instrument could actually make a real musical sound. "I expected it to sound like a toy, but it's beautiful. Come on, sit down here and play a song."

She moved over and patted the log next to her.

"This is called a recorder or vertical flute," John explained, "but it's traditionally been called a sweet pipe because of the warm tone. Some people think that shepherds used an early version of this instrument to calm their animals. This one is an alto recorder. It's an F instrument. Some of the other sizes are C instruments. I think I can play something simple. Let me try a scale first to see if I remember the fingerings."

John experimented, and after just a couple of minutes, he produced a credible scale. Then he launched into "Mary Had a Little Lamb" and "Jingle Bells." Casey clapped after each and asked for more.

"Let me try something minor. I'm going to play an old tune that will be familiar to you. It will sound a little strange because this is basically a diatonic instrument, and it sounds better if I just stay in a modal scale. That gives it kind of an ancient flavor. This tune will be in Dorian mode."

When Casey looked confused, John smiled and said, "I know, just think of it as a tune played a long time ago by a shepherd watching over his sheep."

With that, he played a slow soulful rendition of the old traditional tune "Greensleeves." The rich woody and slightly breathy tone of each note blended into the landscape around them, enhancing the beauty of the moment; it was as if the wind had been given a melodic voice. John's interpretation of the simple song with its long phrases, flexible rubato, and slight vibrato lingered in the air long after the last note was played. The two teens sat in silence. Finally, Casey took the instrument from

John's hands. She placed it on her lap, then took John's hand in hers and held it.

"That was beautiful. I can't even tell you what I am feeling. What is inside of you to be able to turn a simple tune and a simple instrument into something rare and wonderful?" She leaned back against the log and sighed.

John felt her warmth beside him, and her hand was warm in his. If this was just a dream, he did not want to take a chance on waking up. He sat in silence and absorbed the totality of his happiness at this moment. Smiling, he channeled his happiness into an impulsive gesture by turning toward Casey. He put his free hand on her cheek and turned her face toward him. He looked directly into her eyes and kissed her gently, a slow and simple kiss that held itself within the limits of tenderness and friendship for now, but held a promise of future passion. They sat quietly for a moment, content to live within their own individual thoughts. The mood was broken by a sound of far-off barking. John sat up, suddenly alert. That sounded like Rocky.

"Hey, I think my dog is coming up to find me. Come on, let's head down the trail to see." He took her hand and guided her through the fire ring to the path that led to his home at the lodge. When they reached the edge of the fire ring, Casey stopped and dropped John's hand.

"I better be going back the other way. I think it's getting a little late." Casey didn't look as if she wanted their time together to end. John took her hand again and sat with her on the log where he nearly fell asleep a short time before.

"When will I see you again? I went sailing on Tuesday, and I missed you. Can we meet again soon?" John did not want her to fade from his life again.

"'I'm sorry about Tuesday. I couldn't get away. But I'm going horseback riding on Saturday morning, early. I like to be on my way when the sun is barely up. I'm planning on going up to West Springs. Maybe I'll see you there? I like to sit up there and write in my journal. But I have to be home in time to help get everything ready for the Fall Festival Masquerade Square Dance on Saturday night. Maybe you could come to the dance? Everyone is welcome. There will be hundreds of people there.

"Do you think you could come? It starts at seven. You have to wear a mask of some sort that disguises who you are and that's comfortable enough to wear for an hour or so. There's a prize for the best mask. People get pretty creative. Other than the mask, we just wear comfortable clothes for square dancing, but you don't even have to know how to square dance. The caller teaches everyone as we go along. It's always fun. What do you think?"

"I'm not sure. You know about Papa Jacob. I'm trying to get more information from my folks and grandparents about our problems with the sea camp, but everyone seems reluctant to talk about it. Anyway, I might be able to get up to the springs. My parents want me to get better at riding so I can take guests out on riding tours soon."

John checked his phone for the time. It was a little after five thirty. "Hey, I better get going. I have less than a half hour to get home for dinner."

Casey, realizing the time, jumped up. "Omigosh! I have to get back too!" With that, she leaned into John's arms, wrapped her arms around him, and kissed him quickly but fully. John felt the contours of her body against him for the briefest moment, then she was gone. He waved at her retreating form as she disappeared from his life once more, this time into the woods on the other side of the fire ring. He stood still for a moment, clinging unsuccessfully to the rush he had experienced just moments ago. Sighing, he turned and started down the path toward the lodge. At the bottom of the hill, he met up with Rocky. Before long, they entered the gate to the herb garden. John checked the time. It was five minutes before six.

Chapter Eight

At dinner, the family was noisy and excited. Everything was ready for the guests who would arrive on Thursday afternoon. Grandpa Fred, Daniel, Christina, and the twins had taken the Mirabella noontime ferry over town to shop for some special food and groceries at Costco and at Trader Joe's. Most of their staples came by barge from the restaurant supplier who handled Mirabella food servers, but about once each month, Fred liked to go look at bargains at Target or Costco. He always found interesting items, although some were not particularly useful. He also had a list of things that he could not order through the supplier.

He always encouraged others to go with him because he needed help carrying all of his purchases back onto the ferry. Since each voyager could only bring as much as he or she alone could carry or tote down the gangplank, Fred needed as many hands as he could gather. When they arrived back in Mirabella, they loaded up the *LaZBoat* and came back up the coast, arriving at the lodge in the late afternoon. Nana watched with amusement as the big clumsy overloaded boat entered the cove. She was pleased that everyone would be on time for dinner.

When everyone was served, she shared her thoughts with them. "I was just finishing working in the herb garden when Rocky, our escape artist, dashed through the gate and ran off to find John, who was taking a nice long walk. That dog zigzagged back and forth for a hundred yards until he caught John's scent. Then he howled and ran lickety-split down the coast on the bluff trail. Honestly, I think he is part bloodhound as well as the lab and pointer that you all claim are in his ancestry. What a dog."

Mariel laughed with the family, then she encouraged everyone to eat up. She had prepared the food for the evening meal, and she made a point to include everyone's favorite. The result was a potpourri of mismatched but savory dishes: pizza, tossed green salad and fruit salad, pasta, and a plate of sweet and sour pork with steamed rice. She made a special chicken schnitzel for Jacob, but from past experience she knew to make four times as much as she thought she would need because the schnitzel always seemed to become everyone's favorite food after just one taste. The mood was festive and happy. Mariel looked around the table and thought how fortunate she was to have such a fine family.

"Looking at each of you sitting here at the table, I am so overwhelmed by the wonderful people that make up my family." Nana sounded thoughtful. "But I must tell you that I would never have claimed you as mine if I saw the *LaZBoat* in Mirabella loaded the way it was this afternoon when you chugged into the cove. It looked like the *Leakin' Leena* meets the Beverly Hillbillies. Fred, dear, did they have a special on toilet paper at Costco? And girls, I know you are identical twins who do not dress the same, and that is to your credit, but Lord, deliver me from ever seeing the two of you wearing matching lampshades on your heads again.

"And Christina, next time I would just let all the bags just blow into the ocean rather than throw myself over the giant heaps of merchandise as you did. Please! Next time, at least be sure your slacks are high enough to cover up your Day-Glo pink bikini underwear. It's a good thing your bottom faced the bow. I'm sure, like Rudolph's nose, your undies were a guiding light in the mist."

"Yes, Christina, as the captain of the ship, I meant to thank you. You, my dear daughter, light up my life. " Fred smiled at his daughter. When the teasing and laughter subsided, Christina asked a question that was on everyone's mind.

"Mom, what can you tell us about the guests who are coming tomorrow? Are they returning or new?" Christina knew that over half of their annual guest tally included returning guests. Some had been coming every year for decades.

"These are returning guests. We call them the bridge bunch. There are twelve women in the group, all from the Pasadena area, and they play bridge on the patio or in the clubroom for hours each day. They do manage to get in some other activities during their stay. They take a couple of long hikes each day, morning and evening. A few of them like to go horseback riding, and some of them get up very early to do yoga or some other exercise stuff."

"That means very early," Fred added, "you'll see Ruth and Phoebe at breakfast in the kitchen before six. Be sure you are wearing something decent if you come wandering in the kitchen looking for food. I seem to remember that Anne and Elizabeth, and maybe Rhonda, all raid the fridge during the night. We ordered plenty of extra ice cream this week. Anyway, continue on, Mariel. I didn't mean to interrupt you."

Fred smiled and nodded to his wife.

"Thanks. I feel like we are constantly giving speeches lately, but it seems to be the easiest way to get a lot of information to you in a short amount of time. Anyway, back to the bridge bunch. Like I said, a couple of them like to go riding. We'll have to really organize the schedule so that we have enough horses for everyone who wants to ride this weekend. Remember there are fourteen more guests arriving on Friday. They are also returning guests, and many of them enjoy riding. With twelve saddle horses available, it isn't possible to accommodate everyone at once."

"Are we allowed to talk to them? I mean the visitors? What about meals? Where do we eat?" Emma asked. She was definitely the social half of the twins. She liked meeting new people and talking to them. Lucy was more inclined to hang back and listen to whatever conversations were within her hearing.

"Of course you are welcome to visit with the guests, but remember that any conversation should be initiated by the guest. If someone asks you a question that you cannot answer, come and get Fred, Jacob, or me to help. Please do not offer information unless you know it is absolutely accurate. And there is something very important to remember: we never, never talk about politics or religion or money." Nana sounded friendly but adamant about this restriction.

"And dinner?" Emma reminded Nana about the rest of her question.

"Oh, yes! We eat dinner with the guests in the dining room. We do not have to sit down with them at the same time. The tables are arranged now for big and smaller groups, but they can be moved to create whatever space we need. We always have two entrées to offer the guests, but when our family eats on those nights in the dining room, we don't get a choice. Cook will fill our serving plates in the kitchen, and we will usually have whatever entrées are left. We open the dining room for guest dinners beginning at five thirty, but Fred and I are used to having dinner at six thirty every evening. Guests are expected to begin their dinner by six thirty, although we can make special arrangements for a later time if they let us know in advance."

"So we should plan to have dinner at six thirty in the dining room with the family on Tuesday through Saturday night. Is that right?" John wanted to know so that he could arrange his practice time.

"Yes, how does that sound to you all?" Nana could sense that there was general agreement to the plan.

When dinner was over, Christina, Emma, and Lucy said that they were in charge of cleanup tonight. They shooed the rest of the family out of the dining room and forbade anyone from entering the kitchen until everything was washed and put away. The kitchen staff would be responsible for preparing dinner, serving, and cleaning up on guest dinner nights. On Sundays and Mondays, the family would prepare dinner and clean up after themselves.

Mariel sat in the parlor near John's piano. The parlor was pleasantly dark except for the light by the piano. The effect made it look as if John was on a stage with the houselights dim. John was working on his Rachmaninoff prelude. Nana listened carefully. She was aware of a new dimension in his playing, and it pleased her. Where did this young man's depth of talent come from? Mariel had pondered this question many times over the past few years, but now she was surer than ever that John was not just gifted. No, that word was inadequate to describe the depth of his potential.

As he grew intellectually and emotionally, his ability to communicate through music grew as well. She listened and was moved. She leaned back into the cushions of the comfortable couch and let herself be drawn into the piece. This was a Rachmaninoff that she had never played, but she could hear the longing and the pathos woven into the piece by the interacting lines and resulting harmonies. Was it Rachmaninoff's music or John's interpretation that touched her? It took a moment for her to realize that John had stopped playing. She turned her head and saw that John had left the bench and was sitting on a couch across from her. Even in the shadows, she saw that he was in a thoughtful mood. She smiled at him.

"Nana, may I ask you some things about the lodge and our family? I'd really like to know, and Mom either didn't want to tell me or she doesn't know everything." John's voice was controlled, but Mariel could hear the eagerness in his question.

"Well, John, I will share what I can without breaking any promises or confidences that may still be relevant. What is it you want to know?"

"Lots of things. I've heard little references all week about different things that have happened, but it's all kind of a jumble. Maybe we can start with last Sunday morning on the boat, you know, when Papa Jacob got so mad? You know, when we were in the boat on our way to church? Was he still so angry over the fire ring? Because if that's it, I don't understand how he could just leave it for all these years. I mean, I went up there today, and it could be a beautiful addition to the lodge."

John stopped for a moment to see if Nana would volunteer any information. When she stayed silent, John continued. "I know the hill was probably beautiful in its natural state, but lots of trees still grow around the ring, and the stumps are long gone. The ring itself is like another world. It's overgrown with plants and flowers. But seriously, the fire ring isn't really the big problem between the sea camp and the lodge, is it?" He looked intently into her face as he spoke.

"You're right, of course." Mariel was quiet for a moment before she continued. "The fire ring was the beginning of the problems here on the island, but the beginning of the trouble between Jacob and Peter was long before that. It started back in Minnesota where both of them spent their early years." Mariel stopped suddenly. She smiled sheepishly at John before she continued. "You know, John, I learned most of this from Sofia. Most likely, she put her own spin on everything to make Jacob the hero. I'm sure there is another interpretation of this early family history. Keep that in mind as you listen to the story."

"I understand, Nana." John leaned forward and looked eagerly into Nana's face. She laughed, then she composed herself. After a few moments, she began to talk.

"Well, Jacob's family lived on a farm, and Peter's family owned most of the small town that was near the farm. The boys were one year apart in age, but they were in class together in their small rural school. Jacob, who had nothing, excelled in everything, academics, sports, farm projects, games, dancing, everything. But he was most gifted in designing and constructing things made of wood. It was like the wood spoke to him. On the other hand, Peter, who had everything, excelled at nothing. Oh, he was good enough in school, he was on a few sports teams, and perhaps he was involved in other activities. But Peter was just kind of average in everything he tried.

"He envied Jacob for his talents, and he feared Jacob for the indifference Jacob showed to the wealth and power that Peter used to control his other schoolmates. I think Jacob thought of Peter as a gnat, annoying but not worth worrying about. When Jacob graduated from high school, he moved to California with only one suitcase and a box of woodworking tools. Before long, he found a job with a furniture company. Soon he was designing custom orders for them. Then it wasn't even a year before he launched out on his own. He met Sofia at Our Lady of Miracles Church, and they married six months later. Her family had recently arrived from Poland. You know the story of the war and the poker game."

"I wondered about that, Nana," John said, "Did things really happen that way? This land, was it really won in a poker game?"

"You know, Fred has told that story so many times, I'm not sure if the tale as Fred tells it is all accurate, but you only have to go into the clubroom here at the lodge to see the Kodiak bear hanging on the wall, and then look at the silver dollar that is mounted over the registration desk in the foyer. It supposedly is the one that Rudy threw into the poker pot."

"When I was really little, I was afraid of the bear rug, but Mom said it was a magic bear that chased away nightmares. After that, it never scared me again." John smiled at the memory.

Mariel smiled too. She remembered how she had told Christina about the magic bear many years ago. Then she exhaled with a loud sigh. She took a few moments to collect her thoughts, then she began to speak again. "After the war, Jacob and his family moved to the island, and the rest is lodge history. What is not so well known is that Peter convinced his father to give him enough money to buy the land next to Jacob here on the island. His plan was to go into business with Jacob. He thought if he owned the oceanfront property and substantial acreage that was contiguous, Jacob would welcome him as a partner. But Jacob had no interest in Peter's plan. If he had been seeking a partner, it would never have been Peter anyway.

"Well, Peter built his sea camp. Ironically, it was successful, not because of Peter, but because of the woman he married. Harriet was a very smart, very shrewd woman from Los Angeles. Hers was the brain behind the plan. They catered to rich families who wanted their children to experience camping. The camp offered a full array of activities. It is really quite lovely there. As years passed, their clientele dwindled, mostly because camps did not appeal so much to the modern family. But Harriet made a wise move when she affiliated with the private and public schools of Southern California to bring groups over to the sea camp for a three-day marine life study camp.

"Now the California Marine Life Adventure Camp is an institution, sort of a rite of passage for many school kids throughout Southern California. If I am remembering correctly from their brochure, the Sorensons run four groups every two weeks during the school year warm months: September, October, April, May, and June. They run a very successful family camp during the month of July. The rest of the time, they rent the campsite and staff to a few church groups and businesses for camping or retreats.

"I think from the very beginning, Jacob felt Peter was interfering with his life. He resented the ease by which Peter got the money and had the camp built. Peter got the message when Jacob continued to refuse invitations to visit or dine at the Sorenson home." Mariel stopped and looked over at John. He was listening intently to every word she said.

"That is the background. You can understand Jacob's resentment of Peter. But the story gets more complex as the two couples begin to have children."

"But I thought Grandpa Fred was an only child." John looked confused.

"Well, Fred was born before they moved to the island. A few years later, Sofia gave birth to Anne Marie. She was a beautiful child. Being a girl living on a remote island, her experiences were limited, and she was very sheltered. Sofia and Jacob did the best they could. One thing they postponed was telling Anne Marie about her body and how it would be changing.

"Anne Marie was young when she started her first period. Sofia hadn't yet explained the facts of life to her. I guess it was quite traumatic. Fred remembers how his sister screamed and cried, convinced that she was dying. Nowadays it seems so easy to explain these things, but poor Anne Marie was an innocent, and her early maturation caught Sofia off guard. Feeling terrible, Sofia made a real effort to explain the rest of the story about sex and babies to Anne Marie. And remember, they had animals on the farm. Fred would agree even now that as farm kids, they knew about birth."

"Did Fred and Anne Marie go to school in Mirabella?" John asked.

"Yes. The school was small because the island had a very small permanent population. Up until the sixties, there were fewer than a thousand people who lived on the whole island. Many didn't have families."

"But didn't schools have those movies, you know, about bodies changing and babies and stuff? We all saw them in the sixth grade." John smiled and added, "The teachers split up the girls and boys so we couldn't watch the movies at the same time."

"I suspect there were no such films here in the fifties. Parents just explained things in their own way and on their own time. Well, as it happened, when Anne Marie was fifteen, life took another unexpected turn. Sofia noticed some physical changes in Anne Marie that could only mean one thing. Anne Marie was pregnant. It seems that Peter Sorenson's second son, eighteen-year-old Phillip, had been secretly meeting Anne Marie. Jacob and Sofia were sure that Phillip had seduced their daughter, but Anne Marie insisted that she loved Phillip. She insisted that he loved her, too, and they planned to marry. Marriage was a good solution, but Phillip had other plans. He left the island before the baby was born. Anne Marie was left to deal with her pregnancy alone.

"Fred said that during that time, the family and the lodge dream almost crumbled. But Jacob somehow directed his anger and resentment into making the lodge the very best vacation spot in all of California. And he did. For many years the lodge was rated first in nearly every listing of California vacation destinations. Even today, it sits at the top or near the top of every rating list.

"Meanwhile, Anne Marie gave birth to a beautiful child, Kara Cecile, and promptly immersed herself in motherhood. She read every book about child rearing, and she discussed the pros and cons of every new theory with Sofia and Jacob. The three of them, Anne Marie, Sofia, and Jacob, served as parents for little Kara Cecile. The child was showered with loving attention. Anne Marie never tried to locate Phillip. In fact, she had convinced herself shortly after the birth that Phillip was not ever worthy to be a part of her life.

"Certainly Kara Cecile was much better off without the influence of an absent father who had run away to escape his fatherly responsibilities. Then right around Kara Cecile's third birthday, Phillip suddenly appeared back on the island at the sea camp. Anne Marie spent many hours preparing the exact words she would use to tell him that he was not welcome to become a part of her life or that of her daughter. You can imagine how insulted and, yes, even embarrassed Anne Marie felt when Phillip made no effort to contact her. Instead, the stories about his escapades with other women in Mirabella gradually made their way down to Eagle Cove and Three Ships.

"Anne Marie had one good and loyal friend, Rebecca, who was the niece of the cook. Rebecca and Anne Marie had played together as children. Before we moved here, we came to visit a couple of times each year. Anne Marie and Rebecca were inseparable. When they were young, they called themselves salt and pepper because Anne Marie was a very fair blue-eyed blonde, and Rebecca was dark haired with big brown eyes.

"Anyway, Rebecca carried several message to Phillip, but he refused to read any letters from Anne Marie. He even turned his back and walked away whenever Rebecca tried to tell him about Kara Cecile. Anne Marie smoldered with a deep resentment for months. Finally, she decided to drive to the sea camp to confront

Phillip. She left the lodge one Tuesday about eight in the morning. Nobody really knows what happened when she first arrived at the camp, but at about nine thirty, some of the kitchen helpers heard a man and a woman shouting at each other.

"Then Anne Marie was seen running to her car, which she had left in the camp service yard. Phillip, who was following close behind, grabbed the passenger door handle, yanked it open, and jumped in. All the while, the two were yelling at each other. Anne Marie fishtailed out of the sea camp yard and headed back toward the lodge.

"The next anyone heard about either of them was a little after twelve noon. Phillip wandered into the sea camp kitchen and said he needed to talk to his father, Peter Sorenson. Peter was in Mirabella and not expected back for several hours. Nobody could get Phillip to say anything, but there seemed to be a general sense that something bad had happened. Eric, Peter's oldest son, finally called Sofia at the lodge and asked if Anne Marie had returned home yet. Jacob and Sofia were already a little worried because she had been gone so long. But when Eric told them about the argument and the car ride, they decided to go out and search for Anne Marie and the car. They alerted the sheriff in Mirabella in case she showed up there.

"But it only took about a half hour to find the car. It was parked carelessly up by the old campfire ring on our hill. The driver's side door was open, but there was no sign of Anne Marie anywhere near the car. They called out her name but heard no response. They searched the area around the fire ring and found nothing. Jacob and Sofia knew how angry Anne Marie had been when she left the house earlier that day. They knew that it would be just like Anne Marie to stomp away in anger, leaving the car and Philip behind. In fact, Sofia told us later that she kept looking up toward the trail leading back to the lodge. She somehow felt sure that Anne Marie would appear on the trail at any moment.

"It wasn't until Jacob spotted evidence of a narrow mudslide near the cliff that he began to feel any sense of alarm. You see, there was that small natural spring that seeps from under the moss and fern grove high above the fire ring. It gradually works its way like an invisible stream under the soil down toward the cliff where it sends a fine misty spray out over the ocean. You remember how beautiful it was when we passed it last Sunday? Anyway, the ground there was very slippery."

Nana stopped for a moment, then sighed and continued. "Now I need to back up a little to explain about Jacob and his original plans for the hill. Well, before Peter Sorenson had ruined the hill with his fire ring project, Jacob had planned to build a pair of small stone walls to enclose the path of the spring as it headed toward the cliff. He wanted to be sure that nobody would accidentally step onto the slippery earth and lose their footing. The cliff is very high there, almost ninety feet, and it is a sheer drop to the rocks below.

"Somehow, that day when they searched for Anne Marie, Jacob knew what he would see if he peered over the cliff. He looked back toward Sofia and shook his head slowly. She knew then what must have happened. Carefully, she walked over and took Jacob's hand. They circled around the slippery earth, always being careful to stay on firm dry ground. They figured that from this vantage point that they might have a clear sight line to the shore below. Neither could look down. Finally, the screech of a gull coming from far below drew their attention, and they gazed downward. There, the bird was gliding in circles above their daughter. Anne Marie lay face down in one of the tide pools close to shore, her blue scarf fluttered like a flag in the breeze.

"After her burial, Jacob did build those little protective walls around the spring. When he finished, he never set foot up there again. Of course he blames himself for not building them earlier, and he especially blames Peter Sorenson for ruining the hill in the first place. Surely it was Peter's fault that resulted in the delay of building the walls."

Mariel leaned back and looked up toward the ceiling. After a few breaths, she continued. "When Phillip was questioned, he told how they had argued in the car as Anne Marie drove up the road toward the lodge. He finally insisted that she stop to let him out. By then, they were close to the old fire ring. The car skidded to a stop, and Phillip got out as Anne Marie stormed out of the driver's side and walked briskly past the fire ring toward the cliff. Suddenly, Phillip heard her scream as she slipped and fell onto the wet grass. She continued to scream for help as she slid down toward the edge, unable to catch anything solid that could stop her.

"Phillip ran to help her, but she was almost fifty feet away. In less than five seconds, she skidded off the cliff. He rushed back east along the cliff line until it dropped low enough for him to reach the shoreline, but once he was at the water's edge, he found that when he tried to follow the rocky shoreline back toward the place where she must have landed, the shore disappeared into the cliff. It was impossible to reach her from that aspect.

"Finally, he said he went back up to the fire ring and sat on a log for a long time, just waiting. For what, we don't know. He finally hiked back to the sea camp to find Peter. At first, the sheriff wanted to arrest Phillip for something, but there was no evidence of a struggle and no unusual physical signs on Phillip. Everyone finally agreed that Phillip's account was truthful."

Mariel stopped talking and looked over at John. She could see the question was there, waiting to be asked. She went ahead and answered without a prompt from him. "I must admit that I truly believe it all happened just as Phillip explained. Deep down, I know that Jacob believes the same."

Chapter Nine

Mariel was deeply immersed in the memories. She took a few moments to collect her thoughts, then she smiled at John and continued her story. "Fred and I moved to the island in 1972. Your mother was six years old, and your uncle Matt was four. Little Kara Cecile was nearly four. The three children played together, and Christina loved her little cousin dearly. By then, Anne Marie had been gone for a while. Christina doesn't have any memory of her at all."

Mariel smiled as she remembered her earliest time on the island. Most of her memories were positive, especially those of the times when her children were young and new to island life. How much they changed and grew with each passing month! Her excursion into a happier branch of past events was short-lived because John, who was anxious to hear the rest of the darker story that paralleled her good memories, asked another question.

"What about Anne Marie's friend? You know, Rebecca. Is she still around here?" John was curious about the loose ends of the story. His grandmother looked thoughtful as she continued her musings.

"Rebecca is still on the island. We really do not stay in touch. At first it was very hard for Jacob to see her because his sad memories came flooding back. But now we see her sometimes at church. She makes it a point to talk to Jacob after Mass, and he is always content to see her. I think his stroke smoothed over some of the terrible memories, and I am thankful for that. But I've been talking for a long time. Does that help you see some of the lingering animosity that Jacob holds for Peter Sorenson and his sea camp?"

John was silent for a moment. He shook his head then leaned forward and rested his forehead on his hands. Finally he sat up and looked at his grandmother as he began to speak. "I guess my little part of the family doesn't have a monopoly on bad stuff," John said. "Now I think I understand why Papa Jacob acted the way he did." John knew there was more to know, but he sensed from Nana Mariel's body language that it was hard for her to talk about the sad events of the past.

"You're right, John, although your loss is more recent. Healing is a long process, and there are no shortcuts in grieving." Mariel looked at her grandson. She hadn't noticed how handsome he was becoming as he grew up. For the past few years he was all arms and legs, and his face was thin and angular. Now that he was filling out, he didn't have that gawky look any longer. His face was really quite attractive, a lot like Fred when he was young.

The older son, Paul, had always been considered the handsome one, and John was the smart one. Perhaps John was destined to be both. Until just a few days ago, Mariel had thought that John was overly serious, even dour. Now that she had worked with him and talked about many things, she saw him in a new way. He was serious, certainly, but equally sensitive and kind. She knew that she would learn more about him each week. John and Mariel continued to sit comfortably together in the darkened room, each awash in private thoughts.

Mariel looked toward her grandson. He was staring through the dark window, obviously lost in thought. Mariel sensed that John was thinking about his immediate family and the troubles they had faced in the past two years. Christina had called so many times, often late at night and evidently after several glasses of wine. Mariel tried to stay supportive and positive while Christina would rant on about her life. Since the tragedy—that sudden, terrible accident that claimed their firstborn son, Paul—a dark sadness had draped over the Garrett family in Sierra Glen like a heavy quilt. It changed the dynamics in the home, of that Mariel was certain. She remembered how she believed that Daniel and Christina were a solid match from their first meeting at a freshman orientation at USC.

Their twenty-year marriage before the accident was strong and happy. The days were filled with affection, love, humor, shared responsibilities, and shared goals. But the accident caught them unprepared. Daniel especially could not reconcile the terrible loss with the daily demands of living. As time passed, he became more intolerant and angry with the remaining members of his family. He hated that he could not shed the awful depression that threatened to consume him and destroy whatever chance of happiness was left for him.

Ever since that awful day two years ago, Mariel often thought of the impossible situation Daniel had to confront. If his story had been a work of fiction, there would have been a dramatic turn of events at the last minute, and Daniel would have risen to the occasion to save the day. But real life allows that failure is just as likely an outcome. And Daniel failed. He tried, but his best effort was not good enough. Now he lived with the results of his failed efforts. Mariel knew about the demons that hold the soul captive after such a tragedy. The demons laugh at platitudes offered to comfort: "You did your best," "There was nothing more you could have done," "It was out of your control." And all the while the demons whisper, "But you know you could have done better."

Oh, we are so vulnerable to terrible sadness and disappointment when we become parents, Mariel mused to herself. As a parent and grandparent, she did not want to even imagine having to make a decision that would determine a child's fate. How in the world could time progress or normal life continue after being forced to deal with such a catastrophe? She continued to consider how she might feel if she had been responsible for choosing a critical course of action then see it fail. Mariel thought about poor Jacob and Sofia, who never really knew what had happened to their daughter.

It took years to overcome the guilt they felt because they did not go searching for her earlier. But at least they faced the tragic experience together. Christina and Daniel were coping with their own individual sets of emotions. Mariel felt Daniel had grown a special pouch right next to his heart. The pouch was stuffed with remorse, guilt, anger, and resentment mixed with an unending supply of sadness. Conversely, Mariel imagined her daughter was clinging to a different set of jumbled feelings.

Christina seemed to keep a supply of dark, smoldering anger inside her that erupted when she was stressed or tired. But the thing that troubled Mariel most was how Christina was consumed by the need to blame someone for her terrible loss. It saddened Mariel to realize that Christina ultimately placed equal blame on both Daniel and God.

John and Mariel sat in silence. The day had faded completely from the sky outside. Without the final vestiges of daylight streaming through the wide windows, the shadows inside the lodge deepened to dark velvet. John flipped his phone display. It was ten o'clock. He leaned over to switch on a lamp that sat on the end table. The diffused light warmed a small area around where they were sitting.

"I know it's getting late, but I wonder about the baby, Kara Cecile? Did she grow up and leave the island?" John started thinking about the story that Nana had shared with him. "You know, it is really amazing to me that I had these relatives once upon a time, and I never knew it until a few minutes ago."

"I've been sitting here thinking about the various sad events in our family history, and it seems that we have had more than our share." Mariel smiled to herself. "But I also realize that every family has good and bad things happen. I don't think we are unique in that regard."

"But does knowing others are suffering make our suffering any easier?" John mulled that one over, even as he spoke. "Think about the saying 'Misery loves company.' Is it true? I don't know, but maybe it depends on the degree of misery."

John stopped talking for a moment. Then he asked, "Nana, could you finish the story? I'd really like to know the rest if you feel like telling me now, or if you want to wait until another time, I'll understand." John sat on the edge of his couch and looked at Mariel expectantly. It made her smile to see his precious face looking eagerly toward her.

"All right, Johnny. I'll tell you the rest, but I must warn you that I may need to backtrack sometimes. I haven't thought about those days for a long time." Mariel also leaned forward so that the two of them were facing each other across the coffee table.

"Hmm, where was I?" Mariel tried to think of the best way to tell all that happened. She took a big breath and let it out slowly. Then she began to speak once more.

"Well, after the loss of Anne Marie, little Kara Cecile became the responsibility of Sofia and Jacob. We all adored her. Christina was her heroine. Kara Cecile was a very pretty little girl. With each passing year, she became more beautiful. At fifteen she was tall and slender, with thick blonde hair that she pulled back, sometimes with barrettes or maybe in a braid or ponytail. She had the same little wispy, blonde strands around her hairline that Sofia and Anne Marie had, and those little tendrils were always blowing in her face.

"But the thing I remember most about her is how her voice sounded so happy. I can still hear her laughter. She was full of fun, and she saw life as a wonderful adventure. You would never guess she had shadows in her past. Even though her mother lived in the same house with her in the early years of her life, she considered Sofia her real mother. For years, her paternal genealogy was kept vague. I believe that when Kara Cecile finally asked about her father, Jacob and Sofia simply told her that her father had left the island years ago." Mariel felt a tiny chill wash over her, and it made her shiver. She stopped talking for a moment.

"Are you okay, Nana?" John asked. "Do you want to stop now? We can wait till another time if you 'd like." John was worried that he was taking advantage of his grandmother's good nature, but he was fascinated with the story she was telling him.

"No, I'm fine, Johnny. It actually feels good to talk about this. We've kept too many things secret in this family. There was a reason I stopped talking a minute ago. I started to feel the pull of the cosmos," Mariel said with an inflated sense of drama, then she laughed. "Well, what I mean is that sometimes it just seems that everything we say and do is for a reason. It's like the randomness of the million little events that occur around us each day happen to cause certain outcomes in our lives, so when we look at the overall picture, we ask ourselves if the events were really random in the first place.

"Sometimes I think there is a master plan that controls every tiny nanosecond in our lives. I used to think that somehow our family was being tested. In the Bible, Job's faith was challenged over and over." Mariel shifted in her chair and sighed. It was several seconds before she spoke again. "Oh, I don't mean to imply that Jacob is like Job, but it is hard to ignore the similarities in their lives. Well, the next chapter of our family history is very painful to think about. It is the time when the persona of tragedy with a capital *T* came to visit, stayed too long, then fled the scene, carrying away the hearts of Jacob and Fred in a satchel. I had to give them plenty of time and space, and plenty of nurturing, as well. I fed them, I took over most Lodge responsibilities, I cried with them, and I wrapped them in all the love I had to give. It took a long time for me to bargain for the return of those hearts, and I had to work hard, but a sense of equilibrium was restored. Thankfully, Fred sees the good and bad as part of life, and he chooses to dwell in the land of good. Jacob has not been so fortunate. Generally speaking, the happiness we had all held so casually before the big event has never been recaptured, that is, until now since your family arrived. I truly feel that there is hope for our family after all, and I sense that you feel the same way."

"I do, Nana, especially about my dad." John looked away as he continued to talk. "He seems happier here, and he and Mom seem happier with each other too. Maybe there is a chance for them after all. But what about the tragedy with a capital *T*?"

"Yes, this is where it gets hard. It was late September, and Kara Cecile's seventeenth birthday was coming up in just a few weeks. She had always wanted to go to a real Broadway musical, but it is very difficult to arrange something like that from the island, especially when we have so few consecutive free days here at the lodge. Jacob and Sofia decided that Sofia would take Kara Cecile up to the Curran Theater in San Francisco to see *The Man of La Mancha.* On her birthday, a Tuesday, they took the early morning ferry from Mirabella to Long Beach and hired a taxi to Los Angeles International where they caught a flight to San Francisco. It was the first time Kara Cecile had been on a plane.

"They stayed at the Inn at the Opera, an exquisite little boutique hotel near the civic center. They dressed up for dinner, took a taxi to the theater. They loved the show. Afterward, they went out for dessert. All was quite posh and elegant. They called the next morning to tell us how much fun everything had been. I remember it was such a delight living vicariously through the phone lines. They were going to do some shopping before their flight back to Los Angeles. Their flight back was delayed about forty minutes.

"Because they had purchased some large items, they had to check a couple of pieces through the checked baggage service. Well, by the time they arrived in Los Angeles and claimed their luggage, it was almost 3:30 p.m. It took a few minutes to get a taxi, and time was getting tight. They had reservations on the last ferry of the day. It was scheduled to leave the Long Beach dock at 4:30 p.m. They got stuck in the afternoon commuter traffic. The San Diego Freeway was like a parking lot. And it was soon obvious to both of them that they would be late for the ferry." Mariel shook her head and sighed deeply.

"Now we come to the land of 'what if' or 'if only' where we second-guess every decision and still don't understand why things happen the way they do. It is the controlling element of the cosmos. Sometimes, I believe that free will is a myth. What happened next required the whole set of factors to follow a prescribed course, from the delayed plane and the heavy traffic to the open seat on the seaplane to the failure to call home before booking the flight, and so on and so on. Kara Cecile was anxious to get home because she had to finish her big biology project that was due at school the next morning. An excellent student, Kara Cecile had just missed two days of school, and she was worried about missing any more. Sofia understood how important it was to get home that evening, so she had the taxi driver head directly to the Long Beach Airport. It was already after 4:30. They rushed up to the Channel Seaplane Service window and found that there was one seat open on the final flight that left at 4:55 p. m. Without any hesitation at all, Sofia booked the seat for Kara Cecile. The seaplane would arrive in Mirabella at 5:05, about forty minutes earlier than the ferry was due to arrive. Kara Cecile could just wait at the harbor landing until Fred arrived to pick her up. Sofia would stay in a hotel in Long Beach and then take the 9:00 a. m. ferry back to the island. A very grateful Kara Cecile gave Sofia a ferocious hug then rushed out to the tarmac where the seaplane was waiting. Five minutes later, it was taxiing out to the runway.

" When Sofia booked the seaplane flight, she did not know that the Channel Seaplane Service was in trouble financially, necessitating cost cutting in every way. She didn't know that the planes were built decades ago, or that the planes flew with one pilot instead of two. She didn't know that there had been ongoing criticism about the maintenance of the various planes in the fleet. These were prewar planes that had no replacements parts being manufactured. The planes had duct tape sealing leaks in the pontoons. And finally, Sofia did not know that the planes landed in a section of ocean where floating kelp often covered the surface.

"It was the day after Kara Cecile's birthday. That day was the day the left pontoon came loose upon landing, got tangled in the thick kelp, and caused the bulky plane to flip end over end twice before it sank in the shallow water. That was the day that five passengers and the sole pilot lost their lives in a terrible crash that was witnessed by hundreds of people."

Mariel stopped speaking. She sighed once more and wiped tears from her eyes. She continued to speak. "And those who died perished slowly—terrified, unable to escape, and aware of each second that passed until finally, the water filled their lungs, and each of them slowly drowned. And then, visible through the plane windows were the boaters hurrying to assist but too slow to help. That was the last thing the victims saw. That was the last day of scheduled seaplane service to Santa Teresa Island. And that was the day that changed our family forever."

When Mariel stopped speaking, she had tears running freely down her cheeks. When she looked over at John, she saw that his face was also streaked with tears. John and Mariel rose from the couches. They walked toward the family wing. Neither felt like talking. Both were deep in thought. When they reached their rooms, John turned to his grandmother and gave her a warm hug. He said nothing. She hugged him back and spoke to him quietly.

"John, I am so thankful that your family chose to join us here at the lodge. You and the girls bring such spunk and spirit to us all. I know that KC's spirit is somewhere near, and she is filled with happiness. You would have loved her. Good night, dear child of my child."

But John could not speak. His mind was whirling with what he just heard. Finally, he opened his mouth and willed himself to ask her what she meant. "Casey?" That was the only word that escaped his lips.

"Oh, that's what we often called Kara Cecile, you know initials, KC. She thought it was easier than Kara Cecile for people to remember. Well, I'll see you in the morning. Tomorrow morning, the piano still belongs to you. Sleep well." As she walked toward her room, she blew him a kiss.

Chapter Ten

John was reeling. Casey or KC. What was going on? John wondered how his brain could concoct a girl who was obviously fashioned after someone who lived in this house thirty years ago, someone he had never heard of or knew existed until a short while ago. How could he possibly know? Was her spirit somehow entering his subconscious? He rejected that idea as soon as it flashed through his mind. He did not believe in supernatural phenomena. There must be a clue somewhere. Perhaps he heard his parents talking sometime, and it didn't penetrate his consciousness.

He brushed his teeth, stripped down to his boxers, flipped off the overhead light, and climbed into bed. He turned over to stare out the window. He was confused. He yawned then sighed slowly. His eyelids felt heavy. He was drifting from the real world into the place of dreams when suddenly he sat up. His heart was racing, and he felt a sudden wave of nausea tear through him. He wanted to purge everything from his system. He felt sick!

It had just dawned on him that in all likelihood, assuming his Casey was some sort of reincarnation of Kara Cecile, he had kissed his mother's cousin and enjoyed it! Worse even than that, he got turned on by a dream image of his mother's cousin. His mind brought up an image of his father's cousin LeeAnn, who was at least fifty years old and nearly two hundred pounds. How about her, Johnny boy? Want to get it on with her too? He couldn't control his imagination as it got more and more graphic. If he didn't feel so slimy, he would be laughing hysterically. Maybe it was for the best that his Casey was a figment of his imagination.

But what had Nana said about how she thought things happened for a reason? John tried to think of all that had happened in his life since he moved to the island. Which random events could have contributed to the formation of Casey? What had he done or what had he seen that could have introduced some suggestion of a beautiful girl from his ancestry? He turned over on his back and started retracing all the things he did since arriving on the island. Suddenly he remembered something from last week that might shed some light on the mystery.

He reached over and turned on his desk lamp. He looked at all the built-in cupboards and drawers and the small hanging closet that filled the entire wall across from his bed. It had taken him hours last Friday to clean everything out of the storage areas so he could have room for his own stuff. There had been paper bags, Christmas wrap, envelopes, nails, screws, newspapers, school papers, random junk, and many photos. Where were those papers and pictures? When he was cleaning everything out, he remembered putting all the papers and photos in a big shoe box.

He climbed out of bed and started opening drawers. He looked under the bed, under and on top of his desk, and in the small single-bar clothes closet. He could not find the box. Sitting on the bed, he closed his eyes and tried to relax himself back to the moment he put the lid on the box and placed it somewhere out of the way, yet safe from being thrown out by mistake. At least he had the presence of mind to put the box aside in a safe place for someone else to sort and cull. John felt that anything important enough to save for years and years should have a second look before discarding.

He went into his little bathroom and checked under the sink and in the two large drawers in the cabinet. The box was nowhere in his room, at least not where he could find it. He flopped back onto his bed in disgust, thinking to himself that if he had this much trouble remembering things when he's seventeen, what'll happen when he's seventy? He closed his eyes and tried to picture what the box looked like. Just a standard shoe box, kind of brown or tan, with stripes around the long way, irregular stripes all the way around.

He jumped out of bed again and went to the big bookcase by his desk. He had packed his music in it along with his large collection of reference books. He had already searched for the box here, but then he was looking for a box. Now he was looking for a box that was imitating a few thick books. There it was—right in the center in plain sight! The stripes disguised it enough to resemble four thick books, so he missed it when he searched.

Hey, hiding in plain sight. I'll have to remember that if I ever need to keep something secret, he thought to himself. *Kind of like the Poe story of "The Purloined Letter."* He sat on his bed and took the lid off the box. There were things stuffed in it, not very carefully, but at least it was all there. He dumped it out onto the blanket and began to search. He separated all the postcards and letters out and put them on the corner of his nightstand. He wanted to read all of them soon, but right now he was searching for pictures. There were many photos that had faded over time, plus several were torn or bent.

He picked up each and looked for clues about the family. He recognized just a few of the people. He thought there were a few candid shots of Nana and Grandpa Fred, but they were much younger. There were lots of pictures of the lodge with unfamiliar people in groups posing and making happy, silly faces. They were probably guests. He was disappointed to find nothing in any of the photos that helped him understand anything more clearly than he did before he looked at them.

He stood up, stretched up toward the ceiling, then sat back down and attacked the newspaper clippings. First, he pulled out articles without pictures and stacked them in the lid of the box. Then he started on the newsprint pictures. There were over a dozen that featured some aspect of the lodge building and surrounding property. There was a pictorial spread that featured the animals of Eagle Cove Lodge and Family Farm.

The largest picture showed Milton the Mule sitting down next to Nana Mariel and eating a carrot from her hand. John stopped for a moment to figure out how old Milt was. The caption under the picture said, "Mariel Engstrom rewards three-year-old Milton the Mule with a carrot." The date on the corner of the page said 1978. After a little figuring, John determined that Milt was about thirty-three years old now. "How long is a mule supposed to live?" he wondered.

There were many pictures from various newspapers all around the state and even from Arizona and Nevada that depicted groups of visitors enjoying the lodge and its activities. The dates on these varied from the 1960s through the mid-1980s. Apparently, guests sent in pictures from their hometown papers. Many of these made John smile. The quality of the writing varied widely. John snorted out loud when he read the caption from a central California weekly that said, "The Lambert girls, decked out in their Easter finery, celebrate the holiday at beautiful Eagle Cove Lodge on Santa Teresa Island." The picture above the caption featured Milton, two teenage girls, and a cow all posing happily on the front lawn of the lodge, all four proudly wearing their Easter bonnets.

John was getting tired of staring into the grainy reproductions of fleeting fun from the past. Nothing so far had triggered any idea of his current dilemma—where did his Casey come from?—and he was about to give up. Without much thought, he picked up a smaller piece of paper that looked more like something from school. Sure enough, it was a Santa Teresa High School newspaper that most likely had been partially reproduced by using a stencil and a revolving drum. Leafing through it, he suddenly stopped and stared at the fifth page. There in the center of the page was a picture of Casey standing with a few other girls. The caption said they were decorating a float for homecoming. The date in the corner was 1983.

John gasped and put the paper down quickly as he looked up and then all around his room. He had felt a chill when he saw the picture, and now he was shivering as if the temperature in his room had dropped twenty degrees. How could this be? Was it really Casey? He read the caption under the picture. "Ninth grade girls decorate the freshman float for the parade on Saturday. (From left to right: Annie Shaw, Carol Rogers, Mary Beth Darrow, Kara Cecile Engstrom, Patty Jenkins, Carolyn Peterson)."

John stared at the picture. The fourth girl from the left certainly looked like Casey. Since this picture was of a freshman girl, John did some quick figuring. That would make them fourteen or fifteen years old. His Casey seemed older than that, probably closer to his own age. John decided to continue looking through the remainder of the pictures. He put the school newspaper up on his pillow so it wouldn't get misplaced. He looked through every remaining newspaper carefully. There was nothing more about Casey that he could find until he picked up the last paper. It was the metro section of the Long Beach daily paper.

When he turned to the final page, he saw it. There was the solution to the mystery. He stared at the picture that was at the center of it all. On the top of the page from October 10, 1986, was a feature called Afterthought. Apparently, it was a daily feature that showed an eye-catching picture with a small commentary under it. Today's picture showed two girls laughing. Both had blonde hair styled the same way, and they wore identical outfits. They looked remarkably alike. Underneath, the caption read, "Santa Teresa Island twins? Look again. These Santa Teresa Island residents, students at Santa Teresa High School, admitted their real identities are Casey Engstrom and Carolyn Peterson, and they are just trying out their plans to dress up as twins for Halloween."

John remembered when he was putting papers away last Friday night, he actually saw this picture and thought, *Hmm, cute girls.* Then he had folded it and put it in the box along with the other papers and promptly packed the memory of it away as well. Looking back, he now figured that the reporter who snapped the shot asked the girls their names. That would account for the discrepancy in spelling: Casey vs. KC. He looked back at the school newspaper and studied the faces of Kara Cecile and Carolyn Peterson. There was a strong resemblance even when they were not trying to dress and look alike. He would have to ask Nana about the Peterson girl.

At least now he was sure that his Casey was truly a dream girl in the most literal sense of the word. John stacked the papers, letters, and photos altogether in the box, turned off his light, and closed his eyes. Disappointed as he was to learn for certain that Casey was just a very realistic creation of his subconscious, he figured he hadn't seen the last of her. After all, he had to sleep sometime, so why shouldn't he expect to see her again in his dreams? As he drifted farther away from a waking state, he grew more certain that he would see Casey again, and soon.

Chapter Eleven

John woke up abruptly. He could tell it was still very early by the angle of the sunbeams that streamed through the window. Last night, he had fallen asleep almost immediately after his discovery of the two girls in the newspaper photo. He couldn't remember any dreams at all. He hurried through his shower, then he rushed out to collect the eggs. John's hair was still damp, and the morning air felt cool. He wondered briefly when the summer weather would give way to autumn. He had always lived in a climate with four distinct seasons, and he wasn't sure what weather to expect on this Southern California island. So far, each day seemed like the last—perfect: clear skies, warm light winds, average humidity, very few bugs.

John took the eggs in through the service porch and wiped them clean. He packed them in the egg boxes and put them in the cooler. He didn't hear anyone moving around in the lodge yet. He wandered into the kitchen and found a container with Cheerios. Slicing a banana on the cereal, he poured milk on it then grabbed a big slice of leftover pepperoni pizza from the fridge. He sat at the big table and ate quickly. There was nothing to read and nobody to talk to, so John felt a little at loose ends.

He sighed and made short work of the food, then cleaned and put away his dishes. He glanced at the kitchen clock—7:00 a.m. Why did he get up so early? He couldn't practice for two more hours. He had no school projects yet, although he could always start reading one of the books from his great books list for college. That idea floated in and immediately out of his brain. There was time enough for school beginning next week.

He heard scratching at the service porch door. Rocky! John thought a walk would be perfect this morning. He and Rocky could head in the other direction, away from the fire ring, toward the isthmus of the island. At that point, the land on either side of the island curved toward the center until only about three-quarters of a mile of land separated the leeward and the windward sides of the island.

Everyone talked about how beautiful the windward side was, especially at the isthmus curve. There the waves crashed against a wide sandy beach, perfect for board and body surfing. John thought there were sure to be surfers out at this hour. It would be fun to watch them. He grabbed his shoes from the shoe basket on the porch and opened the door.

"Good boy, Rocky, wait! We'll go for a walk in just a second!" John said as he filled a water bottle from the service porch sink. Soon John and Rocky were on their way west toward the isthmus. The sun was warm on John's back as his long shadow led the way.

It took less than thirty minutes at a brisk pace to reach the summit overlooking both sides of the island. The view was breathtaking. On the leeward side, there were three huge rocky crags protruding from the water far out in the natural bay. At dusk and dawn, they resembled old galleons approaching land. The wide inlet was aptly called Three Ships Bay. The tiny colony of shops, homes, and eateries that had appeared gradually over the years on the lee side of the isthmus was simply called Three Ships.

It was only about a fifteen-minute drive from Three Ships to the lodge, but part of the road was unpaved and very steep. Grandpa Fred had told them about how someone at the lodge would have to make an occasional emergency trip down to Three Ships for supplies, usually to satisfy a guest's craving for ice cream, but if the craving set in after dark, the poor guest had to wait for the next day.

This morning, the sun glistened on the calm surface of the bay. Out in the channel, John saw a huge boil on the water surface indicating a large school of small fish—sardines, anchovies, or other bait—that were fleeing in a wild frenzy from some sort of predators. Sure enough, as John watched the ruffled water, he saw several dolphins in pursuit. The dolphins were surfacing and fishing for food, demonstrating nature's food chain. Thanks to Grandpa Fred, John understood that when the dolphin were fishing on the surface, great schools of tuna were likely to be found below the baitfish eating their fill from underneath the traveling supply of food.

John and Rocky looked down the steep dirt road that linked the western end of the Island Summit Road to the narrow paved Isthmus Pass Road. The IPR connected the Pacific Ocean to itself straight across the narrow isthmus. From the aspect of the summit overlook where he was standing, John could see the vastly different character of the water on either side of the island. The ocean on the lee side looked as if an artist had used a brush to paint the ocean from shore and beyond in multiple shades of brilliant blue: sparkling turquoise, shimmering teal, and deep midnight. On the windward side, the water was a wild froth of white translucent foam from shore to beyond the surf line.

The official name on the maps for this stretch of beach was Whistling Wind Beach, but no island native ever used that silly title. Islanders, along with everyone else who knew better, simply called the beach Surfside. There was no easy water access to this beach except by private boat around the west end of the island. Most visitors just walked from Three Ships across the narrow strip of land on the IPR. Guests of Eagle Cove Lodge could either hike directly to Surfside as John had done, or they could arrange to catch a ride to Three Ships then walk across. Islanders who surfed could keep their boards in a shed above the berm of the beach. Stretching out above the beach in both directions was a wide grassy meadow with native trees growing here and there.

A small fire ring with logs placed around the ring for seating had been built about five years before by the Island Lions Club. The service club had placed the ring where the beach met the plateau of grass and trees. The men also provided the area with a few large picnic tables. An eco-friendly restroom facility was built above the berm on the eastern end of the beach. The beach still maintained a rustic and natural look. There were several teams of volunteers who kept the beach and its surroundings safe and clean.

Most of the residents on the West End felt this was a better solution than paying a tax surcharge for a permanent maintenance crew. On their assigned cleanup day every three months, the Eagle Cove owners and as many staffers who wished to join in went to Surfside for the day with big plastic sacks, rakes, clippers, rags, and various other cleaning supplies. It took about three hours to finish the entire project; everything was immaculate when they left in the afternoon.

John and Rocky hiked down the steep road and turned left toward the sandy beach. When he arrived, he slipped his shoes off. The sand already felt warm on his feet. He saw that farther down the beach toward the west was a natural outcropping of rocks forming a low jetty that extended about forty feet out into the water. He headed toward the jetty. Rocky bounded ahead. There were many beach pebbles and rocks at the foot of the jetty. Rocky found a nice round rock. He picked it up in his teeth, carried it over, and dropped it at John's feet. Then Rocky sat expectantly.

"Okay, Rocky. A few times, and that'll be all." John threw the rock along the waterline. Rocky bounded after it and brought it back immediately. John looked out in the water and saw four surfers sitting on their boards. They were crowded together with boards pointed toward the middle of their circle, and they seemed to be deep in conversation. John watched them. The waves seemed perfect for surfing. John wondered why the surfers weren't grabbing every ride. Meanwhile, Rocky waited impatiently for John to continue their game together.

John picked up the rock and tossed it again. Soon he and Rocky were immersed in the endless game. Not for the first time, John wondered just how long Rocky could keep it up. John had to be honest with himself; he had always been first to quit when he and Rocky played. John secretly suspected Rocky would play forever. His mom said playing fetch with a dog is like playing peekaboo with a baby. The baby never stopped the game first. Sure enough, when John saw parents and babies play that game, it was always the adults who made some excuse for stopping.

Continuing to toss the rock, John noticed that two of the surfers were turned to catch a wave. Rocky ran to retrieve the rock at the far end of the beach. He grabbed it and ran back to John and sat without dropping the rock. He watched the boys on the boards as they skimmed along, propelled by the power of the wave. As they grew closer, Rocky began to whimper. He dropped the rock then plopped onto John's feet and covered his head with his paws.

"Well, this is a first, Rocky. I was just thinking how you never quit our game. What's the matter?" The surfers hopped off their boards and unfastened their bungees. They carried their boards up toward John, then put them down in the sand. They looked over at John and Rocky and smiled.

"Hey, nice dog. What's his name?" The surfer who spoke looked about John's age. The other was younger.

"This is Rocky. Something spooked him. He's usually slobbering dog kisses all over a new person. Actually, I think you're lucky." Rocky had perked up a little when he heard his name, but he didn't budge from John's feet.

"What brings you here? It's pretty early in the day for a visitor."

"Yeah, I live at Eagle Cove Lodge. We just moved in with our family about a week ago. I'm John Garrett." John was glad to be talking to someone his age.

"Oh, yeah. I heard there were going to be more of you. I'm Sam Peterson. Good to meet you."

Just then, Rocky began to bark. He jumped up off John's feet and ran to the water's edge. He barked wildly, then he dashed into the water and out again. He made a horrible racket. The surfers who were outside the surf line looked toward shore. They waved. Rocky continued to bark and carry on. John, Sam, and the other boy got up and walked toward the barking dog. By now, Rocky was in a frenzy. John tried to calm him, but Rocky continued to run in and out of the water, barking continuously. Suddenly, Sam pointed to a spot out beyond the two surfers. There was something near the horizon. Sam waved frantically at the two on the boards.

"Come in! Shark! Shark!" He waved them in, pointing behind them. Soon John and the other boy were yelling as well. The two on the boards, realizing something was wrong, headed toward the surf line and prepared to catch a wave in. They had no idea what the problem was, but both could see that everyone ashore, including the big black dog, seemed anxious about something. A small wave was forming, and both surfers were about to pass it up for the next one when the smaller surfer caught a glimpse of something very big and very close. He started paddling frantically. He had to catch this wave.

"Shark! Ian, shark! Get in now!" With that, the two paddled as never before. They caught the small wave and prayed it would propel them all the way into shore. They did not dare look back for fear of turning out of the little swell that was already threatening to disappear. They saw the figures on the shore become larger and clearer with each second that passed. The black dog continued to bark and dash in and out of the water.

As soon as the surfers reached waist-deep water, the dog paddled out to them and began to herd them into shore and safety. When they were standing on the solid ground, Rocky continued to circle them and sniff them. He nuzzled each of them even as he grumbled and growled in a scolding manner under his breath. Finally satisfied that everyone was safe, he turned three circles, plopped down, yawned widely, and promptly fell asleep.

"Did you see the size of that monster?" The boys were all talking at once. "I can't believe that it was so close! Lucky that the dog sensed the danger. How did he know?" Everyone was giving Rocky lots of attention, most of which he slept right through.

The boys were Sam and Ian, Monty and Mark. John learned they were all some combination of brother and cousin, but he wasn't sure who was which. They were from the Sorenson Sea Camp. John tried to act casual when he heard the camp name.

"Oh, Sam, did you say your last name was Peterson? Are you related in any way to Carolyn Peterson?" John asked.

"Yeah, she's my aunt. Her name is Carolyn Anderson now." Sam pointed over to Ian and Mark, who were putting all of the boards in the storage shed. "She's their mom. Why do you ask?"

"Well, when I was cleaning out the old cupboards in my room so I could put away my stuff, I found some old pictures and newspapers. I saw some with my second cousin and Carolyn Peterson together. The name just stuck in my mind, I guess."

"Oh. You must mean Kara Cecile. Yeah, Aunt Carolyn had lots of pictures of them together. We have one picture from when they were planning to dress up like twins for Halloween. They looked identical. That was just before, you know, before the crash."

"I think we have that one too. That's what caught my eye, I think." John checked the time on his cell phone. It was almost nine. "Oh no, I've gotta get home right away. I didn't know it was so late. They're all probably really worried. I didn't even leave a note. Do you know if there's phone reception out here?" John felt like he was sinking into another stew pot that was simmering to feed Dad's wrath.

"Why don't you come with us?" Monty volunteered. "Our van is parked just past the meadow. We drive right by the back of your orchard on the way home. You'll be home in ten or fifteen minutes."

"Good idea," Sam added. "And the answer about the phone reception is yes. You can call from here usually, well, unless you have some odd server or something. I'll go tell the others that we're in a hurry." Sam turned to get Mark and Ian.

"Come on, the van is this way." Monty started walking up through the meadow toward the small parking turnout at the end of the IPR. John and Rocky followed along. The other boys were on a diagonal path that would intersect with theirs in another fifty yards. Rocky was happy to be moving again. He ran back and forth between the two groups of boys. When they merged, he ran ahead and returned so many times that John figured Rocky had probably completed a five-mile hike by the time they reached the car.

John had called the lodge phone and left a message that he was out walking with Rocky and would be home soon. He mentioned that he left over two dozen eggs in the cooler. Ian got in the driver's seat and Monty sat in the front passenger seat. Sam, John, Mark, and Rocky crowded in the back. Before Ian started the car, Rocky jumped over to the front seat and sat on Monty's lap.

John said, "I forgot to tell you, Rocky likes to ride shotgun. He thinks it belongs to him, but he doesn't mind sharing. I hope that's okay." Everyone laughed and called Rocky the hero of the day. The mood was festive as they relived the shark tale. With each telling, the shark was bigger and closer, and Rocky ventured farther and farther out to warn them. Ian was a careful driver, and the trip on the steep dirt road up from the isthmus was uneventful. They reached the western end of the Island Summit Road, a two-lane road paved with slurry that meandered down the center of the island all the way past Mirabella. As they were nearing the lodge orchard that abutted the ISR, Sam turned to John.

"Say, John, I hear you're really good on the piano. You ought to come over and play ours sometime. Nobody plays it except for camp kids who play chopsticks. Oh, once in a while there's a kid who plays real music, but mostly the piano just sits in the dining hall and gathers dust."

"Yeah, I play. How did you know? I'd like to come over sometime. Maybe you all can come over to the lodge sometime too." John was curious about who could have said anything about him.

"I don't know where I heard it, maybe from the rug cleaners who work at both our places. Anyway, here's your orchard. Thanks again for having a great dog."

Mark got out so John could climb out of the backseat. Monty opened the front door for Rocky. The dog jumped out, then turned around and sat. Ian leaned over and talked to John through the open door.

"I don't know who will be in charge of getting the Baldwin girls down to the camp for the dance this Saturday, but maybe you could drive them and stay. It's a blast every year."

Ian spoke as if John knew all about the Baldwin girls. When John looked confused, Ian clarified. "Maybe you don't know about the Baldwins. They stay at your lodge every year for a family get-together. We met the girls last summer, and we stayed in touch during the year. Anyway, they are planning to come to the dance. You'll probably hear all about it when they get to the island tomorrow. So maybe we'll see you on Saturday."

"Yeah, see you Saturday, and thanks again for saving our lives!" Monty laughed and leaned down to scratch Rocky's ears. "See ya, boy!"

He sat up and shut the car door just as Ian started the car. John waved and headed off through the orchard toward the lodge. He was anxious to use this time to practice on his piano before the bridge bunch arrived. As he walked, he wondered how his family was going to react to the news about the Baldwin girls. Papa Jacob was a firm believer in doing everything possible to please the guests.

John knew that it would be tough for Jacob to accept that some of his loyal lodge people would even want to travel into enemy territory, but he would accept it all the same. The question in John's mind was how would the girls get over there to the dance? John fully intended to tell Nana Mariel about his adventure at Surfside. She would know the best way to share the information with Papa Jacob. John was still deep in thought when he opened the herb garden gate.

CHAPTER TWELVE

John was deeply immersed in his music when Nana came to interrupt him. She waited until there was a natural break in his train of thoughts. She tapped his arm and mentioned that it was almost noon. Fred and Daniel left the lodge over an hour ago in the *LaZBoat*. They had gone down to Mirabella to pick up the twelve ladies, and they would be arriving anytime now. Nana gently suggested that maybe John would like to go to his room and get cleaned up. After his morning adventure and then over two hours of practicing, he was spent, both mentally and physically.

He told Nana that sometime soon he would like to talk with her, but right now he'd better get organized for guests. He went to his room and showered again. He brushed his teeth then shaved off the stubby whiskers that were beginning to appear with more regularity. He found that once a week was not often enough any longer if he wanted to look neat. He could only get by skipping one day now, two at the very most. He wondered when he'd have to shave every morning.

As he pondered all of this, he dressed in a white polo shirt and tan shorts that were cut long as was the style. After combing his hair carefully, he checked himself in the long mirror in the hall outside his bedroom. His hair had a lot more blonde highlights from being out in the sun and ocean air for just these past few days. Even with sunscreen that he put on daily, his skin was well tanned. He thought he looked okay and could be a passable bellhop. The last thing he did was clip on his family name tag. He stepped out onto the veranda and looked out over the water.

Just as he looked at the cove, he saw the *LaZBoat* come around the point, cross the cove, and head toward the pier. He had to smile when he saw the passengers. It looked like a boatful of grandmothers. All of them were wearing matching green baseball caps on their heads and green and white sweatshirts. Then John heard voices singing. It was the bridge bunch, and they were singing a camp song he had learned from his mom when he was younger. It was a real oldie—"Floatin' Down," complete with harmony.

They sounded great across the water. John knew this group was going to be full of fun. They finished their song as they drew nearer the pier. Their laughter floated across the water. Some of them were pointing to the shore and the lodge. He secretly hoped that sometime they would need a substitute in their bridge playing. John loved all card games, and bridge was his favorite. Unfortunately, not very many young people learned to play it anymore. The women saw him and started waving. He waved and smiled, then he started across the lawn to the bluff steps. He was eager to meet this group of guests.

It took a good half hour to get the women settled in their rooms. There was some last-minute shuffling because Phoebe and Ruth, who were signed up as roommates, were having an argument. Apparently Ruth left the Sudoku puzzle book in the car. Phoebe woke up early each morning and looked forward to doing a couple of puzzles while she took care of her bathroom business. Soon the bickering encompassed other perceived slights and problems that had occurred during the past year.

At the height of the argument, both insisted that staying in the same room with the other was simply intolerable. Myrna and Patsy offered to trade around so that the two warring women could be separated, but neither Phoebe nor Ruth liked the room that Myrna and Patsy had been assigned. After further consideration, Phoebe and Ruth decided to try staying together. If it didn't work out, they would just arrange an extra single room and pay the extra fees.

"It's too bad those two women are having a problem, isn't it? It could cost them a lot of extra money if they can't get along," John said to his mom.

"Oh, don't worry about them, Johnny. Mom says these women are always pretty tired and cranky when they arrive. And this is not the first year Phoebe and Ruth have had a tiff. The word is they argue all the time. We should just wait and see how things are after the cocktail hour."

"Well, it would be a shame if this ruined their visit," said John.

"It will be fine, Johnny. After all, they are sisters. They've lived together all their lives. Their basic values are the same. Mom told me that the other women told her Phoebe and Ruth bicker every day at home. But then, most sisters argue. In fact, I think siblings just naturally fight and argue and tease and generally spend a good portion of life trying to get the best of one another. I wouldn't worry about the bridge bunch. They're much better than many groups. Now, I did tell them that if they ever need a substitute, you are available." Christina smiled at her son. He looked happy and rested.

John was still thinking about the altercation he had witnessed. "I didn't know they were sisters. How weird to get so mad over something so small." John smiled back at his mother. "I'll remind them this afternoon when I see them around the lodge that I can sit in if necessary. I need to see Nana about some things before too long. Now about school starting on Monday, ten is a good time. Have you decided who will supervise the AP calculus and AP history?"

John hoped his father would take charge of the math categories. It might be a good way for his dad to see John in a different light.

"Daniel will definitely supervise your prep for AP math. When we looked through the test samples, he was the only one of us who understood any of the questions. Nana wants to guide you in all the music, literature, and art classes if that's okay with you. She taught me all my advanced level subjects since the AP tests and classes didn't exist then. I was able to take the university class equivalency tests and test out of several basic freshman classes.

"I plan to work with you in writing, history, government, and sociology. Grandpa Fred will teach physics, chemistry, and life sciences. We're using the University of California Education Commission guidelines in choosing study materials for you and the girls. It's the most demanding program for homeschooling we could find. I think you will be well prepared for anything you must face when you're getting ready for college."

While Christina was excited about the possibilities for her children in the homeschool movement, part of her was nervous about the decision to keep them home from the school in Mirabella. She asked herself if homeschooling was to give her children every possible advantage, or was it simply a convenient way to take care of school and still have help in the lodge operation. She hoped this was going to be the best solution for her family.

John met several of the bridge players in the kitchen. It seemed that everyone was hungry all at once. An assembly line of sorts was formed to put together sandwiches. There was a large bowl of fresh fruit salad with a sticky tab pasted on it that simply said "Enjoy!" The women searched through the snack cupboard and found bags of chips. There was a large plastic container filled with homemade ginger cookies. Phoebe and Ruth seemed to be over their tiff. They were laughing with Patsy about something that had happened on the ferry from Long Beach.

John laughed along with them. They all carried their food out to the veranda. Some found chairs around the tables. Others sat in the Adirondack chairs that were set in groupings along the porch. Christina followed close behind with a large pitcher of iced tea. John jumped up when he saw her and hurried to get a supply of glasses. His mom poured while he returned to the kitchen and sliced a couple of lemons, grabbed the sugar bowl and some spoons, and returned to the porch.

"Your mom tells us you play the piano, John. How about if you play some while we're having our lunch?" Ruth seemed to be the leader. Everyone nodded and smiled.

"Sure." John gulped down his sandwich then went in to the piano. It took a few minutes to find his music folders. Someone had placed them in a big square basket under the piano, arranged neatly in alphabetical order. John grinned. He recognized the hand of Nana in the arrangement. His mother had warned him before they moved to the island that Nana was a compulsive organizer and tidy-upper. It was a constant problem between mother and daughter, but John thought it would be great to have somebody organize his stuff.

Maybe he would ask Nana to help him get his room in order. So far, he just had shoved everything into the cupboards and closed the doors quickly. The room looked neat, but he had no idea how he was going to find anything in the chaos. Sorting through the folders, he found his pop notebook that was filled with lead sheets and scores for background and sing-along music. He had prepared it a few years before and added to it periodically. Back in Sierra Glen, he had played piano at the Sierra Glen Grill a couple of times each week. He learned the music that was most requested by patrons, and his mom had suggested several standard pieces to include as well.

During every evening, he was asked to play "Fur Elise," the first movement of the "Moonlight Sonata," "Clair de Lune," and something by Bach. After a year of playing at the grill, John could almost always predict which songs would be requested just by looking at the clientele. The retired folks usually asked for beautiful old standards, songs like "Always," "Smile," "Unforgettable," and "September Song." People who looked about the same age as his parents asked for Billy Joel, Motown, show tunes, and disco or country.

Parents often came up and demanded that their child have a chance to play the piano. Luckily, the owner of the grill had a strict policy that barred anyone besides John from playing during the evening. If the parent was a regular local customer, Mr. Raines invited the parent to make an appointment with him during the day for an audition. If a child was average or worse, Mr. Raines would not even let the youngster finish the tryout. If the child sounded good and the piece was polished, he would ask the child to repeat the piece. If it was not just as polished the second time, he stopped them and said, "Sorry, no thank you."

When John was eleven, Christina made an appointment with Mr. Raines. John played for over a half hour, piece after piece with segues between. His playing was mature and stylish. Mr. Raines listened for errors. He knew there must be a mistake here and there, but he couldn't hear any. Mr. Raines wanted to hire John on the spot for a ninety-minute block four days each week during the dinner hour. Christina allowed John to play on Friday evening from six to seven.

John developed a loyal following. As he grew older, he played for longer shifts, and when he left Sierra Glen, he had been playing four nights for two to three hours. The result was an eclectic combination of popular tunes from several decades, show tunes, familiar classics, some novelty and camp tunes, and several beloved and familiar hymns. John segued from song to song when he played, resulting in a seamless stream of appealing music that enhanced the atmosphere of a pleasant social gathering.

As he sat at his instrument, he decided to start with a medley of show tunes. The bridge women shouted and clapped after every song. Soon, they started drifting in to join John around the piano. When John launched into "Big Spender," Myrna and Maxine belted out the words and acted out the whole piece with gusto and skill. Soon John was surrounded by green sweatshirts and gray hair. The bridge ladies were singing and dancing all over the parlor.

When he played "I Feel Pretty" from *West Side Story*, they all danced just the way Natalie Wood had in the movie version. Then they begged John to play the "Jet Song" from the same musical. As he started the first notes, the women all started snapping their fingers. When he got to the first line, they were right with him and launched into song. John marveled at the combined talent in the room. As he drifted into "Cool," the women gathered in a cluster and crouched down to imitate the wonderful movie scene where the Jets ran together toward the camera snapping fingers and jumping in tiny unison hops.

When they finished, everyone including John clapped and congratulated themselves for a remarkable performance. The fun continued for nearly an hour. The women gradually headed off toward their rooms to rest up from their travels. When John put his notebook back in the storage basket below the piano, his mother came over and sat down on the piano bench.

"Johnny, that was so nice of you to join in with the ladies. They had such a great time, and you all sounded so good. Nana and I were listening from the kitchen. I am glad you'll be able to use your talent like this. It's kind of a new dimension for you to explore in music. Also, I was listening to you as you were singing along. It was easy to hear you since yours was the only male voice. But, John, I didn't know how beautiful your singing voice had become. I guess I really haven't heard you for a few years since the family drifted away from singing in the evenings." She looked away wistfully as if searching for a memory from long ago that she could somehow catch and hold close.

A similar vision floated into John's consciousness. It was of his family in the living room back home. They all had instruments of some kind. This particular memory must have been from one of the last times they gathered to play together because the twins looked as if they were in grade school, probably about ten years old. As always, Emma had a kazoo. She could hum into the little tin instrument louder than anyone in the family. As he did frequently, John's father was reminding Emma to keep it quiet between songs, and she tried.

Lucy usually chose unobtrusive, quiet instruments like the triangle or the tiny bells. This evening she held the little finger cymbals; the girls called them Barbie cymbals. Lucy played them very softly. Each time she clinked them together, she jumped a little as if startled. After a while, the rest of the family used the cymbal as a cue to bounce up and down quickly. When she noticed how the family was teasing her, Lucy started playing on every beat, causing the rest of them to bounce out of control. Soon the whole family was laughing. It was a good memory.

On every family music evening, John's father had an old clarinet that sounded okay if they were playing one of the eight songs he knew. When they ventured into something unfamiliar, Daniel switched to the bongo drums. He almost always kept the pulse steady. John's mother usually played the piano while John played a variety of other sounds on his synthesizer. John felt his breath catch as he remembered his brother Paul singing or whistling.

The two skills were attractively interchangeable for Paul. His thought processes were simple: he sang if he knew the words, he whistled if he didn't. John was lost in a haze of reminiscing when his mother suddenly jumped up from the bench and rushed toward the kitchen. She looked back over her shoulder and spoke quickly to John.

"'Oh Johnny, I'm sorry to rush, but I forgot I have cookies in the oven. I hope Mom took them out for me!"The sentence faded as she went through the kitchen door. John was pleased to hear a muffled "Oh, thank goodness!" coming from that direction. He smiled to himself as he left the piano and headed for his room.

Chapter Thirteen

He wanted to have some time alone to think through a few important ideas that were forming in his mind. As he entered the family wing, he sensed that he was all alone. The hallway was cool and quiet.

The twins are probably off doing something with the horses, John thought to himself. *I wonder where Dad and Grandpa Fred are this afternoon?* John realized he had not seen them since they had delivered the bridge ladies from Mirabella before lunch. He knew his mother and Nana Mariel had been in the kitchen baking cookies. When John opened the door to his room, he could feel a gentle breeze brush across his face. The breeze was coming from the bank of windows and the door across the room.

The windows were wide open, and the glass door opening to the veranda was ajar again. John figured he would have to use the dead bolt to secure the door until he remembered to get the latch fixed. John could see the legs and feet of someone who was resting on a chaise lounge outside the door. When he looked outside, he found Papa Jacob sound asleep. Jacob looked peaceful enough, but his face still held vestiges of the scowling frown lines etched onto his brow. John often heard Jacob moving about in his room late at night, so it was good to see him sleeping so soundly this afternoon. Closing the door quietly, John went back over to his bookshelf to retrieve the shoe box with all the papers in it.

He wasn't sure what he was looking for, but he thought he could learn more about his family history by reading through all the materials that had been stored in his room. Slipping his shoes off, he flopped down on his bed and started to read. Last night, he had only skimmed through the news articles with pictures. This time, he read through every page. Someone had gone to the trouble of saving these things for years, and John wanted to know why. Many pieces were from the *Los Angeles Times*. John found ten different articles from the travel section describing the Eagle Cove Lodge and Family Farm. The earliest was from 1955 and the latest from 1995. All the reporters wrote highly favorable articles. John learned that many celebrities had been guests. Apparently, the secluded location appealed to those who wished to enjoy a family vacation without being hounded by autograph seekers.

One article that intrigued John was from the metro section of the *Long Beach Press Telegram*. The story described a daring rescue that had occurred at Whistling Wind Beach on Santa Teresa Island. It was a very windy day in September 1982 when a young boy who was climbing on the rock jetty was apparently swept into the water by a rogue wave. His friends who had been making a sand fort up on the beach did not notice that he was missing until one of his shoes washed up onto the beach beside them. There was a strong rip current that day siphoning water from shore straight out toward the open ocean. Several of the boys thought they saw someone far out from shore. Two fourteen-year-old girls who were supervising the youngsters at the beach found three rescue tubes in the storage cupboard. The girls told a couple of the boys to run across to Three Ships for help. Then after commanding the remaining boys to stay up on the beach, the girls ran into the surf and rode the rip tide out to sea. According to the boys who waited, it was a very long time before they heard a truck coming over the IPR from Three Ships. Before the truck arrived, the two girls could be seen out in the water about a half mile down the beach. The boys ran down the beach, and the rescue crew followed. Three of the crew members dashed out into the surf and dragged the two girls and an exhausted young boy up onto the shore. Except for cuts and bruises, all three of the adventurers were healthy and very happy to be on dry land. The Three Ships rescue crew had nothing but praises for the quick-thinking girls. But Captain Bill Small of the Santa Teresa Fire Department noted how the outcome could have been a triple tragedy. "I'm happy that all three are safe, but the lesson we learn here is that adults need to supervise youngsters at the beach. It is unfair to expect a couple of fourteen year olds to be responsible for a large group of children at a beach like this one. Santa Teresa is a wild and beautiful place, but it can be a dangerous place as well."

The article went on to describe the prevailing tendency for a strong rip current to develop at Whistling Wind in stormy weather. The local surfers were interviewed. They all stressed that the waters just west of the jetty were always treacherous, especially in windy weather. As John read, he realized that he had seen the rock jetty described in the paper.

Whistling Wind Beach was the official name for Surfside. He and Rocky had stood by the same rocks to watch the surfers hurry away from the shark. The article identified the young boy as Timothy Little, eleven, of Norwalk. The two girls were Carolyn Peterson and Kara Cecile Engstrom, both students at Santa Teresa Island High School.

John wondered who had this room before; who had saved all of this stuff? John was startled to hear someone knocking quietly on his door. He jumped up to open it. Nana was there.

"Hi, John, I'm sorry if I woke you," she started, "but the bridge players are all in a funk because Myrna has a sick headache, and she doesn't think she can play bridge this afternoon. They need a sub." She looked expectantly at John.

"I wasn't sleeping. I've been looking through some old papers I found in this room." He opened the door and beckoned her to come in to see the papers. "I'll go and fill in at the bridge table. But do you recognize these papers? Do you know who saved them? Who had this room before me?" The questions rolled out one after another.

"Well, this room has been vacant for years, but Jacob has used it on and off as a study of sorts." Mariel paused for a moment then continued. "At one time, this was KC's room. Jacob built her that little bathroom where the walk-in closet was originally, but she really missed her big closet. After a few months, she moved across the hall. Gradually, this room became a catchall for Jacob. We all stored some craft materials and wrapping paper in here. I bet you found a million toilet paper rolls in the cupboard." Mariel looked over the news articles and pictures. "These look like things that Jacob may have saved. Most of these articles are in the lodge scrapbooks over in the clubroom."

"Well, I guess I better go play cards. Where are they meeting? Are they starting right away?" John was putting on his shoes as he spoke. But Mariel did not respond. She was busy reading the article about the rescue. When she finished, she sighed and turned toward John.

"Remember how you asked why Jacob hated Peter Sorenson and his sea camp?" John nodded as Mariel continued. "Well, this incident added more reason for Jacob to be angry. Carolyn and KC were best friends. I secretly thought, at least I hoped, their friendship might help to end this awful feud that plagued us for decades."

"Were the girls able to visit each other at their homes?" John was curious how much control the adults had over the teenagers on the island.

"Actually, the girls did show up at each other's home once in a while. It was a little awkward, but Fred and I thought things were thawing a little bit." Mariel sighed again and held up the newspaper article. "But then this happened. Jacob had allowed Kara Cecile to go over to the sea camp for a visit just before lunchtime. He said he would pick her up at three. Peter Sorenson called to say he had to drive over to the marine store at Three Ships, and he would drop off KC at the lodge orchard's back gate. Sofia was the one who answered the phone. The plan seemed straightforward enough, and she agreed."

"If Papa Jacob had answered, would he have agreed?" John asked.

"Most likely Jacob would have agreed grudgingly. But Sorenson didn't tell Jacob or Sofia about the whole plan. Apparently, he had a small group of campers at the sea camp who were there with their church fellowship group. I believe there were ten boys, age ten to twelve. Their group director had an upset stomach during the night and was unable to lead the group in their planned activities the next day. Well, when KC came over to see Carolyn, Peter Sorenson asked if the two girls would like to supervise the boys for a couple of hours while he drove the camp van down to Three Ships. Since Peter was planning to take the fifteen-passenger van already, Carolyn asked if they could all go with him and hike over to Surfside. Peter agreed, and they left a few minutes later.

"The two girls were aware that the wind had come up. So they warned the boys to keep out of the water. They all decided to build a sand fort. KC went to the storage shed and borrowed a couple of shovels and some plastic buckets. They all worked together to build a very elaborate fort with a moat and huge buttresses on either side. Carolyn and KC never even missed Timothy. They just assumed everyone was with them. When Jerry saw the shoe wash up next to the fort, he recognized it, most likely because it was marked on the side with two big letters, TL for Timothy Little.

"The girls asked if anyone had seen Timothy in the past few minutes. Joey said he saw Timothy standing on the rocks by the jetty. Joey thought Timothy had gone over to the rocks to pee. You see, the restroom facilities and the picnic grounds hadn't been built yet. The whole beach was pretty primitive. Anyway, they all stopped building and began to shout out for Timothy.

"You can see in the article what happened. The girls were recognized as genuine heroes, but everyone agrees that they were remarkably lucky. When Jacob learned about the incident, he was livid."

John and Mariel were quiet. Each was thinking the same thought: how unfair to saddle that responsibility on two young teenagers. Finally, Mariel sighed again very audibly as if to clear away the sad memories. Turning her thoughts to the present, she told John what she knew of the bridge plans for the afternoon.

"They've set up three tables around the fountain out on Sofia's flower garden patio. It's lovely out there this afternoon. Anyway, the bridge girls plan to play from 4:00 p.m. until 5:30 p.m. If the weather is nice, they may have dinner out there as well. They don't plan to play cards again until tomorrow morning." Mariel looked at her watch and smiled at John. "You have about ten minutes before you have to be there."

"Okay, that'll be fine." John then remembered about Jacob. "Oh, Papa Jacob is taking a nap on the veranda just outside my door. Do you think he needs a blanket or something?" John was worried because Jacob was in the shade, and it was breezy on this side of the building. Fortunately, Sofia's flower garden patio where they would be playing cards was sheltered from the wind.

"I think Jacob will be okay. He sleeps really warm, and I'll be waking him for cocktails before too long." Mariel thought about the cocktail hour the family had each day, often with the guests. The lodge kept a ready supply of beer, ale, and wine as well as soft drinks and juices for guests' enjoyment. Usually, the family just had water over ice with a sprig of mint or a lemon slice. Special occasions were celebrated with sparkling cider. Once or twice each week, Mariel would open a bottle of wine to enjoy at the dinner table, but except for Fred and Daniel, most of the family members did not have much in the way of alcohol. Fred liked his beer or wine every afternoon, but it did not seem to have much effect on him. Daniel, who drank wine every afternoon, actually seemed more pleasant after a glass or two.

Once in a great while, there would be a guest who would overindulge and behave inappropriately, but Jacob would take care of things quietly and decisively, using great discretion and tact. Jacob decided long ago that he would not threaten the family friendly reputation of his lodge by tolerating alcohol abuse. The most effective deterrent to overindulgence was a simple policy that Jacob adopted decades before. It stated that his family friendly establishment would not reserve rooms in the future for any guests who bothered other guests with loud or rude behavior. Since no one wanted to be blacklisted from the Lodge, most guests monitored themselves. Mariel was thankful that she did not have to deal with the out-of-control behavior of heavy drinkers.

Several of the innkeepers and restaurant owners that she knew in Mirabella had told her horror stories about drunk patrons who started fights, got sick, peed the beds, destroyed furniture, and generally made life unpleasant for other people. In fact, when she and Fred first decided to come to the island to run the lodge, Mariel had worried about the environment in which her children would be raised. Did she really want her children to see other people only in vacation mode? Would her children think that the behaviors they observed in guests on vacation were the normal behaviors of day-to-day living?

She had talked with Fred for hours and weeks about her fears. But he only had to remind her that he himself had grown up on the island. His parents had instilled a strong work ethic in him. His parents had also given him a firm grounding in good manners and good scholarship. They had been active in church, and they encouraged him to seek experiences over town whenever possible. He had represented Mirabella High School at Boys' State, he went on the annual church mission trips, and he traveled many times each semester to athletic competitions over town.

He entered the science fair every year in junior high and high school and three times made it as far as the regionals in Los Angeles. When Mariel realized that the man she loved was the product of an upbringing at the lodge on Santa Teresa, she felt confident that she could give her own children the same wonderful albeit unusual opportunities.

She only had to reflect on the status of her two children to see how her decision decades ago was a good one. Although the teenage Christina had been a challenge in many ways, the adult Christina and her family were a source of joy now. As even tempered and cooperative as her son Matt had been growing up, he and Fred had still suffered through some battle of wills during Matt's high school years. Mariel had to smile at the memory of Matt's senior year in high school.

It was a rough year. Somehow, it seemed to Mariel that Matt suddenly had to question every vestige of authority in his life. He challenged every rule at home and at school, he argued with teachers who could not provide him with proof to substantiate their assertions, and he even challenged his baseball coach when the team was required to sell candy to raise funds for the athletic program.

Mariel and Fred had admitted secretly to each other that they were thankful for September when Matt left to attend Santa Clara University. But now, Matt was a parish priest up in San Jose. He loved his life and his church. The parish school was a vibrant reflection of Father Matt's stewardship. He encouraged all children to learn at least one other language. He himself spoke English and Spanish fluently, thanks to his upbringing on the island.

Mariel talked with him each week, and he kept her informed about his life as a priest. The island had provided a rich environment for both of her children. She was pleased to think that the three remaining children in Christina's family, Mariel's only grandchildren, would have the same opportunities. And as always, Mariel grappled with the unwanted thought of how life might have turned out differently if Daniel and Christina had come a few years earlier, but she shooed the ideas from her head. Paul was gone, and that was that.

Chapter Fourteen

John grabbed a pullover cotton sweater as he left the room. He was looking forward to playing some bridge. He hoped the women were patient. Were they expert players? Did he really know enough to sit in? His mind raced through all of the worrisome self-doubt, but as soon as he stepped onto Sofia's flower garden patio, he relaxed. The women greeted him warmly and thanked him for substituting. They assured him that they all played bridge just for fun.

The patio, flanked on two sides by wings of the lodge, was pleasantly warm. The eaves along each wing stretched out to form covered walkways supported by posts. Huge basket planters were mounted on each post, and a profusion of colorful flowers cascaded from each. Several guest rooms had French doors opening onto the patio along one of the wings. The guest rooms across the hall from the bridge ladies faced out on the other side of the building wing toward a natural meadow.

In one corner of the patio, an ancient wisteria grew up past the edge of the roof and hung gracefully down over a sturdy arbor that Jacob had built decades before. Surrounding the rest of the patio was a short plastered wall with thick clear glass mounted above, allowing an unobstructed view of Eagle Cove. The tile fountain in the center of the patio featured a bronze statue of an eagle ready to take off into the sky. His wings were arched gracefully with feathers set wide in a fan. One talon was touching the landing site.

John always felt good when he was here on Sofia's patio. Although he had been nearly five years old when Sofia passed away, he had only a vague memory of her. He felt as if he knew her because of all the Sofia stories he had heard from Grandpa Fred and Papa Jacob. Jacob made it clear that Sofia's flower garden patio was his favorite part of the lodge. Jacob told John how Sofia had lovingly selected, planted, nurtured, and trained every mature plant in the garden. She had chosen the pots for the annuals, and she had designed the fountain that he constructed.

And it was Sofia who found the magnificent bronze eagle in a shop over town, then convinced Jacob that they had to purchase it, though it cost more than the fountain on which it was mounted. Jacob had spoken so often about his memories of Sofia here in the garden that when John looked at the eagle and the fountain, the borrowed memories of Sofia crowded into his own mind, and he had to smile.

"Well, John, do you play a short club?" Trudy was anxious to get started. Before John could respond, she continued. "How about conventions? Have you ever played duplicate?" John sat across from Trudy at table number two. Apparently, the ladies were going to play just two rounds of party bridge this afternoon before dinner.

"Mom taught me short club. So do I need five or four in a major suit to answer?" John spoke quickly when Trudy stopped for a breath. When she didn't continue, John finished his thought. "I play the move where you bid four, no trump, then your partner lets you know how many aces or kings he has." John waited for someone to say something, but the ladies just smiled at him. He continued to talk. "And finally, I never did play duplicate. I'm not sure what it is."

"It sounds like you'll be just fine with us. We table talk when we're not sure what to bid or play, so just have fun," Hazel reassured him. Then she giggled as she added, "And remember, every time you say a bad word, you have to put a quarter in the kitty." She pointed to the pink cat-shaped ceramic bowl on the snack table. There were already a few quarters in it.

"Some of us think you need a four-card major, but a few think five is necessary. Since you and I are partners, four is enough for me." Trudy turned to the group and said, "Well, let's get started!"

They dealt and played without stopping until dinnertime. John was surprised how fast the time passed by. There was a lot of laughter, and John heard several swear words and cuss words deemed bad enough to require a quarter in the kitty. Trudy paid at least two dollars worth of quarters before the end of the first round, mainly because of her habit of saying "Oh, pooh" when she got bad cards or missed a finesse.

She claimed it was spelled with an *H* like Winnie the Pooh, but the women finally voted that since it sounded exactly like what you call the stuff in a baby's diaper, it would be categorized as a bathroom business word. When the vote came in against her, she muttered, "Damn it to hell! Pooh is a great word!" which cost her three more quarters. After that, she controlled herself and paid no more that afternoon. She resorted to saying "Oh, pooh with an *H*!" which everyone chose to ignore. John was thankful he never got in the habit of cussing and swearing, so he never worried about feeding the kitty.

"What do you do with the money from the kitty?" John asked Trudy as he helped her collect the cards when they had finished for the afternoon.

"We usually go out for a nice lunch later on in the fall. We call it the Hell-Raiser's Luncheon, and then we play a small tournament and use the remainder of the money for bridge prizes. The kitty grows all year long. Right now we have almost two hundred dollars in there. The first couple of years we had over five hundred by the end of the year, but we've cleaned up our mouths since then." Trudy packed all the cards and scorecards in a large picnic basket. John picked it up and carried it into the lodge.

"Thanks, John. We just leave it here in the corner at night because we use it all again each day. No sense in schlepping it back to our rooms." Trudy grinned. "And thanks for filling in today. You played very well. I hope you had a good time. See you at dinner." With that, she patted him on the arm and turned to join the other ladies who were heading toward their rooms to clean up for dinner.

John waved at the group, then he headed for the kitchen. A blend of wonderful aromas was drifting into the dining room from the kitchen door. John's mouth watered in anticipation. As he walked through the door into the kitchen, he felt a blast of warm moist air on his face. The air was thick and wet, practically dripping off the kitchen walls near the stove. The Escobars were speaking in rapid Spanish, and Grandpa Fred was up on a ladder, holding the fan components in his hands.

Mariel held the ladder while she handed tools back and forth to Fred. After a few moments, Fred slipped the lighting unit back into the ceiling frame and snapped it in place. He grumbled some as he climbed down the ladder, but as soon as he flipped the switch and heard the trusty purring of the fan, he broke into a wide smile.

"That should help get some of this wet air out of here." Fred folded the ladder as Mariel packed away the tools. "You know, Mariel, that's the same fan that we had to fix last month. Maybe we should replace it? This unit is over ten years old. I think they make much better ones now anyway."

"Good idea. We can order it tomorrow." Mariel looked over at John. "Hi, Johnny. Say, could you help Grandpa put the tools and ladder away? I'm going to help get the serving dishes ready. We've crowded into Marina's space and time, so we'll need to hurry so dinner isn't late."

John nodded and picked up the large toolbox. He fell in behind Fred, who was carrying the ladder toward the service porch. Soon, the tools and ladder were stowed. John thought this would be as good a time as any to ask about the Baldwins who were arriving tomorrow.

"Grandpa, about the family that's arriving tomorrow, you know, the Baldwins?"

"That's right. They've been coming for at least fifteen years. They are great people. You'll like them. Say, they have a couple of cute girls who might be just about your age. Might be kind of interesting, hmm?" Fred smiled at John.

"Well, actually, I wanted to know about the girls. Well, that is, I met some guys at Surfside this morning who live at the sea camp, and they told me about the Baldwin girls who will be going to the big dance or whatever they call it at the sea camp on Saturday night, and Ian, he's one of the guys I met, wondered if I could drive the girls to the dance, and if I could come to the dance too?"

John felt like a little kid asking permission to stay up late. Somehow, the whole idea sounded stupid now that he said it out loud. He started to shrug his shoulders and turn away, but Grandpa Fred smiled and put his hand on John's shoulder. Fred looked directly into John's face, then he laughed out loud.

"Well, it's true. The quiet ones seem to learn the most information in the shortest amount of time. You know, John, you've asked a simple question that deserves a simple answer. But I can tell by the way you seem kind of nervous and worried about the whole sea camp subject that you know something already about our little dilemma. Who have you been talking to? Mariel? Your mom?"

John started to answer, but Fred interrupted him. "No, John, you don't need to tell me. I think it would be a fine arrangement for you to take the Baldwin girls to the party. Heck, I might just take my girl to the party too. I get an invitation every year, and I have to say that from what I hear from year to year, it's the best damn party on the island!"

Fred smiled at John. John couldn't believe what he was hearing. His grandfather's words were encouraging. However, John's relief was short-lived as Fred continued to speak.

"The only problem we have, of course, is Dad. You know your Papa Jacob has this ongoing problem with old man Sorenson.

There's not much we can do about it, but I have to respect his position as much as possible, especially in light of his health. I'm sure you've noticed how fragile he is." Fred watched John's shoulders slump in disappointment.

"Yeah, I know. It's okay, Grandpa." John started to turn way once again, but Fred reached out and placed his hand firmly on John's arm. "But wait just a minute. We have these Baldwin girls to think about. It seems your new friends from the sea camp are pretty smooth operators. They must have met the girls last year and stayed in touch all year long. Well, if the girls are counting on going to the party Saturday, it's only fitting we provide transportation. Who better to take them than you?

"I've watched you when you've been driving the pickup during this past week, and I'd say you are the second-best driver around here, certainly better than your parents and a little better than your Nana Mariel. You shouldn't have any problem handling the van. It's a stick shift, but it doesn't have four-wheel drive. Just be extra careful on hills." Fred stepped back and started to turn back toward the kitchen. John took a quick step and fell in beside him.

"Does that mean I should plan to take the girls on Saturday, and I should plan to stay at the party too?" John asked tentatively.

"Well, you can't stay if you don't have a mask, at least that's what I've heard, so you better get to work on it. I'd keep it kind of quiet though. You've got a noisy sister in that Emma, and Lucy doesn't miss much of anything. Maybe we'll just start quiet, and if things work out this year, we'll all go next year." They reached the kitchen door and stepped through. Fred turned to John and whispered, "Ready to be a waiter and maybe a busboy? Let's wash up. We get to do it all, you know.

Friday morning started out as a typical day at the lodge. Four out of five days were like that: relaxed, predictable, following the schedule with no unexpected surprises. Grandpa Fred and Nana Mariel explained to the Garrett family that they should welcome the days that ran smoothly because the other days could be overwhelmingly stressful. It was the unforeseen circumstances—medical emergencies, unpredictable weather, problems with guests, equipment failures, animal issues, barge delivery problems—that made those days so challenging. It seemed to average about one day in five, or about 20 percent of the total schedule, took up far more than 90 percent of the total energy the family spent working at the lodge. Jacob stressed to all of them that if they handled the unexpected problems well and without panic, everything else would fall into place.

John was ready for anything, but he was secretly hoping the Baldwins would arrive on a day free of problems. He'd like to meet the girls casually, and then he could direct the conversation toward the masked party at the sea camp. He had a fleeting idea that this kind of social calendar planning is what girls do all the time.

The bridge ladies were busy playing a session of bridge in the clubroom. It was a little chilly on the veranda and on the patio, so the women took a vote. All but one wanted to stay inside, at least until after lunch. John waved at the group as he passed by the clubroom. They waved and shouted out greetings to him. He smiled to himself as he realized how relaxed he was around the older ladies. Three months ago he thought there would have been no way he could have filled in so easily for the ailing player. Had he changed so much since arriving on the island? He knew the answer was yes. He could feel his confidence grow each day as he became more familiar with his surroundings and his responsibilities.

The Baldwins were arriving in Mirabella on the midmorning ferry. Grandpa Fred and Christina were going to meet them and bring them back in the *LaZBoat*. Nana said they would be returning a little before noon. John was to watch for their arrival and then help them with luggage. It was nearly eleven, so John decided to use the next half hour to plan for his mask. He went on the Internet and found some news articles about previous fall festival masquerade square dances at the sea camp. John realized it was a much bigger deal than he had thought.

Apparently, most of Mirabella came. The camp had a live band, a square dance caller, plus a great spread of food and drink. There were several pictures of the guests wearing masks. Most of the masks stood tall on the head, and many of them draped over the shoulders as well. John saw a few people who had very simple "Phantom of the Opera style" masks, but he decided those who wore the small masks seemed somehow to be cheating a little bit. He started to worry about the time factor involved in designing and building a mask. Could he get it done in his spare hours between now and Saturday afternoon?

Well, worrying about making a mask doesn't matter if I can't decide on what I want to make, John thought to himself. He ran several ideas through his mind and rejected them all almost immediately. He wished he hadn't thrown out all the arts and crafts supplies that had been stored in his room for decades. He knew he had a limited amount of time, but he wanted to make something better than just minimally adequate. He thought of Shakespeare characters but immediately dropped the idea. He figured that over the years, people had done everything of interest. He thought about other literary characters, then people in the news, politicians, monsters, animals …

Animals! I know what I'll do, he thought to himself. Now, sometime last week he had packed away the perfect item. Where had he put it? He looked through all the drawers, cupboards, and cabinets in his bedroom and bathroom but found nothing. There were lots of things tossed under his bed, but nothing that resembled the thing he sought. Then he had a brainstorm. Lucy! His quiet sister loved stuffed animals of all kinds, and she could not tolerate the abuse of any stuffed animal.

She fixed ripped arms and missing button eyes, she washed and ironed any little jackets or nighties, she fluffed up fur with her hairbrush, and she generally treated her stuffed animals with loving care. John crossed the hall and knocked on the girls' door. Hoping that noisy Emma was not in the room, John was relieved to see that it was Lucy who opened the door.

"Hey, Luce," he said, "did you see the stuffed animal that was in my room last week when we first got here?" John tried to act casual.

"Um-hum." Lucy made one of her regular ambiguous sounds. John wondered if that meant yes or no. He decided to just assume it was a yes.

"Well, I need to see it for a little while. I'll take good care of it, I promise."

"It's not an it, it's a she, and she has a name, Ba-a-a-sheepa. Why do you need her? I spent one whole evening repairing her arm and her neck. She's still kind of tender. If you take her, will you be sure that she gets plenty of rest?" Lucy spoke with a great sense of solemnity, but John saw a twinkle in her eye. Suddenly, he had a flash of insight. He didn't even know his sister. He realized that Lucy was not such a pushover after all. Earlier, John had decided not to tell anyone about the mask project. But he found that he just couldn't lie to Lucy. Instead, he had another idea.

"Well, can I come in for a minute? I could use your help on something." Lucy stepped aside. John entered the room and closed the door behind him. He found it easy to talk to Lucy. She listened carefully to him while he told about the masks and the big dance at the sea camp. But when he told about his idea to use the stuffed animal as a part of his costume and mask, she shivered then glared at him. Her voice had an edge to it when she finally spoke.

"You can't do that! What you're saying is that you'd kill Baaasheepa and cut her up just to make you a mask that you'll use for an hour or so. If you want to be a sheep, why don't you just make a sheep mask from something else and leave Baaasheepa alone?" Except for the sheep voice that she made each time she pronounced the name of the stuffed animal, Lucy sounded very reasonable.

"No, you don't understand. I don't want to cut her up, I want her to become part of my mask. You know that little statue we have from the Holy Land, the one of a shepherd who has the lamb?" John paused for a moment, waiting for Lucy to respond. The silence stretched out for several seconds as John continued to wait for an answer. Finally, Lucy broke the silence. It was clear she had been waiting for John to explain in more detail what he had planned.

When she spoke, it was hard for her to keep a straight face. "Well? You mean you want to carry a sheep around? What are you supposed to be anyway? How are you going to dance with a sheep in your arms?" Lucy smiled. "I'm sorry, John, but for someone who is pretty smart, that makes you sound pretty dumb!"

"I don't want to carry it, I mean her, around. I'd like to carry her over my neck like that shepherd."

"The shepherd in our Christmas crèche has a little lamb draped around his neck, but the wooden one from the holy land is carrying a big sheep in his arms. I seriously doubt if he could square dance." Lucy smiled. "So you want to be a shepherd? Why not just take Rocky? He can be a sheepdog just as well as he is a retriever, pointer, bloodhound, or whatever else he wants to be."

"Yeah, right. Our well-behaved dog is just what I need." John was thoughtful for a moment. "You know, he is considered a hero at the sea camp. Remind me to tell you a neat story sometime. But yeah, I really wanted to be a shepherd so I could carry a little wooden flute as a prop. I thought the sheep would help establish what I was. I don't want to look like a terrorist or anything."

"I think we can make a pretty good shepherd headgear and mask that will look authentic, even without the sheep around your neck." She looked at him for some indication that he heard and agreed.

"You're saying you'll help me? That would be great!" John was relieved. He felt that a load had been taken off his shoulders. "Just let me know what you want me to do sometime for you 'cause I'm in your debt now." John was about ready to say good-bye and thank his sister again because in a few minutes, he needed to be at the dock to greet the boat and help with luggage.

"Well, I do have something you can do for me, and for Emma too." Lucy looked directly at John. "We already have our masks done, and we were going to have to sneak down to the sea camp for the dance, but now we can ride with you!" John was quiet for a moment while the whole scenario became clear to him. With a laugh and a wave, he turned and hurried out the door in the direction of the dock. As he left, he called back to Lucy, "Sure, the van carries eight passengers. So far we have two Baldwin girls, a set of twins, and a shepherd. I guess you and Emma got invited when you were at church last Sunday."

John was nearly out of earshot when he heard his sister answer. "Um-hum." He just shook his head and smiled.

Chapter Fifteen

John arrived on the dock before the *LaZboat* was in sight. He was looking forward to meeting the Baldwin family. He had a fleeting thought about the two girls he would be driving to the dance, but he also wondered about who else might be in the group. After all, there were a total of fourteen Baldwins. It seemed likely that there might be a boy around his age, and maybe there was a musician in the group. Well, John was going to find out before long. He saw the *LaZboat* come around the point and enter the cove.

According to his cell phone, it was exactly twelve noon. He could hear the squeals of young children as the boat got near. How was it that no matter what language was spoken by the family, young humans make the same kinds of sounds when they are excited or sad or angry or tired? There must be a universal maternal reaction to a fussy baby, or a whining tired toddler, or the cries of a terrified child. The happy sounds that flowed across the top of the choppy water made John happy too.

It was easy to be infected with such straightforward expressions of joy. John smiled as he looked out at the boat. Peering out across the bow were three preschool-age children in life jackets. They were the source of the squealing, but there was plenty of other noise being generated by the other passengers. John decided right away that the Baldwins were a loud fun-loving family.

Fred had cut the speed at the buoys, and when he was about a hundred feet out, he cut it again. Without the loud full-throttle engine noise, it was easy to pick out individual voices. John heard the girls before he saw them. He hoped his ears were not bright red from blushing as he pretended to busy himself with the lines on the dock. Probably because he had the exceptional hearing of a musician, he caught snippets of words and phrases from the entire group. "He's really cute!" "Mmm, good!" "I'd like a piece of that one!" mixed with "Look how beautiful the lodge looks!" "I can hardly wait to go riding." "Hope we get in soon, I gotta pee!" "Well, here we are again." "Well, yippee." John noticed the yippee voice sounded bored or angry. He couldn't tell which woman had said it, but her voice was low and hard sounding—a whiskey voice is what his mother called it.

Once or twice a month back at the Sierra Glen Grill, there would be a drunk woman with a voice like that who would come up and try to drape herself on his shoulder while he was playing, and one time when he was just barely fourteen, there was a woman who actually put her tongue in his ear.

He remembered with a wave of fresh embarrassment that he had squealed like a pig and stood up abruptly, causing the woman to fall off the bench with a loud splat. Her husband threatened to sue the Grill, but Christina quickly countered with a threat of her own, involving the police getting DNA evidence from saliva and then pressing child molestation charges. Although they were a local couple, they never set foot in the Sierra Glen Grill again.

When the *LaZboat* was alongside the dock, Fred stepped lightly off the boat. He and John coordinated their efforts to secure the launch. As soon as they finished, Fred turned and announced that John was here to assist anyone who needed help disembarking. He reminded them that their luggage would be carried to the lodge.

"Now, be careful standing up and moving about. We'll take one row at a time beginning with this row." He pointed to a row near the rear where four women sat together. As soon as the boat was empty, John and Fred took a few moments to wipe out the dirt and bits of paper trash that had been mashed underfoot on the short ride from Mirabella.

John had the big dolly ready to load with suitcases and other gear. Once they had it packed and secure, they started rolling it slowly toward he lodge. After stopping several times to rest, they finally wrestled the cumbersome load up the wide stone stairs to the lawn level. John was so out of breath he couldn't form words for a couple of minutes. Fred was leaning over with his hands resting on his knees. After several false starts, he finally gasped out a sentence.

"Well, that was kind of dumb. It might have been a lot easier to bring this stuff up in three loads. Whattaya think?"

"I think you're right. How long are they staying anyway? A month?" John finally could speak without gasping between words. "I wonder what they could possibly have in these big crates?"

"Actually, those crates are for the lodge. Jim Baldwin is the distributor for all those fancy products we use for guest toiletries and also all the stuff we use for general cleaning. He brings us a generous supply each year in exchange for letting him use our endorsement of his products in ads. So suck it up and act grateful." Fred had recovered sufficiently to grin at John. John couldn't help but smile back.

It was after one thirty when John and Fred finally got all the suitcases and gear delivered to the Baldwins' wing in the lodge. John put the three large crates of gifts from Mr. Baldwin in the pantry with the promise that he would unpack the materials later that day. Nana Mariel, at least according to Grandpa Fred, was eager to get into the gift boxes to organize everything.

John was starving. He hurried into the kitchen from the pantry only to find four teenage Baldwins there making peanut and jelly sandwiches. They looked up as he entered. Without stopping the production line of sandwich construction, one of the girls handed him one.

"Here," she said, "you look like you need this right away. Eat first, then talk."

"Thanks!" John ate the sandwich in a flash. He went to the fridge and took out a gallon container of milk. He grabbed a tray of glasses from the cupboard and put it on the square table with the milk. After pouring himself a second glass, he sat down at the table and wiped his mouth with the back of his hand. "Wow! Thanks for the sandwich. I needed that!" John smiled at the others, and then he added, "There's milk here for anyone who wants it."

The boy Baldwin poured himself a glass and drank it down in one gulp. Then he poured himself another. He smiled at John. "Hi, I'm JP. You must be from the Sierras. We heard your family was coming down to help with the lodge. You are so lucky. What a great place this must be to live year around. Anyway, these two blonde Baldwins are my sisters, Gina and June. The dark-haired one is my cousin Ana." John smiled at each girl as he heard the names. He tried to cement identities on each so he would be able to call them by name right away.

"Hi, I'm John, and I did move down from the Sierras about two weeks ago. And yes, I think I'm going to really like living here." John felt at ease with the Baldwins, and he was comfortable making small talk. He was curious about the dance. "Which of you are going to the party tomorrow night? I'm your driver, so we should probably decide on times and everything."

"June and I are going." John figured it must be Gina who was talking. "We have our masks ready. I think Ian wrote that we should arrive by 7:00 p.m. The masks are judged, and then everyone takes them off at 8:15 p.m." Gina looked over at Ana then turned back to John and said, "Ana was invited, but she didn't want to go. Now she has changed her mind, but it's too late to make arrangements for another guest!"

"Oh, it's okay. Ana, if you want to go, you can. Everyone is invited. Almost everyone on the whole island goes. All you need is a mask. And what about you, JP? Don't you want to go?" John felt a little strange talking about the dance just like an authority. "We have room for eight in the car, and so far with all of you and my sisters and me, that's only seven."

"What about your brother? Last year when Jacob was talking about your family, he mentioned two boys." JP was curious. "I remember because he said John played the piano, and Paul sailed. See? My name is John Paul, JP for short."

"Well, I did have a brother, but he died a couple of years ago. Papa Jacob gets confused since his stroke." John tried to say the words without any particular inflection or emphasis. He did not want to admit to anyone that this was the first time since that day two years ago that he had spoken out loud of Paul's death. All he wanted to do now was to run to his room and slam the door. How could he get away from these people?

"Oh, damn! I'm sorry! I didn't have any idea, John, I'm really sorry, but how, or what happened—"

Gina put her hand on JP's arm to quiet him. JP was fumbling for something else to say, and John suddenly felt compassion for the discomfort he could sense in all the Baldwins. Ana had turned away so nobody could see that her eyes were shiny with tears, but John saw them. When he felt his own lower lip begin to tremble, he pushed his lips tightly together for a moment before he tried to speak.

"It's okay, you couldn't have known," John said sincerely, then he took a deep breath and changed the subject abruptly back to the dance. "Well, anyone who is going tomorrow night needs a mask. My sisters are pretty good at stuff like that, so you might want to get them to help. I've got to get back to work now, but I'll see you at dinnertime. My sisters Emma and Lucy are twins. They're thirteen. If they aren't anywhere in the lodge, you'll find them in the stables. Both of them are a little bit horse crazy."

"Sounds like they'll get along with you, June." Gina spoke to June then turned to John. "Junie just had her fourteenth birthday a couple of months ago, and she's horse crazy too."

"I'm guessing your birthday was in June?" John said.

"That's right, June twenty-first, the first day of summer. It's the longest day of the year," June told John with a sense of pride. "But don't tell Monty that I'm only fourteen. He thinks I'm fifteen."

John was surprised when June said she was really fourteen. He had thought to himself that she was maybe thirteen at the most. He tried to keep a straight face and an even voice when he answered her. "Oh, I won't say anything about anybody's age. But you might just tell how old you really are. Nobody much cares anyway, and then you don't have to remember which fib you told and who you told it to. It's hard enough to remember all the true stuff."

John noticed that the other Baldwins were smiling and nodding. He continued his thought. "Plus, fourteen seems to be a pretty mature age. I'm seventeen, and if I liked a girl and found out she was fourteen, I don't think I'd care." All but June burst into spontaneous applause. June tried to look mad, but soon she started laughing along with the rest of them.

"Okay, okay!" June said. "I guess I'll tell him, but I'd better fix up my mask a little to make me seem older. Right now I'm supposed to be a royal princess, but I think I look more like Bo Peep!" As she spoke, June rinsed out her milk glass then turned to go out through the service porch. As she put her hand on the doorknob, she turned back toward John and asked, "You think your sisters are out with the horses? I'm going out to find them and see if they can help me fix up the mask!" With that she hurried out, and the door slammed behind her. The rest of them heard a faint, "Sorry! Didn't mean to slam it!" coming from the path on the way to the barn.

John smiled and turned toward Ana. "Ana, if you want to go, it'll be fine. Maybe my Nana Mariel knows where there are some things you can use for a mask. I'll ask her if you want." John felt kind of sorry for this quiet dark-haired girl. She seemed out of step in every way from the other three Baldwins who all had fair complexions and blonde hair. Built like athletes, they were noisy and outgoing and seemed comfortable saying whatever came into their minds. In contrast, Ana was slender and dark haired, and she was slow to say anything at all out loud. John suspected that she had plenty of long, detailed conversations running in her head, just like he did.

"Thanks, John. That's really sweet, but I'm not sure if I really want to go. Plus, I'm going to play my violin for a little while. I have an audition next week, and I should practice."

When she smiled at John, her face lit up in a surprisingly vibrant way. John was intrigued by this quiet girl who was obviously bright and probably musically talented. Wasn't that what he was hoping, to find a musician in the group? John thought to himself and made a quick decision. He said, "Do you need an accompanist? I'm a pretty good reader, and I've played a lot of ensembles. What are you working on?"

"You've got to be kidding," Ana said. "I have been trying to find somebody, anybody, to play the piano parts. I've never heard what the ensembles sound like. I'm playing pretty standard stuff, but I'm told some of the piano part are challenging." Ana was cleaning up after herself and her cousins as she told John about the accompaniment parts.

"Hey, if you guys are going to play classical music, then I'm saying good-bye for now." JP rose quickly from the table, turned away toward the pantry, and called back to challenge Gina in a game of horseshoes. They waved at John and Ana and hurried out toward the horseshoe pit. John looked over at Ana, and they both laughed out loud.

"I guess some people will do anything to avoid hearing classical music," John said. "Come on, let's get your violin and music. Do you have it packed? How about if I meet you at the piano?"

John was eager to play some ensemble. Piano solo work is by its very nature a lonely activity. John envied his friends who played orchestral instruments. While he practiced for hours by himself the orchestra and band members had a great social time whenever they met to rehearse. Even sectionals seemed to be a lot of fun, at least from John's viewpoint. But then he thought of how much he loved the sound of his instrument and the music that was written for it, and it didn't seem bad at all.

As John headed for the front parlor, he tried to guess which violin scores Ana would bring. Certainly there would be a Bach, Vivaldi, or Telemann. He decided in his mind that it would most likely be the familiar Bach Concerto in A Minor. Then there was sure to be a Mozart or Beethoven and then a Romantic or more modern work. *It could be Meditation from Thais*, John thought as he reached the piano and sat down. Audition pieces seemed to go in and out of fashion every few years. One piece that was in vogue now was the Massenet. John hoped Ana was working on that piece primarily because it was beautiful, and also because he had been coached thoroughly on the work by his former piano teacher back in Sierra Glen.

John remembered how his teacher described the Massenet piano reduction. He told John that the piano accompaniment was easy to play, but not so easy to play well. John had performed the *Meditation* with Nicole, a gifted twelve-year-old violinist who was a member of the prep division at the university. She won a big regional competition with John accompanying. When Nicole proceeded to the state level finals in Los Angeles, she and her violin teacher chose to use a staff accompanist who was available in Los Angeles for much less money than it would have cost to take John and pay his stipend, plus his hotel and meal expenses. John smiled to himself when he thought of how Nicole had stormed into his practice room at the university on Monday following the finals. With tears of frustration streaming down her cheeks, she told John how she could have won first place instead of second if only John had been there to accompany her.

John was jolted back to the present when he heard Ana hurrying down the hall from the Baldwins' guest wing. As the steps grew louder, John stood and opened the door that led from the foyer to the south wing. Ana had her hands filled with a jumbled collection of musical scores, a portable music stand, and a violin case. Balancing the loosely stacked scores on her hip, she was reaching for the doorknob when John opened it from the other side. Ana nearly fell down as she struggled to keep her balance, but the whole pile of scores dropped to the floor and slid in every direction across the smooth terra cotta tiles.

"Uh-oh! Hey, I'm sorry! I should've been careful opening that door. I knew you were somewhere close because I heard your footsteps in the hall." John finished picking up the music and turned to hold the door open for Ana. He followed her through the door, then they both headed for the piano. Ana set up her music stand next to the treble end of the piano. She adjusted it slightly so she would be able to see John's face when they began to play. John saw the Bach concerto resting on the top of the scores that he held. He lifted it up and asked, "Are you doing the first movement here?"

"Yes, I'm really anxious to hear that one with the piano accompaniment. I've only heard it on a CD with a chamber orchestra. I guess you'll be playing an orchestra reduction. Your part looks kind of hard." Ana looked worried that she was asking John to do something impossible. She was surprised to hear his response.

"Let's give it a try. How fast do you take it?" He was already spreading the music across the piano music stand. Ana got her own violin score out and spread it on her own stand. John continued, "I'm not sure how much in tune the piano is right now. I hope it's not too bad." As he spoke, he played an A. They didn't speak for a few moments while they tuned. Since Ana hadn't answered about tempo, John chose to play it about half as fast as he thought the piece should be played when it was finished. Ana's entrance was correct, but it wasn't long before John could sense that she was struggling to maintain the tempo.

She was missing notes, and the rhythms were becoming more ambiguous with each phrase. Finally, the piece came to a grinding halt. A loud sound, something between a sigh and a groan, escaped from Ana's lips. She turned away quickly so John couldn't see her face. John knew that she was feeling both frustrated and foolish. Her neck was blotchy, and her face was flushed with embarrassment.

"That was much faster than I play it. I'm sure it could be fine a little bit slower. Can we try it? I never quite felt the pulse that time." She sighed audibly once again, then she gave a weak but hopeful smile. "Can we go about half that speed for now?"

"Sure, we can practice it slower until you're ready to play at tempo. The finished tempo will move a lot faster than we were playing just now," John said.

"Oh no, I heard the CD and it wasn't that fast, it couldn't have been! I'm sure you must be thinking of another piece."

John didn't say anything, but Ana could see from his expression that he did not agree. She tried to ignore his reaction as she continued to speak. "So okay, let's start about like this," she said as she played the first two phrases at a very slow speed. John just nodded and prepared to start once more. They continued through without mishap. Ana seemed satisfied, but John had a few ideas. He wasn't sure if anything he said would be welcome, so he just asked if she wanted any suggestions. She agreed.

"Well, that went pretty well. Your tone is warm, and your pitch control is really nice. Now, you'll want to adjust your bowing in certain places to make the phrases clear and well shaped. Also, try to carry your tied notes out to full value and lighten up on the passagework."

The two of them spent the next forty-five minutes discussing and playing sections of the Bach. Finally, they decided to play it through once again. When they finished, Ana grinned.

"Wow! That was so much better! Thanks, John. How do you know so much about music? And you don't even play the violin, do you? How do you know all this stuff?"

"Well, I heard a lot of coaching in my ensemble sessions. I'm just trying to remember everything that could help you. What other pieces are you playing? Maybe we can practice again sometime tomorrow?" John was enjoying himself, but he knew he was probably needed by Grandpa Fred or Nana Mariel to help with the lodge.

"Well, I have a Mozart sonata movement. Then I have a really pretty piece called *Meditation* by Massenet. I don't play it very well. I can't seem to keep it going. I've never heard it in finished form, but I know it's going to be beautiful." Ana stopped talking when she noticed that John was laughing. "What's so funny?" She started to laugh as well.

"It's just that earlier, I was playing a little game with myself about what pieces you might be playing. I guessed the Bach, and I was hoping for the *Meditation.* It's one of my favorites. Let's just try it through one time right now, okay? I can feed your part to you if you get lost. What do you say, want to try it?" John was already searching through the stack of music for the Massenet score.

"All right, but don't expect much." Ana found her music and spread it out. "Let's take it really slow, okay?"

John nodded, and he counted out a measure before starting. He was surprised when Ana began to play. Obviously, this was her kind of music. She played with a sense of maturity and a warmth of tone that was not so evident in the earlier piece. She had difficulty with some of the subtle rhythmic variations, but she was able to recover when John doubled her part with the piano in some of the more intricate passages. John was impressed with her easy command of rubato. They came to the reprise of the A section, a natural breathing spot, and brought the work to a halt. Ana was breathless. Unable to contain her enthusiasm, Ana laughed out loud.

"Oh my gosh, John, that is the most beautiful thing I've ever played! I can't believe how much it helped when you played along with me. I'm not very good at figuring out how to play the funny rhythms without slowing the whole thing down, but you kept me kind of honest. Really, what an incredible experience."

Ana still held her violin and bow. John was glad because he sensed that Ana was exuberant enough to hug him, and he was anticipating how that could create an awkward moment for both of them. Thankfully, her excitement subsided, and the two of them were able to talk rationally.

"Ana, this piece is really going to belong to you. I can hear how well you're going to play it, just as soon as you get confident playing all the notes and rhythms right. Let's work on it tomorrow sometime. I can show you some ways that will help you with deciphering rhythm patterns. But now, I better get hopping. I'm sure my Grandpa Fred is looking for me. There are always things that need to be done this time of day."

John stacked the piano scores neatly as he spoke. Turning, he headed toward the family wing. "I'll see you at dinner. That was fun, Ana. I hope we can find time to play together again."

"Absolutely! And thank you again, John, for your help. You're a great teacher! I'll see you at dinner. Say, can we sit together?" Ana looked hopefully at John. He stopped at the dining room and turned back toward Ana.

"Sure, I'd like that, but I'll have to find out what the family policy is about how much we are supposed to interact with our guests. The first night we were here, we had a couple of big lectures from my grandparents and parents about what they expected from us. The message I got was that we were supposed to be quiet and speak only to answer questions. Oh, and never talk about money, politics, or religion. So I guess except for the being quiet part, I've mostly followed the rules."

He smiled and started to turn away. "Well, I'll see you later." They waved at one another across the span of the large room, then each headed toward the opposite ends of the lodge.

John looked around for his grandparents and his parents. Where was everyone? Was this a time where the whole family was supposed to be somewhere and he had somehow forgotten? Was there another training class in rug cleaning or harvesting the herb garden or using the new barbecue? John began to feel uneasy. He thought, not for the first time, that maybe he should get a master calendar to keep his lodge responsibilities straight. Certainly, before he started his homeschooling, he needed to get a grasp of his day-to-day schedule. Otherwise, he might be in trouble most every day.

As he passed his parents' room, he heard some muffled sounds. John 's first inclination was to pass by and ignore it, but it sounded like someone was crying. He stopped and listened for a moment. He was certain that his mother was in her room crying. Actually, it was more like his mother was sobbing uncontrollably into her pillow in an unsuccessful attempt to be quiet. John was unsure about what to do. Was his father in there? Did Mom need help? Would she be embarrassed if he knocked on the door? Finally, John thought it would be cruel to ignore such obvious unhappiness. He stood close to the door and knocked lightly.

"Mom, are you in there? Mom, it's me, John. Are you okay?" John heard the bed squeak as his mother rose abruptly. He heard her footsteps approach the door. She blew her nose noisily. The door opened, and his mother gave John a tentative smile. She stepped back into the room, offering John a nonverbal but very clear invitation to enter. When he was in, she closed the door quietly behind him.

She waved him toward the captain's chair that was pushed halfway into the knee cubby of the ancient rolltop desk. The massive piece nearly filled the whole wall across from the queen-sized bed. This furniture had come with them from Sierra Glen. John remembered when he was little how he would stand on this chair to investigate the big desk. He had been fascinated by the endless rows and columns of miniature drawers and tiny doors that snapped shut with a distinctive click. The fleeting memory made him smile as he scooted the chair around to face the bed. Meanwhile, Christina had climbed back onto the bed and sat cross-legged, facing toward John.

"I'm sorry, John. You must be worried to hear me sobbing my eyes out, but I assure you, everything is okay. Sometimes I need to clear out a brain load of things that seem to pile up inside, and I've learned that once in a while, a good session of serious weeping helps." She smiled at John. "I think it's a girl thing. Most every girl and woman I know has moments like this, although I guess my sobbing today was a little over the top. Did I frighten or alarm you?"

"Not really," John started to say, but then he decided to tell the truth. "Well, yeah, I was really worried that something awful had happened. You know, really awful."

John was sure his mother was glossing over something. He looked at her face closely for evidence of secrets that were sheltered behind her expression. Although her eyes were puffy and red, there seemed to be no sign of furtiveness or guile. Did women really cry like this on a regular basis? John found it hard to believe, but he figured that his mom wouldn't tell him something that would give him false information about the psyche of all women. Still, he felt a certain amount of skepticism when he thought about her answer. Surely something must have triggered the tears.

"Well. What sort of stuff was piling up? I thought things were going pretty well since we got here. Especially with Dad. Do you think we made a mistake, you know, about coming to the island?" John was unsure about how much he should say. He realized as he spoke that he was really glad the family had moved to the island, and now he worried that his parents would decide not to stay.

"Oh no, Johnny! Your dad and I think this was the best decision we've made since, well, since, you know, a couple of years ago. And you and the girls are thriving in this life. Can't you see the changes in yourself? Look how comfortable you are with the guests. I can't believe the difference in you after such a short time. And Lucy! She has somehow decided that her own opinions are as important and valid as Emma's. Have you heard them talking lately? It used to be Emma talked and Lucy listened. Now they chatter and they argue and they yell at each other, but they still present a formidable united force of two when anyone or anything challenges them. I pity anyone who crosses either of them."

Christina had morphed into her mothering role and seemed to be done with her crying, at least for now.

"Yeah, I've noticed some changes in the girls." John realized this was a good time to find out about the implied rules and customs of the lodge. "By the way, Mom, I met four of the Baldwins today at lunch. They're really nice. I'm going to be driving at least two of them down the sea camp for the dance tomorrow. You probably already know that the twins are going too. I'll be taking them as well. Anyway, Ana asked if I could have dinner with them at their table tonight. Is that okay? Are we allowed to sit with guests at dinnertime? I'm sure June Baldwin and the twins are best friends by now, and they'll probably sit together without even thinking about it. Say, did you happen to hear us, Ana and me, practicing?"

"I have to confess that I was listening to you from the kitchen while you worked on the Bach. John, you are a natural teacher and coach. I was proud of how you were helping her. Your thoughtful suggestions made a big difference in her playing."

Christina was obviously ready to prove to her son that she was in control of her emotions and her reasoning ability. Her manner demonstrated clearly that the crying was over, and John should not worry one bit.

"You know, Mom, Ana didn't seem to understand about how to read rhythm."

John stopped talking for a moment to collect his thoughts. He didn't want to sound critical, but he was puzzled about Ana and her training. "How could she be playing advanced music when she hasn't mastered the basic concepts of meter or rhythm? Also, I noticed her Massenet score had accidentals marked all through it. I'm not sure she understood what it meant to be in a particular key. Maybe she never had a chance to take violin lessons with a private teacher. Do you think maybe she gets all of her training in big group ensembles at school? Maybe there isn't enough time to make sure every student really learns how to read music, especially students with a good ear like Ana."

John was curious what his mother would say about Ana's apparent deficiencies in training.

"Unfortunately, Johnny, lots of teachers neglect to give students the tools they need to decipher a musical score. Those teachers must believe that the student will always have a teacher or mentor to unlock the secrets in a new piece of music."

Christina smiled at her son, remembering him as a young student. "That's why we insisted that you stay in evaluations every year. It was a way to make sure that you understood all of the notational concepts in your music as it got more complex."

"Thanks, I guess. I always thought it was fun anyway." John changed the subject abruptly. "So it's okay if I sit with Ana at dinner tonight?"

"Sure, Johnny, if she asked you. Mom and Dad have known the Baldwins for years. They are easygoing and will certainly welcome you into their group."

Christina was thoughtful for a moment before she added, "But don't assume that you will be spending every moment and every meal with Ana. Try to maintain a friendly relationship, but limit your time together. You will have lodge responsibilities, and Ana will be expected to interact with her family.

"Also, keep in mind that there will be new guests every week, and beginning next week you will have school responsibilities as well. We are the constants here at the lodge. It's like a giant television series that is being staged at our house. The members of our little nuclear family are the stars who are under contract with the network, and all the other characters change around us.

"You have seen only a tiny fraction of the revolving cast: first the bridge ladies, and now the Baldwins. Think of how much you have enjoyed your time with them. Most likely, you will find some really interesting and intriguing people each week. Mom has told me about lots of nice families that come year after year. Many of them include teenagers, so just relax and enjoy all of the guests."

Christina stretched out her legs and slid to the side of the bed. She stood up and walked over to the adjoining bathroom. Leaning in close to the vanity mirror, she took a long look at her face and laughed out loud. "If I didn't look so funny with mascara dripping under my eyes, I think I'd start to cry all over again. What a mess!"

"Oh, you don't look that bad, Mom." John realized that didn't sound exactly the way he meant it. He tried to explain that he thought she still looked okay, but everything sounded insulting.

"Thanks, Johnny, I know what you mean." Christina leaned over and gave him a hug. "I'm going to fix up my face and change for dinner. I'll be down in the front parlor in about a half hour. I'm reading a good book, and that long couch is really comfortable. If you want to play a little piano, I'd love to listen." John smiled as he rose to go.

"Okay, Mom. Maybe I'll see you then." John left the room and turned toward his own room down the hall. It wasn't until he had entered his room and shut the door behind him that he realized that he never really discovered what had caused his mother to sob into her pillow. He didn't buy her answer at all, even for a moment. John sat on his bed and thought about the past few days. Everything was changing. The dynamics in his family were different now.

His parents still maintained a sense of reserve with each other that robbed them of the spontaneity that used to define their relationship. But recently, there had been times here on the island when John saw them working comfortably side by side on a task. Granted, the easy interplay of light conversation that John remembered from the past was missing, but at least the rancorous animosity was fading. There were times that everything seemed normal. But his thoughts kept going back to what he had observed just minutes ago. Why was his Mom crying?

John sighed and turned his thoughts inwardly. He had met two really interesting girls: a dark-haired musician and a blonde phantom. He had learned many details about his family history, details that explained the ongoing feud between the lodge and the sea camp. But then when he met the guys from the camp, he wondered why things were still so raw between the two owners. Time is supposed to heal all wounds. But then, why could he not speak about his own brother when the Baldwins asked about him?

Paul, Paul, I couldn't even say your name out loud! he thought as he sat there quietly. John knew that he and his father were destined to become bitter and angry like Papa Jacob if they didn't deal with their feelings about the bad time two years before. And what about Mom? Was she crying about Paul? Did she cry often about him? John did admit to himself that some good things were happening to him since he moved to the lodge.

His mother was right when she said he seemed more comfortable talking and interacting with new people. The old self-consciousness that plagued him until just a few weeks ago must have fallen off his shoulders when he walked off the ferry in Mirabella. John wondered if his new attitude was the result of leaving some of the old emotional baggage behind in Sierra Glen. It was as if a reset button had been activated, giving him a brand new opportunity to understand and react to new people. He leaned back onto his pillow and stared at the ceiling. *Well, I guess I shouldn't worry too much*, he thought to himself, *because life seems pretty good so far here on the island.*

Chapter Sixteen

John was mired in the gauzy net of twilight sleep when he heard loud knocking on his door. He looked at the clock on his wall. It was a little after six. Oh no, dinner had started! He opened the door and found Lucy about to knock once again.

"Hey, are you going to sit with the Baldwins? Ana's saving you a place, and she feels kind of stupid. Did you have a date with her?" While Lucy was talking, John had wiped his face with a wet towel, rinsed out his mouth and gargled with mouthwash, and combed his hair.

"I was just waking up when you knocked," he said. "Let's hurry back to the dining room. Are you sitting with June?"

"Yeah, the three of us had a lot of fun riding the horses in the corral. Grandpa Fred was showing us how to ride bareback. Emma fell off when her horse started to trot, and I almost did, but I didn't."

"Is she, Emma, okay?" John spoke without paying much attention. He was anxious to get to dinner. Lucy answered just as they reached the dining room. "Yeah, she's okay, but she has a big bruise on her behind." Lucy giggled. The two of them smiled at the folks gathered in the room.

John's parents and grandparents hadn't yet arrived, but the twelve bridge ladies were seated at one long table, and the Baldwins were all seated at two round tables, each with nine place settings. Lucy sat in the place between June and Emma, and John quickly slid into the empty chair beside Ana at the other table.

"I'm sorry to be late. I fell asleep in my room." John thought that sounded pretty lame, but it was the truth. Now that he was sitting down, he remembered why he had been in such a fog when Lucy was pounding on his door a few minutes ago. He had been totally immersed in a dream adventure, but as soon as he had awakened, a misty nothingness shrouded any access back into the exciting plotline. John listened as bits of disconnected conversations swarmed around and between the two Baldwin tables. The Baldwins were not quiet. The older ones along with all but the smallest Baldwin family members contributed to the discussions that filled the space over the tables like a smoky cloud.

Those who did not speak were still fully engaged in the conversation. John watched the group dynamics carefully. As the family members listened, they nodded in agreement or frowned and shouted "No!" John found himself laughing at the appropriate places and responding whenever necessary. He was unaware that a good portion of his unconscious brain was sifting through his memory banks to recall the elusive dream.

Ana leaned over slightly and directed her voice to John. "It's always like this at every meal in our family. Everyone talks and laughs a lot. I hope we don't drive you crazy. You seem kind of quiet. Are you okay?"

Ana was concerned that John really didn't want to be at their dinner table. John noticed that she looked particularly vulnerable as she waited for his response. When she tilted her head like that and smiled, Ana was very pretty in a classic, well-bred sort of way. He liked her manner too. She was quiet and observant, and those were traits that he understood very well. He turned so that Ana could hear him over the noisy conversation at the table.

"Hey, your family is really great. I'm glad to be here tonight. It's just that I had a weird experience a little while ago. When I got to my room after we practiced, I leaned back on my pillow, and I guess I fell asleep. I had a strange dream, but when I woke up, the details eluded me. The more I thought about it, the foggier everything was. It's driving me crazy because there was something really important about the dream, like a message or warning."

John smiled at the sound of that. "I guess that sounds kind of melodramatic, but I have a creepy feeling that the message is important. Now I've got an odd sort of feeling that won't go away."

John stopped and took a long drink from his water glass. He tried to explain how he felt. "Well, it's almost like the way I feel just before I go on stage to perform. You know, that mixture of terror and exhilaration. But I guess what I'm feeling right now is closer to the awful butterflies-in-the-stomach feeling, not the excited anticipation feeling."

"What do you mean, anticipation? I never had an excited anticipation kind of feeling," Ana said. "I'd say that every single thing about waiting to perform can be summed up with two words: pure terror! I'm sorry, John, but performance anxiety puts a stampeding herd of buffalo in my stomach. Giving a speech is the worst, but playing my violin is pretty awful too."

"Well, maybe I feel anxious right now because I have no control over my brain." John smiled as he tried to explain things more clearly. "I'm assuming some part of the old bean is sifting through the memory banks to find the dream."

He watched Ana's face as he spoke. "You know how it is when you have to stop trying to remember where you left your wallet or stop trying to remember someone's name? Well, whatever you forgot usually comes to you at some odd moment when your mind is a million miles away."

"That's how my brain always works when I'm under pressure," Ana responded. "Honestly, I can't even play Boggle if someone insists on using that little egg timer. As soon as there is a clock running, I freeze up."

Ana shook her head and smiled. "I love to watch the TV show *Jeopardy!* but even though I know most of the answers, I can't seem to blurt them out before anyone else. My uncle Bart says I'm one of the only Baldwins left that takes after my great-grand Lacey's side. They were the daydreamers, kind of like readers and poets. You know, very different than the family today."

With that, she looked around the table then rolled her eyes. She laughed and added, "Uncle Bart says I'm programmed like a distance runner instead of a sprinter. Slow twitch muscles, he says."

"I do remember feeling like that during those math quizzes where the teacher had a stopwatch and yelled 'Go!' That was back in elementary school." John hadn't thought of those days for a long time. "I could never do well on those. Do you remember how there were a zillion little problems on just one page, and you had to finish before the teacher said 'time'? I really hated those tests," John said. "I knew the answers cold, but I could never finish in the time limit allowed." John smiled.

Turning toward Ana, he said, "I guess our brains are built the same way. Your family says you have slow twitch muscles, huh? Well, my family says I have a baseball brain."

When Ana looked confused, John clarified, "That's right, baseball. It's the only major league team sport without a clock controlling it. And you know, I really do like to watch baseball better than most other sports. I guess that both our families think we're the odd ones. They just explain us in different ways."

The food was delicious, and the mood in the dining room was relaxed. About halfway through the meal, John heard his parents and grandparents enter the dining room. His mother had put on makeup and fixed her hair. She was wearing a blue dress that John hadn't seen before. John thought she looked really nice. He marveled at her ability to make her guests feel special. Always poised and relaxed, she greeted each person warmly. She knew most of their names, and several times she took a few moments to lean close in order to ask about some unique factor in the guest's life.

There seemed to be no evidence of sadness in her appearance or her demeanor. She finished circling the bridge ladies, then she turned toward the Baldwin tables. She welcomed them and thanked them for inviting her children to share dinnertime with their family. She smiled at John and the twins then turned to the lodge family table.

The dinner plates were cleared, and there was no evidence of the heaping stack of Toll House cookies except for some crumbs left on the serving platter. Guests and lodge family members were everywhere. Several were playing cards in the clubroom. A few were in the front parlor visiting. Someone had turned on the music out in Sofia's patio; some of the younger Baldwins and a couple of bridge ladies were dancing. A few had partners, but most were just dancing. Nobody seemed to care about how they looked or what kind of dance steps they were doing.

There was plenty of good-natured teasing, and as always, when one person tried a new dance form, the others were quick to copy the new steps. The electric slide lasted several minutes, giving everyone a chance to master the steps and turns. Still, as often as not, June turned the opposite way from the group. Twice she bumped into Phoebe, who suggested that June would be just fine if she just thought "Left foot is right!" when she wanted to turn. June was bewildered, but the other dancers started laughing and making suggestions of their own.

"Left foot might be right," said Ruth, "but the right is the only foot left!"

"Step right ahead or you're left behind," JP said, and without missing a beat, Gina added, "Think left right left right, you'll be fine." Phoebe and Ruth mulled that one over for a moment, then they both agreed those instructions were confusing and probably not even correct. By then, the dancers had moved on to trying the jerk, the twist, and the surfer stomp.

John and Ana sat at one of the outdoor tables and watched the dancers. They had both joined in the chicken dance, and now they watched as Ruth and Phoebe taught the Baldwins and the twins how to do the bunny hop. Before long, there was a conga line of Baldwins, bridge ladies, Garrett twins, Grandpa Fred, and Nana Mariel snaking around the patio and singing an almost tuneless rendition of the bunny hop music. They all sang random syllables in time to the music until it was time to hop three times. At that point, the whole group seemed to know instinctively to shout "Hop! Hop! Hop!" After several minutes, the bunny hop line dissolved into a mass of out-of-breath individuals who collapsed into chairs all around the patio. When Christina and Daniel staggered out of the lodge with a large ice chest filled with juice, water, and soft drinks for the dancers, there was a spontaneous round of grateful applause.

"Would you like to practice again tomorrow?" John asked Ana. "We should probably arrange for a time now because of the dance tomorrow night. I have a few chores that need to be finished before noon, and then Grandpa Fred will probably need me for something in the late afternoon. What do you think? Is there a time that's best for you?"

"How about eleven?" Ana answered. "By then everyone will be out of the house, and we won't bother people with our classical music."

"The bridge bunch will be playing cards out here on the patio. If we shut the windows by the piano, I don't think they could hear us at all. So eleven is fine. I'll tell my mom tonight so there won't be any surprises tomorrow. Have you decided about the dance at the sea camp?"

"Not really," Ana said. "I haven't given any thought to a mask. And I'm not too sure about square dancing. I got confused with the electric slide and the chicken dance tonight, and those are easy compared to following a caller." Ana smiled. "I'll tell you what though. Tonight, I'll decide. I promise to have an answer when we meet tomorrow morning at eleven. Okay?" Ana stood, then she picked up her sweater and tied the sleeves around her waist.

John watched her as she scooped up the stack of cookies she had wrapped in a napkin. Again, he thought how attractive she was in a soft and gentle way. He liked the way she moved with a pleasant blend of grace and efficiency. He liked the way she pushed her hair back from her forehead. He began to list in his mind all the qualities in Ana that he found attractive. After a couple of minutes, however, John realized that Ana was waiting patiently for an answer.

With a start, he stood up next to her and stammered, "That'll be fine. I guess I better go clear things with Mom and then hit the sack. It's going to be a full day. So I'll see you at eleven?"

"Okay, John. Oh, and thanks! I really appreciate your help with my music. I can hardly wait to work on the other piece. So I'll see you tomorrow."

With those words, Ana turned toward the lodge, waving to John as she entered the wing where the Baldwins were staying. John waved and headed back toward the kitchen. When he passed through the back hall, he heard his parents' voices in the dining room. John poked his head in through the door. His folks were sitting at a table far across the room. Their heads were close together, and Christina's voice had an edge to it. John couldn't hear the words, but it was obvious his parents were arguing, or at least bickering. John hated to hear them. Daniel heard the door and turned toward John.

"Oh, hello, Son. Come on over and join us." Daniel's voice said the words, but John could tell that his father was not particularly interested in having John join them.

"We were just talking about Emma and Lucy and the horse incident," his mother said. "Did you hear about Emma's little mishap?" John was sure his folks hadn't been talking about the twins.

"Yes," John answered. "Lucy told me that Emma had a doozy of a bruise on her butt. No, wait. That's not exactly right. She said Emma had a bruise on her behind!" The obligatory chuckling to such a declaration emanated from their throats, but the mirth did not reach below the surface, and the laughter stopped quickly. John decided to just take care of his business and leave.

"Mom, I'm going to practice with Ana tomorrow at eleven. We figure that would be a good time, and it wouldn't interfere with anyone's day. What do you think?"

"That should be fine. Just be finished a few minutes before noon, you know, in time for lunch." Christina smiled at John then turned to her husband and rapped him on the arm. Daniel nodded and turned to speak to John.

"Fred told me you were driving to the sea camp dance. How many people are going so far?" Daniel asked.

"Well, there's me, Gina, June, Lucy and Emma, maybe JP, and maybe Ana. So at the most we'll have seven. I would bet that JP won't go, so I'd count on six. Why do you ask? Do you want to join us?" John was teasing, but both of his parents nodded thoughtfully.

"Good. We were hoping there would be room," his mother said. "Do you mind if we join you? I dug out a couple of old masks that were in a box in the attic. Nothing too original, just a couple of jokers. You know, they are the kind that you find in a deck of cards. By the way, if anyone else needs a mask, there are several up there."

John was surprised and pleased to learn that his folks were actually going to do something together, something by choice. He was curious to see how they would act tomorrow night. It had been so long since John had seen evidence of the warm affection that defined their relationship up until the accident a couple of years ago. John tried to see vestiges of those days, but he could not see past the protective shells they both wore. John stayed a few more minutes in small talk with his folks. Then he excused himself and headed toward his room. What a curious evening it had been. Tomorrow was sure to be very interesting.

John reached his room and opened the door. There on his bed sat a large cantaloupe wearing an exquisite mask. The mask consisted of a piece of creamy linen that had been draped and then sewn so that it would fall to the middle of his back in soft pleats. A gold-and-silver braided rope held the headpiece on the cantaloupe. The little lamb, Baasheepa, rested in a cozy sling on the right side of the mask. John could see how the contraption would fit nicely over his shoulder like a baby sling.

The upper part of the cantaloupe's "face" was covered with a papier-mâché forehead and nose. Lucy had attached a flowing mustache underneath the nose. John was surprised at the workmanship. Once again, he felt a pang of regret over the way he had ignored his sisters as individuals.

Well, my little sister really came through, John thought. He was grateful that he didn't have to do anything more about the mask. He was going to tell Ana about the extra masks in the attic. Maybe she would decide to go after all. His mind wandered as he got ready for bed. He turned off the light and rolled over onto his side. Suddenly he sat up. The dream! He remembered it all. John reached to turn the light back on, then sat on the edge of his bed.

"Oh no! Tomorrow morning, I was going to ride one of the horses up to the springs to meet Casey." John frowned as he sat and thought about what he should do. Should he go out riding really early to meet a girl who might not even exist at all? Should he forget about it and just wait for tomorrow night at the dance to see if there really was a Casey? And if she was real, who was she? Then there was Ana. What if Ana decided to go too? What if both girls expected to be at the dance with him? Would they fight over him? And if they forced him to choose between them, who would he choose? *What a mess!* John thought. *And to make it worse, my whole family will be there to see it all.*

After considering his options, John turned the light out once again and sighed. *I guess there's nothing I can do about tomorrow night until it gets here.* With that final thought, he closed his eyes and fell asleep. At least his subconscious was kind enough to avoid any more dreams from forming. He'd had enough mystery in his life already.

Chapter Seventeen

John woke up just before dawn on Saturday morning. He stared at the ceiling for a few moments while he sorted out his thoughts. With an audible sigh, he sat up then pivoted so that he was sitting on the bed with his feet on the floor. He leaned over and grasped his forehead with his palms. He could feel his temples throbbing; in fact, his whole body shuddered with each heartbeat. He felt miserable. Was he getting sick? John sat for a few minutes more, then with another long sigh, he stood and stumbled into the bathroom.

Fifteen minutes later, he emerged from the steamy, hot room feeling much better. He knew that he had just wasted a big supply of fresh water with his hot shower, but he justified the use of it by thinking he washed away the flu or whatever he was on the verge of getting. John dressed quickly. He wore his comfortable old Levi's and a T-shirt. He grabbed some socks and his hooded sweatshirt and headed for the kitchen. Nobody was around. John quickly put on his socks then grabbed a couple of bagels and a plastic bottle of orange juice and headed out the door.

Gathering up his old Adidas from the shoe basket on the back porch, he slipped them on and hurried up the path toward the barn. His plan was to take Cherry up to the West Springs where he just might see Casey, then return home by 8:30 a.m. so that he could take care of the chickens before 9:00 a.m. When he arrived at the barn, however, there were already three bridge ladies and a few Baldwins milling around. Fred and Daniel were working with Christina to saddle the horses. They all looked a little frazzled. John made a quick decision and hurried over to his mother's side.

"Hi, Mom. I thought I heard something out here, so I came out to see if you needed any help."

John knew he'd said the right thing when his father nodded approvingly and answered him. "Son, we could use your help getting these horses ready for our guests." Daniel swept a hand toward all of the horses who were out of their stalls and tied to the barn railing. "Thanks for getting out here so fast."

"It's fine, Dad. Are they all going out for a long ride? Do we need to pack lunches?" John wondered if Ana was going riding. He didn't see her yet, but there were still a few Baldwins arriving from the lodge each minute or two.

"No, I think they are just riding up to the springs for a little while. They all had a quick, early breakfast. Mariel fixed it for them. Didn't you see the spread in the dining room?" Daniel looked at the bagels and juice in John's hands.

"I didn't even think to go in the dining room since it's so early. I thought I was the first one up." John smiled. "I guess I should know better. Nana Mariel always gets up really early, doesn't she?" John put his juice on the fence post by the barn as he ate one bagel. He tucked the other in the pocket of his sweatshirt. John followed his mother into the saddle room. She got a saddle blanket and the bridle gear for Cherry; John, following her out of the barn, carried the awkward western saddle. Together, they prepared Cherry for the morning ride.

"Thanks, Johnny. This is so much easier with two people. We have eight more horses to go. Thank goodness a few of the Baldwins decided to ride tomorrow instead. I wish we had a few more horses. Mom says they often run out of mounts on the weekends when the lodge is full. Maybe we'll start shopping around for a few more good saddle horses." Christina sighed, knowing how hard it would be to buy animals from over town and ship them across the channel. "You know, maybe I'll talk with the sea camp people tonight. I hear they breed some pretty nice horses. Also, there's Rancho Buena Vista, the big ranch in the island interior down towards Mirabella."

"You ought to take the twins when you go shopping for horses," John said. "They'd love it. Maybe eventually, they can become your equine experts. They're interested enough in horses, at least for now."

"You may be right. It would be nice to delegate the whole stable operation to the girls when they are a little older," Christina said as she finished with Cherry and headed back to the tack room. John followed close behind. It was twenty minutes before all of the horses were ready for the guests. Since there were expert riders in both the bridge group and the Baldwin family, Christina did not feel it necessary to send a guide with them. The trails were well marked, and the riders had ridden to the springs every year for at least the past five years.

The bridge women left about ten minutes before the Baldwins. They were laughing like junior high students. John had to smile when he watched Gurtha use her reins and knees to guide Two-Door, the only pinto in the entire stable. The old gelding was a favorite because of his attractive markings and his dependable behavior. Gurtha might think she was in command, but John knew that Two-Door could follow the trail up and back without any help or guidance. After all, he had walked that trail hundreds of times. John watched until the last horse turned out of sight at the junction up past the orchard. The dust swirled up around the horses' hooves. The bridge ladies planned to be back before half past nine. The group was scheduled to start playing bridge at ten. The Baldwin group all expected to be back before lunchtime at noon.

Christina and Daniel looked hot and tired. John felt as if his shower that morning was a complete waste. Sweat was rolling down his back, and his arms felt leaden from the continuous chore of lugging the western saddles from barn to mounting corral. His second bagel had fallen from his pocket onto the stable floor, and Rocky grabbed it from the dirt and chomped it down in two bites. Now it was nearly eight, and John was starving.

He followed his parents in through the back porch where he slipped off his sweatshirt and tossed it in the laundry hamper. Dropping their shoes in the basket, the three of them went to the dining room and found that Mariel had made some banana muffins to add to the breakfast spread. John grabbed a hard-boiled egg and a handful of crispy bacon. He scooped up two muffins and carried his food treasures into the kitchen where he poured a huge glass of milk and sat at the table.

A few minutes later when he finished eating, he sat still for a moment. The morning had not progressed the way he had planned, and his head was beginning to throb again. As John was about to return to his room to lie down, he remembered the eggs that still lay in the nests, waiting for him to collect them. *Stupid eggs!* he thought to himself. *Stupid horses, and stupid everything else, too!*" He felt a little better after blaming his headache on his morning encounters.

Then with a sigh, he got up and rinsed out his glass. He was going to get the stupid eggs and then return to his stupid room and sleep. Walking out the door toward the chicken coop, he thought of Frank Sinatra singing with his daughter Nancy Sinatra. Their most famous collaboration was a song called "Something Stupid." In John's opinion, it ranked as one of the worst five songs ever recorded. The tune lodged into his mind, and as he walked past the barn, the infernal melody began to play a duet with his throbbing forehead. He sighed again as he entered the coop, thankful at least that he hadn't felt compelled to sing the stupid song out loud.

John was meeting Ana in the front parlor at eleven. He felt much better since taking a nap and another shower. After leaving his room, he stopped in the kitchen to make a quick peanut butter and honey sandwich, then he grabbed a half-filled carton of milk and drank it down without bothering to get a glass. *That's better*, he thought as he entered the parlor. He felt ready to enjoy some time working on beautiful music with an attractive girl. What could be better? So what if his plans to ride up to the springs didn't work out this morning? Who knows if Casey would have been there anyway? *Well, there is always tonight at the dance*, John thought to himself. *Maybe Casey will materialize there.*

Ana arrived a few minutes after eleven. She seemed a little flustered and out of breath. She put her violin case and her music down on the couch and plopped down beside them with a sigh.

"I'm so sorry to be a little late, but I've been up in the attic looking at old masks. If I can find one that will work, then I think I'll go to the dance tonight." She looked over at John and continued, "That is, if it's okay, or if, you know, there's enough room. Oh, I hope there's still room in the car."

Ana was clearly uncomfortable, and John thought he knew why. She seemed to have the same set of insecurities that he had. It was a mystery to John how someone as poised and gracious as Ana could possibly feel insecure. He began to wonder if he looked that uncomfortable when he was in a new situation.

"Ana, I'm really glad you decided to go. Everyone says the dance is really fun. Now I know I'll have a good time because you'll be there. We can make room for everyone in the car. What about JP?"

"JP told me this morning that he's planning to stay home with the boys. I guess the male Baldwins are planning a poker party tonight."

"Well, they just don't know what they'll be missing. Hey, let's try the Massenet. Mom said we need to finish playing before noon, so that gives us a little over a half hour."

Chapter Eighteen

The sun had set, but the sky still glowed with the last twilight of the day. It was a perfect island evening. John drove onto the sea camp property and parked the van on the edge of the makeshift parking lot that had been marked with orange cones. He lagged behind the others as they followed the path toward the lighted social hall. He was still thinking back to the morning practice session with Ana. He could still hear the beautiful melodic line that soared over the gentle accompaniment.

He and Ana had been a little self-conscious at first when various people started to gather in the area around the piano so they could listen. When their audience begged the musicians to play the whole piece for them, Ana and John agreed. Quietly, John reminded her to treat it like a real concert. Ana understood that John meant she should fix any problem without letting anyone know she might be having difficulty. John could still hear the magical performance.

The piano and violin blended the individual lines of music into a lush garden of sound. The two of them seemed to know just when to stretch the melody with either a broad allargando or a gentle ritardando. They felt the music soar toward glorious moments of dramatic intensity, and they recognized the genius of the composer in every note. Their performance paid homage to Massenet.

The room was quiet when the piece drew to a close. No one said a word. Then a rumble of applause started and continued to grow louder while several Baldwins and bridge ladies and staff members, including several from John's family, called out, "Brava! Bravo!" John was lost in the good memories of the morning as he walked up the path, carrying his mask.

His group was progressing slowly toward the hall. About fifty yards ahead, guests were beginning to pause long enough to put on their masks. Even from far away, John could see that some of the masks were incredibly ornate and large. He was thankful for a small and comfortable mask. Before long, his group stopped for a few moments to don their own masks. Lucy helped the others align the eyeholes so all could see reasonably well with the masks in place. They walked as a group toward the entrance of the hall.

There were festive lanterns hanging everywhere, and thousands of tiny white Christmas lights outlined the eaves and windows of the social hall front wall. The surrounding trees and bushes had lights defining their shapes. It was like a magic wonderland. The music—fiddles and drums and guitars and instruments of various other timbres—filled the hall and spilled out through the door to the front walkway.

Everyone was filled with happy anticipation. The masks helped to defray any anxiety the partygoers might have had about square dancing. The caller was giving gentle instructions and encouragement. Soon, it seemed everyone was dancing. The masks were cumbersome and a few toppled over, but mostly, the atmosphere was one of timelessness—a unique venture into another era. John felt that a time warp had blended fourteenth-century Verona with Colonial America. For the first set of dances, John's square was made up of the eight who came from the lodge.

His mother, decked out in a floppy red joker mask, was his partner. Daniel, in his black joker mask, stood with Ana across the square. Ana had found a silly Cheshire Cat mask in the attic, and Lucy helped make it small enough to fit Ana. Even so, it tended to slip down on one side, making the grin even more lopsided. The twins were partners beside John. They had decided at the last minute to make new masks, and they finished up just a few minutes before it was time to leave for the dance. They came as a matching pair of lamps, complete with the lampshades they had worn in the *LaZboat* a few days before. John thought they looked great, especially since they had rigged up a little battery light in each mask that could be turned on and off by the lamp switch on the mask.

They had worked out a little routine where they switched the lights on and off together in a rhythmic pattern that fit with an eight-bar phrase of the fiddle music. Every so often, they would insert the routine into the dance steps, causing spectators around the dance floor to applaud and cheer. June and Gina, dressed as a princess and a Queen of Hearts, were across the twins. The caller led them through many traditional square dance steps, and by the end of the set, the group felt confident enough to throw themselves into the spirit of the dance.

The caller said that the squares were ready now to mix it up. He insisted that all the dancers mingle and find new partners. The musicians vamped some travel music while the partygoers wandered around. Soon, there was a full dance floor once again with the masks arranged in new combinations of eight to a square.

John danced two more sets with various combinations of masked characters. The mood was lighthearted and fun. Somehow the masks kept anyone from feeling foolish or clumsy. The combination of anonymity and whimsy contributed to the happy atmosphere. When John sat out for one set and stood at the side of the hall to observe, he was struck by the masterful plan that drove the whole event.

Whoever came up with this party format knew human nature. Hiding behind a mask made it both easy to interact with others and to try new things. The square dance format eliminated the need for matched partners. Male, female, young, old, big, small, shy, outgoing—any combination of eight individuals comprised the square, and the success of the dance steps and combinations depended upon teamwork of the group.

As John scanned the room, he marveled at the creativity and wit behind the masks. Simple animal masks do-si-doed with elaborately constructed masks depicting mountains, waterfalls, buildings, or other man-made structures. Famous people of history linked arms with movie and TV characters across the square. *What a great night!* John thought. *No wonder they do this year after year.* John caught a glimpse of the Cheshire Cat across the dance floor by the back wall. She was standing quietly in front of the large sliding windows, which were open all across to the wide lighted patio. *I guess Ana's taking a break too*, he thought as he started to thread his way toward her around the periphery of the room. It was slow going because of the crowds and the masks that everyone wore.

Finally, he reached the first of the open doors. He stepped outside and felt the cool night air on his arms. There were almost as many people outside as there were in the hall. Since the sound system had speakers aimed outside on the far side of the patio, John saw several squares dancing over there as well. Other guests were seated around tables or stood in small clusters to visit. The outdoor punch bowl was as popular as the indoor one, and the booth serving wine and beer had a crowd of people waiting in line.

Just as John passed the punch bowl, he saw the Cheshire Cat standing in the shadows on the far side of the patio. He hurried toward the mask.

As soon as he was about twenty feet away, he called out, "Hey, you with the big grin, are you ready to dance some more?" He saw the mask turn toward him. All of a sudden, he felt confused. There was something odd about Ana's mask. Hadn't it been drooping toward the left when they were dancing? Now the mask sat perfectly straight on Ana's shoulders, and somehow it seemed a few inches taller. When he reached her, he was surprised when she spoke.

"I'd like to dance, but since I just got here, it'll be the first time tonight. Hello, John." It was Casey's voice emanating from beneath the mask.

"Casey!" John said. "I don't understand. I have a friend who came over from the lodge with us tonight, and she has the exact same mask! Where did you get yours?"

"I found it in the storage room over the camp dining hall across the patio from here." She pointed to the big building adjacent to the social hall. "Mark's mother said she wore it to the dance when she was a junior in high school."

"Is Mark's mother Carolyn Peterson by any chance?" John thought he knew why there were two Cheshire Cats.

"Yes, well, she's Carolyn Peterson-Anderson now, but that's right. How do you know about her?" Now Casey sounded confused.

"It's kind of a long story, but I knew that Carolyn Peterson and one of my relatives used to pass for identical twins when they were in high school. I'll bet anything that Kara Cecile made her mask with Carolyn. They probably had a lot of fun deciding what subject to choose for their identical masks. The Cheshire Cat seems perfect. You know—elusive, strange, funny. Anyway, my friend Ana found the other one in our storage attic and decided to wear it tonight."

A chilling breeze caused Casey to shiver. She stepped toward John. It felt natural for him to put his arms around her and draw her close. The masks bumped awkwardly, making it impossible for anything more than a quick embrace. As they stepped away from one another, John thought he saw another Cheshire Cat staring at him from across the patio, but before he could wave or call her over, Ana turned and rushed in through the doors at the far side of the social hall. John was about to tell Casey that he would be right back, but just then the music stopped, and the microphone squeaked loudly.

"Well, folks," Mr. Simon said. "It's about that time once again. As you've been dancing and having a good old time," he paused, then continued, "You *have* been having a good old time, haven't you?" The crowd clapped and whistled. The caller laughed and said, "Well, while you've been dancing and carrying on, the judges have been carrying on a project of their own. That is, to choose the winning masks for this year. I've been told by all three judges that it was especially hard to decide since there were so many creative masks, but they have reached an agreement on the prize winners.

"As you probably know, we'll award prizes for first, second, and third-place winners. Now, allow me to introduce Dr. Keith Sorenson, grandson of Peter Sorenson. Keith came all the way from San Francisco to serve as festival coordinator this year. Let's give him a nice island welcome home. Come on up, Keith."

Mr. Simon waved him up to the podium as the audience clapped and shouted out greetings.

John stepped back into the hall, curious to see the man his mother had told him about—the one who had a crush on her when they were in high school. Keith Sorenson was a tall man, slim and sandy haired. He seemed friendly enough, and his wide grin lit up his face. With a spark of good humor, he leaned over to speak into the microphone.

"What a pleasure to be back on the island. I think those of us who were raised here never lose the feeling that this beautiful place is where we are truly meant to be. Making the channel crossing showed me how much I miss the island and all of you, my friends. I guess what I'm saying is, it's great to be home!" The crowd clapped and cheered. John could sense that here was a man who was well liked for himself and for his accomplishments in the world beyond Santa Teresa. Keith nodded to the drummer, who produced a short drumroll.

"Now, without further delay, I'd like to begin with our third-place winner. Our third place is actually a pair. Who could resist these two matched lamps with their precision light show? So if Lucy and Emma Garrett could please come up." As the girls dashed to the podium giggling and flicking their lights on and off, Keith continued, "May I present our third-place winners! Congratulations, girls!"

He handed them a bronze trophy and an envelope. John knew that the trophy would be cherished secretly back at the lodge. He felt it was a shame that Papa Jacob would never know the joy and excitement that the girls were experiencing right now.

Second place was awarded to a Chinese dragon mask that had red glowing eyes and smoke coming from its nose. The first place award was for a unique mask that was designed to look as if there were three people sitting totem pole style on the shoulders of the mask wearer. The man had arranged a pulley inside that allowed him to make the topmost figure's arms move. He made the little guy wave and salute to the audience as he accepted his prize. Keith Sorenson laughed and clapped along with the audience.

After waiting a few moments, Keith spoke, "Well, it's another great night on the island. Congratulations to our winners, and let's continue with the fun. Happy dancing!" As soon as he finished speaking, the music started up, and Mr. Simon prepared to call the next set. Masks were lined up around the edge of the dance floor and in a heap outside. Casey had left after the awards ceremony to help organize the masks so they would not be trampled. She told John she would look for him later.

John was about to go searching for Ana, but as he turned toward the big room, he caught a glimpse of his mother sitting at a table in the corner of the patio. She was partially in the shadows, but her profile was clear, and it was obvious that she was furious. John could see the veins in her neck pulsing. John couldn't see who she was talking to because there was a group of people standing in the way, but John suspected his father was feeling the brunt of his mother's wrath.

As the group of people moved beyond the table, however, John was surprised to see Keith Sorenson sitting across from his mother. He was holding his palm up toward his mother's face in a gesture that seemed to be asking her to be quiet for a moment. John could see his mouth forming words. His mother was shaking her head back and forth as if to reject what she was hearing. She rose abruptly, but Keith took her arm and gently pulled her back into her chair. Nobody noticed as tears began to run down her cheeks. Sorenson stood slowly and then leaned over to say something in her ear. Then he walked away.

John could feel his mother's sadness. He knew that whatever Sorenson had said to her was unexpected and painful. But John could also allow himself to feel relief. He had been worried about his mother and the mysterious Keith Sorenson from her past. When his parents said they were coming to the dance, John was secretly worried that Keith might be one of the reasons. But it was obvious that Sorenson had rejected his mother, albeit as tactfully and gently as he could. With a sense of relief tinged with anger, he stared at his mother. Who was she to treat her husband and children so badly? As he looked at her, trying to decide if he should go over and talk with her, she got up abruptly and hurried through the door into the hall.

Just as she disappeared into the crowd, John saw movement from a table farther back in the shadows. There was his father with several empty wineglasses in front of him. Daniel stood carefully and walked slowly and tentatively toward the edge of the patio. It looked like he was heading for the walkway that led to the parking lot. John hurried to his father, arriving just in time to curtail a nasty spill. Daniel hadn't realized there was a step down from the patio surface to the walk. John caught him and guided him toward the car. His father reeked of cigarettes and wine.

"Dad, do you want to just sleep for a while in the car? Or if you want, I can gather up everyone in a few minutes, and we can head back to the lodge."

John was hoping his father would just climb in and fall asleep. Daniel started to answer, but as he reached the backseat, he lay down and almost immediately began to snore. John checked to make sure his father was in a comfortable enough position. It wouldn't do for his dad to barf and choke. John sighed and thought how there was something weird about tending to your drunk father. Wasn't that kind of backward? Jon felt a wave of disgust wash over him when his father belched and coughed.

John closed the door quietly and headed back inside the hall. The party was going strong. He looked for Casey and Ana, half hoping not to find either. He saw the twins as they stood in the punch line with Mark, Ian, Sam, and Gina. They were all laughing about something Ian had said. Scanning the room, John spotted June and Monty dancing in one of the squares out on the dance floor. John thought they looked good together. Everyone seemed to be having a wonderful time.

John was surprised to see his mother dancing with a group of older ladies he had met at church. They were all laughing. His mother showed no sign of her earlier tears. He wondered again how things could look so normal on the outside and be so messed up on the inside. Did he really know his mother? He knew that sometime soon he would need to find out, but it made him tired and angry to even think of dealing with all the problems that hid under the surface in his family. *Is this what they call dysfunctional?* he thought to himself. *Because if it is, I think my family really needs help!*

Finally, the caller announced the last dance of the evening, the Virginia Reel. Dancers of all ages scurried around to find partners. Two sets were organized, and the partners took their places across from one another in line formation. The music started, and after a few wrong turns, most of the dancers caught on to the simple steps. Spontaneous singing and plenty of good-hearted teasing and laughter blended with the familiar fiddle tunes that drove the reel dancers. When the music ended, the crowd groaned in disappointment.

Nobody wanted the evening to end. The crowd acknowledged the musicians with wild applause and whistling. Then a group of young men stormed the stage and lifted Mr. Simon onto their shoulders. They carried the popular caller around the room while the dancers cheered. Just as he reached the stage once again, Peter Sorenson and his grandson Keith climbed the stairs up to the stage. They stood with Simon, and the three took a couple of deep bows. Sorenson thanked everyone for coming, then he closed with a broad invitation for next year—the fifty-fifth Sorenson Sea Camp Harvest Festival and Dance.

John found Ana near the door where they had all entered hours ago. He approached her tentatively, noticing that she was holding her Cheshire Cat mask. Seeing her mask reminded him that he'd have to go back and get his own shepherd mask. It was on the other side of the hall. He started to turn away, but then he turned back and walked up to Ana. He took her arm gently as he spoke.

"Come on with me. I forgot to pick up my mask, and Lucy would kill me if I left it." Although Ana came with him willingly enough, John could feel the tension in her arm. He decided to tell her about Casey. Ana would probably think he was certifiable, but he was tired of secrets. He took a big breath and started to talk softly to Ana as they crossed the big dance floor.

"Look, I'm sorry about not getting back to you after the awards, but it's been a weird night. My mom had a nervous breakdown over some guy she knew in high school, my dad got stinking drunk and is at this moment sleeping it off in the car, and to top everything off, there was a girl wearing a mask just like yours. It turned out she was a girl that I had met in some really odd circumstances before. When I say odd, I really mean it. The first time I met her was a few nights ago—"

"I know, John. You met Casey on the beach, and then you saw her again up at the fire ring. Then you thought she was me just a few hours ago when you saw her here at the dance in the Cheshire cat mask. " Ana laughed. "Honestly, John, you should see your face right now. Anyway, Casey told me how you had been looking for me. She told me all about how you met. She told me to tell you she'd be in touch sometime next week. Now, come on! Let's find your mask."

The tension between them faded to nothing as they found the mask and returned to the punch bowl by the entrance. In that short span of time, they had regained the feeling of easy companionship that had been developing between them during their practice sessions. John knew then that as the first friend he had made from the unending supply of lodge guests he would meet in the future, Ana would always hold a special place in his memory. They rounded up Gina, June, and the twins, who were all talking about the evening and what fun it had been. Nobody wanted to admit that it was time to go home. Gina was just telling the others about how Mark was directionally impaired and how when the caller said, "Not quite, in square number one. Son, use your other left foot!" He was talking to Mark. As they laughed, Christina came up to John.

"Johnny, please gather everyone quickly. I just got an emergency message from Dad. Papa Jacob has collapsed and lost consciousness. The paramedics are on the way from Three Ships."

Chapter Nineteen

Within five minutes, the lodge van was filled with Garretts and Baldwins. Daniel was still sound asleep in the backseat where John had helped him settle almost two hours before. Christina sat in the front seat next to John. Very little was said on the way back home. John drove carefully and deliberately. He realized that his mind was filled with many diverse thoughts. Images from the evening of dancing and visiting competed with concern over what he saw regarding his parents, then the confusion over Casey, and then Ana, and finally, the image of his great-grandfather unconscious and gravely ill.

They arrived back at the lodge, and the Baldwins headed for their rooms. Ana stopped to tell John how sorry she was about Papa Jacob. The air between them seemed back to normal: two friends who genuinely liked each other. John was surprised and pleased when Ana leaned toward him and gave him a warm hug and a kiss on the cheek. The gesture was heartfelt and genuine, offering consolation and hope.

It was close to dawn on Sunday morning when Mariel gathered the family into the family den to report about Papa Jacob. Late last night, the paramedics had wanted to take him in the Coast Guard helicopter across the channel to the hospital in Long Beach, but Papa Jacob had left very clear instructions with Fred and Mariel that he wanted to die at home. Jacob feared being taken away from home much more than he feared death. Fred understood all of this, but he was still a bit uncertain whether he had made the right decision in rejecting the recommendation of the paramedics. Mariel looked around at her family. They were still wearing the clothes from the dance, and they all looked a bit disheveled.

She stood and began to talk quietly. “Fred is with your Papa Jacob now.” Emma yawned audibly, causing Mariel to pause and smile before she continued to talk. "Jacob seems to be resting comfortably enough. He regained consciousness briefly when the paramedics were here, but he's been fading in and out for the past few hours. We're really not sure if he is just sleeping or more like in a coma condition. At any rate, his pulse is weak but seems steady, and his breathing is regular, so I guess we just wait and see. In the meantime, Brenda Hernandez from hospice will be arriving within the next few hours."

Mariel stopped talking. A wave of anxiety made her sit down. She realized that her cheeks were wet with tears. It was no surprise to learn that Jacob was close to the end now, perhaps only a few days were left. It surprised her, nonetheless, to realize how sad she felt to be losing this gruff old man from their midst. Christina stood and walked toward her mother. She sat beside her and put her arms around Mariel's shoulders.

"It's okay, Mom. You and Dad made the best decision. This feels so right. Papa Jacob saw so many of his friends grow old and get sick then get carted off to some strange place to die. If he gets better, he'll thank you in person, but if he doesn't make it, I think you can be sure that you and Dad followed Papa Jacob's wishes." Mariel smiled at her daughter, grateful for the words of encouragement. She stood once again and faced her family.

"I have just a few more things to go over with you." Mariel was surprised at how confident her voice sounded. "Brenda explained to me on the phone how we can't be sure if Papa can hear or understand anything we say when we're in his room. She said we should just assume Jacob can hear everything. She said to keep speaking to him of good things and good memories and to assure him often that he is loved."

Everyone nodded and agreed with the course of action except for Daniel, who had sunk down into his chair and was snoring quietly.

"Now finally, we still have guests in the lodge. They expect a wonderful Sunday breakfast, a meal I haven't even thought about yet. The bridge ladies have a two o'clock boat to catch in Mirabella. Then the Baldwins are scheduled for the five o'clock boat. Johnny, do you think you and Daniel can handle the *LaZBoat* well enough to get both groups and all their stuff to town? It'll take two trips, one after another. The Baldwins always have plenty of luggage, so you'll need to leave extra time to load and unload.

"Oh, I almost forgot! Father Thomas is coming back with you after you get the Baldwins settled on the pier. He's planning Mass for our family and our staff members this evening here at the lodge."

Mariel was pleased to see John nod in agreement with the plan. Then she turned to the girls and said, "Fred would really like to stay with Jacob today, but he would appreciate it if you all would drop in to visit. Now hurry and get cleaned up, and remember to get your chores done. Oh, and I could use some help setting up for breakfast in about two hours. So scat now, but keep Papa Jacob in your prayers, and your Grandpa Fred too."

John stood and walked over to where his father was sleeping. He leaned down and gently shook Daniel's shoulder. "Dad, hey, Dad. Wake up, Dad. Come on, it's time to get cleaned up. I'll walk you back to your room so you can get a shower and some clean clothes. We have lots to do this morning, then you and I have to get all the guests to Mirabella this afternoon."

Daniel's eyes fluttered open and he seemed to be listening, but he did not respond.

"Come on, Dad, let's wash up so we can have breakfast."

John helped Daniel stand up, then he continued to support his father as they made their way toward the family wing bedrooms. When they reached Daniel and Christina's room, Daniel turned to his son and smiled sheepishly. Without a word, Daniel opened the door and slipped in, closing the door behind him. John wasn't sure if his father would take a shower or just fall asleep on his bed. On TV and in movies, drunk people were often portrayed as amusing, even hilarious. As John entered his own room, he thought how his dad's condition was not one bit humorous.

As John stood under the scalding-hot shower, he felt some of his anger and feelings of disgust melt away. He loved his parents and his family, but he worried that they were all heading for some sort of family explosion. He prayed that each family member would have enough emotional strength to weather the storm. John dressed quickly then, on a sudden impulse, decided to go into Jacob's room to sit with Grandpa Fred for a while. When he entered the room, John was surprised to see the twins and Christina sitting around the bed. Grandpa Fred was not in the room at all. John sat in a chair beside his mother.

The girls were keeping up a lively conversation, mostly about the horses. They told Jacob about their new friend June and how she might come and visit during the summer. Christina held her grandfather's hand and told him how glad she was to be back home on the island. As she spoke, she felt a slight pressure on her palm. Then Jacob turned his head toward his granddaughter and blinked his eyes open. Lucy stood and raced out the room to deliver the news to Grandpa Fred, who had gone out briefly to change clothes.

"Papa Jacob is awake!" she told Grandpa Fred. With a sigh of relief, Fred rushed to his father. He asked Christina if she would mind letting him have some time alone with his dad for a few moments. Nodding, she and Emma stepped from the room. John followed them out the door. Fred sat next to Jacob and held the old man's frail hand firmly in both of his own. Fred was the son, but he suddenly realized he was an old man himself. Jacob wanted to talk, and they spoke of many things—good memories, old friends, family members living and dead, and finally of the future.

Both men were products of the past, and they saw in the Garrett family hope for a smooth continuation of the lodge operation into the time yet to be. Fred, however, wanted Jacob to understand that just as the lodge had changed subtly over the years to accommodate new trends and new tastes, they could expect the Garretts to respond to new challenges in the future. Fred wanted to say something about the everlasting feud with the sea camp and how it would be a smart move to mend some fences with the neighbors.

Somehow, he could not find a way to say the words. Then he wondered if it was really that critical to burden Jacob in his final days with such an issue. Then again, he thought how there had never been a time where Jacob and Fred had kept secrets. They always shared their thoughts with each other, and they had disagreed frequently. The only exception had been the relationship with the sea camp. Over the years, Fred and Mariel had maintained a cordial relationship with Peter and his family, but the camp and its activities and personnel were never mentioned in front of Jacob.

The anger that Jacob felt over perceived wrongs and real tragedies gradually matured into a solid chunk of bitterness that affected every aspect of his life. It was clear that Jacob had not received his full measure of happiness upon this earth, but it was of his own making that he missed out on many of life's simple pleasures. Fred wanted to make it clear that the Garretts were going to put the old hate aside. Fred had practiced how to explain his thoughts to Jacob as he bounced ideas off Mariel. He had fully intended to discuss the issue with Jacob before Christmas, but now that Jacob was so sick, the issue could not be postponed any longer. Fred thought to himself, *It's time*. He sat next to his father and willed himself to just say something. He couldn't.

Soon, John knocked lightly and stuck his head in to ask if he could join Fred and Jacob. Fred welcomed John into the room. It made Jacob happy to think of the lodge continuing under the direction of John sometime in the future. Before long, Mariel knocked and entered. She had some broth to feed the old man, so Fred got up and moved to the side of the room. When Mariel searched Fred's face questioningly to see if "the conversation" had occurred, Fred just shook his head.

Mariel gave him a little squeeze on the arm and smiled. She mouthed the word *soon*. She sat down and proceeded to feed Jacob. After three spoonfuls, Jacob turned his head and refused to eat anymore. The hospice nurse had explained that people at the end of life usually stop eating so that their digestive system can begin to shut down. She stated, "Force feeding and natural death are not compatible," then softened her position by adding, "but an end-of-life loved one has the right to eat or drink pretty much what he wants, in moderation. Just follow your Papa Jacob's lead, and you'll be fine."

Mariel remembered that advice, so she put the soup aside. She set one freshly baked gingersnap on the tray next to Jacob's bed. When she leaned over to kiss him, she whispered that there was a cookie for him if he wanted it. She picked up the soup to take it back to the kitchen and had barely reached the door when Jacob asked John to hand him the cookie. Mariel and Fred smiled at each other as she slipped quietly out of the room. Jacob nibbled tiny bites off the cookie, then he slipped the rest under his pillow. Fred sat back down in the chair next to Jacob.

Suddenly, the door opened once again, and Daniel entered the room. He was still a mess. He flopped down in a chair next to John. Daniel's clothes were wrinkled and soiled, his dark hair was sticking up on the side where he had slept in the car, and he still smelled like a fraternity party.

Jacob noticed everything and asked, "What is the matter with you, Daniel? If I didn't know better, I'd think you were drunk or hung over!" Jacob's words held a little of his old fire.

"Yeah, I guess I was a little drunk, and it's wearing off a bit now," Daniel said slowly, and then without thinking, he added, "Went to the dance and had some wine while my wife threw herself at this guy named Keith."

John tried to interrupt the flow of words that spewed forth from his father's mouth to Papa Jacob's ear, but there was no stopping Daniel. He told about the girls winning a prize, he told Jacob about how John was a fine chauffeur. He finished by saying that eight people were there from the lodge, including the whole Garrett family. Fred also tried to stop Daniel's account, but the damage had already been done.

"What do you mean? You all went to that infernal dance? How could you? You know, don't you, how untrustworthy and dishonest they all are?" Jacob's voice shook with anger. Mariel heard the shouts and hurried back into the room. She realized that Jacob has somehow learned about the sea camp dance. She sat beside Fred, who was angry with himself for not speaking up earlier. Now it was as if he and Mariel were part of a conspiracy. Jacob fell back onto his pillow and began to sob. Fred wasn't sure which of Jacob's behaviors was more disconcerting: shouting or crying.

Fred and Mariel had both heard plenty of shouting over the years, but it occurred to Fred that the only time he had witnessed uncontrolled sobbing like this was thirteen years ago when Jacob and the family stood in the Mirabella cemetery and watched as Sofia's coffin was placed in the grave. Sofia had passed away after a long struggle with cancer. During the final weeks leading up to Sofia's death, Jacob was so mired in his terrible sadness that he had no energy or interest in anything beyond his grief. As Sofia's only living child, Fred was left to deal with his own feelings of loss. Thankfully, with Mariel's support, Fred weathered the bad times. In contrast, Jacob buried his sadness away in his heart just as surely as he had buried his wife in the ground. That terrible grief bonded with all the other hurts and disappointments he had encountered during his life. Over the years, Fred finally came to understand how Jacob's cumbersome burden of unhappiness had gradually eroded away any capacity to feel joy and peace. It filled

Fred with sadness to know that his father had missed experiencing the totality of God's gift: the precious gift of life itself.

Finally, Jacob was quiet. His eyes were open, but staring off toward the ceiling. Just as he was about to sleep, there was a light rapping on the door. Fred got up and peeked out. With a gasp, he stepped back into the room with Casey following behind him.

"Casey! What are you doing here?" John was amazed to see her. His Grandpa Fred hadn't spoken since his initial gasp. Casey walked toward the side of the bed and smiled at Jacob. He looked at her for at least a minute before speaking.

"Well, Casey, it's been a long time. How is Sofia?"

John and Fred stepped back to allow Casey full access to Papa Jacob. "I'm not sure who you think I am, Papa Jacob, but my name is Casey, and I've come with messages from many people who love and admire you. Now, Sofia … I think you are referring to your wife? Well, I'm sure she is safe with our LORD in heaven, waiting for the time when we are all called home."

Casey sat on the edge of the bed and took Jacob's hand in her own. He seemed content to maintain the contact. Casey smiled and nodded at John and Fred, then she directed her attention back to Jacob.

"But dear Papa Jacob, I have come to the island to tell you about your relatives back in Minnesota, where I was born and lived for the first five years of my life. Do you remember your second cousin Eva? Her daughter, Imogene, married the son of your old friend Sully. They had five children, the youngest is named Anita. You would be amazed at how much she looks like the pictures you sent long ago of your granddaughter, Kara Cecile. Anyway, when she was in high school, Anita met the man of her dreams. "He was a visitor to town, and he was in his first year of college in California. To make a long story less long, they fell in love, got engaged, then four years later, they got married. Their first child, a daughter, was born while the man was finishing med school in Minnesota. Then they moved to San Francisco. I'm telling you all of this because members of the family have sent me on a mission. Everyone in our old hometown knew about the bad blood between the Engstrom family and the Sorenson family out here on the island. I'm here to ask you to try to end the feud for one simple reason. That child, the daughter I spoke of, is me. Your second cousin Eva is my great grandmother." Casey stopped to allow Jacob to absorb what she had said. She smiled at him as she continued speaking, "Yes, Papa Jacob, we are family." Casey stopped talking for a moment as if to gather strength. Then she took a big breath and said, "And my father is Keith Sorenson." She looked carefully at Jacob to see what his reaction would be to her news.

John was dumbstruck at first over the revelations he was hearing, then he thought everything was beginning to make perfect sense. Grandpa Fred and Nana Mariel had gradually moved to the far side of the room and were standing together quietly. Both were enjoying every moment of the surreal experience unfolding before them. Meanwhile, Jacob was quiet and very still.

"My name is Karole Celine, and they call me KC for short. Dear Papa, I hope you will consider what I have said. There are good and bad people in every family, but both sides of my family, the Engstroms and the Sorensons, have many more good than bad. Please forgive us for the terrible behavior of one or two bad family members."

When Casey smiled at Jacob, she looked exactly like the girl in the twins article. John could not believe how closely his Casey resembled the Casey of the past. Jacob did not say anything, but after a few moments, he sighed, then gently extracted his hand from Casey's and turned over to face the far wall, effectively turning his back on everyone.

"Well, please think about what I've said. I hope you'll find it in your heart to let go of the anger. I'll be thinking about you, Papa Jacob, and I will continue to pray for you. Please know that you are loved by many people back home. I'll just say good-bye for now, but if you want me to return, just call the sea camp, and I'll be here before you know it."

She turned and smiled at Fred, Mariel, and John, then she stepped out of the room and was gone. Mariel left shortly after, and when she returned about twenty minutes later, she found Jacob asleep and John and Fred sitting quietly, staring off into space.

Jacob lingered for three days. He had moments where he was lucid and clear. During those brief periods, he spoke with whichever family members were keeping bedside vigil at that moment. The family took turns rotating in and out of Jacob's room. They sat in pairs and groups of three; once in a while, someone would sit alone in the quiet room with Jacob. On Wednesday evening, Fred was sitting close to the bed where Papa Jacob lay.

Father Thomas had visited Jacob earlier in the afternoon and served communion to the whole family as they gathered around Jacob's bed. Now, Jacob was resting peacefully. Fred put his hand on his father's forehead, gently brushing back the long white strands that had fallen over Jacob's eyes. Quietly, Jacob opened his eyes and turned his head toward his son.

"Tell Casey I'm ready, Son. Tell Casey I'm ready. She's right. Tell Sofia I'm ready, Son, I'm ready. Sweet Jesus, I'm ready." Jacob smiled as he took his last breath. Fred sat for many minutes watching the spirit of his father vacate the shell that had confined it for ninety-three years. Fred could tell that the essential core of his father was soaring toward another place, a place where he would throw off all vestiges of sadness from the past and then bathe in eternal peace of his Almighty Father, surrounded by all those he had loved and lost.

When Mariel entered the room to join Fred in keeping vigil, she saw that Jacob had passed. She sat next to her husband and circled her arms around him as she leaned in close.

"It was a good and peaceful death, and I think Dad is finally happy." Fred felt sad, but somehow, he was also heartened by this intimate encounter with death. He knew now that leaving this world is not something to be feared, for as he had just witnessed, there surely are loving hands waiting to guide you across the dark threshold. And Fred knew when it was his own time to go to meet his Maker, that Jacob's would be the first hand offered.

After the funeral Mass Tuesday afternoon, John stretched out on his bed and stared at the ceiling. Uncle Matt had participated in the service with Father Thomas, and the little parish church in Mirabella was filled to overflowing. John heard that two hundred chairs had been set up in the church patio, and they were all filled. Many of the residents of Sorensons' Sea Camp were there, and there were ten relatives from Minnesota, including Jacob's eighty-nine-year-old second cousin, Eva. Casey Sorenson and her parents, Keith and Anita, sat with Eva.

Fred and Mariel had made sure that all of the relatives, including those with dual ties to the Engstrom and Sorenson families, were invited to sit in the family pews. John sat directly in front of Casey. She leaned forward before the Mass began and told John how much she had been thinking of him and his family. John and Casey had spoken quietly for a few moments, but he excused himself hastily when the parish coordinator signaled that it was time to start.

John walked over to the piano and sat down on the bench. After a few moments, he began to play the opening of the elusive Rachmaninoff prelude. Just a little over three minutes later, he reached the final cadence, and the music whispered away, dissolving at last into the cool autumn air. The entire church was silent. The music, truly a voice from eternity, had said all that John wanted to express in eulogizing Jacob. When the Mass had ended and Jacob's remains had been consecrated and buried, there was a big reception at the parish hall. Almost everyone made it a point to tell John how much his music contributed to the beauty of the day.

As John rested on his bed later that afternoon, he thought about all the sad things that had happened in his family. If he made a list of the tragedies, how many would there be? What constituted a tragedy anyway? Certainly, today was not a tragedy. It was sad to have to say good-bye to Papa Jacob, but the whole family agreed that today was a celebration of Jacob's life. Who could doubt that Jacob was at this moment and forevermore in the presence of his Savior, Jesus?

John knew that Jacob would be sheltered and loved throughout eternity; just as surely, John knew when it was his own time to leave life on earth behind, Jesus would be there to guide and shepherd him from transitory life to life eternal. John thought, *Then I guess death itself is not a tragedy, but maybe it's more of when and how the death occurs.* John mulled this over for a few minutes. Then he realized that the tragedy of death does not apply to the person who dies, but rather the tragedy lives within the hearts of those who are left behind. *Yes,* John thought, *what if, instead of Papa Jacob, it had been Mom who had died? Or Emma? Or Lucy?* John realized then that death follows an expected order. Everybody will die, but it is expected that the old die before the young. John began to think that a tragedy is the result of unexpected or out-of-order death.

In his mind, John sifted through the familiar plots of many books he had read over the past few years. He tried to summon up a plot line with multiple examples of bad luck, bad decisions, bad health, bad choices. The concept of tragedy grew more elusive the longer he thought.

Would there have to be a death to have a tragic situation? John decided that death was automatically a family tragedy, but only when the death was unexpected. As soon as John reached that conclusion, however, he could think of several examples of an unexpected death that would not be regarded as tragic.

First in mind was a news article John had read several months before about a ninety-year-old lonely widower who went out to play nine holes of golf with his son and grandson one beautiful spring morning. There were no crowds, the course was in perfect shape, all played well. On the ninth hole, the old man made a hole in one. It was witnessed by several of his friends who were in the clubhouse eating breakfast. As he was engulfed in hugs, congratulatory laughter, and happy chatter, he sighed once then slumped over. He had died instantly, a smile still on his face. John had to conclude that though the death was unexpected, it was in no way tragic.

Suddenly, John was struck by a novel thought. He was aware of a very tragic unexpected death in his own family. Heck! He had even witnessed it! Every time he tried to think of the details pertaining to the incident, however, there seemed to be a million distracting thoughts that floated into his mind, keeping him from zeroing in on that day two years ago. In fact, just realizing that he had avoided any thoughts about the "incident" made him almost sick with dread and disgust. John knew that he could not even begin to understand the nature of tragedy if he did not come to terms with that fateful time in the Sierras with his brother and his father.

John forced himself to drift back to the fateful spring camping trip two years ago. As soon as his mind wrapped around the notion of the awful accident, John felt a profound heaviness fall over him like a canvas tarp. John was tired, he was frustrated, and he was finally ready to do something about it. He forced himself back into his memory so that he could revisit that trip and study it with the maturity that he had acquired from living two more years.

He remembered getting out of the car, putting on his pack, and following his father into the woods. He could not force himself to continue pursuing the memory linearly. All of his emotions seemed to get jumbled, making the visions blurry. John sighed. Perhaps if he tried to see those events in third person, he could keep the memories straight. He concentrated hard, starting back at the beginning where a father and two teenage boys got out of the car and started to hike into the forest. Yes! John began to see the experience replay in front of his eyes as if he were watching a movie about someone else.

Chapter Twenty

Long before the three hikers saw any evidence of a waterway, they could hear the river roaring down the gorge. The air was fresh and cool, almost cold enough for jackets, but the three had been hiking for over an hour, and they had all worked up a sweat. The packs were beginning to feel impossibly heavy. Fourteen-year-old John was small and thin. Even though his fifteenth birthday was less than one month away, he was still much smaller than his brother had been at age fourteen. John felt like he could hardly take another step, but he refused to complain. His older brother Paul would be relentless in his teasing; John would do anything to avoid the ribbing, no matter how good natured. He was relieved to hear his father speak.

"I'm pretty sure the tent cabin is just around the next bend. Just a little bit more, boys, and we can settle in." With renewed energy, John stayed close behind his father. Paul started to jog up the path, overtaking his brother and father. "Come on! Let's hurry so we can get something to eat, I'm starving!"

Daniel and John plodded along until they turned the bend. They saw Paul stretched out on a cot in front of the modest tent cabin, their borrowed accommodations for the weekend. It was a beautiful setting, secluded and pristine. There were only sounds from nature: birds singing and chirping, the wind blowing the high branches of the trees, and the water rushing down the narrow canyon.

It was mid-May, and the runoff was ferocious. A record snow pack followed by one of the quickest spring thaws in recent years made for some spectacular river watching. Each year, the river carried the newly melted snow from the high elevations toward the lakes and reservoirs below where the water would become docile—ready to do man's bidding. Here in the gorge, however, water was king. Nothing and nobody could stem the will of the powerful flow.

Paul had just turned seventeen. He was eager to experiment with the new camera lens his parents had given him for his birthday. Lately, Paul had been studying the work of Ansel Adams, especially the collection of photographs portraying the section of the Sierra Nevada range where Paul and his family were camping this week. Paul was eager to capture on film the raw energy that Adams seemed to expose and portray so naturally.

It's a good thing the weather turned out to be so clear this week, Paul thought to himself. *I know I'll get some great shots.* Paul approached every challenge with confidence and enthusiasm. In addition to his passion for photography, Paul was interested in a variety of other activities. He seemed to achieve a high level of success in anything he tried: sailing, tennis, soccer, acting, and even video games.

"The Garrett family father and sons camping trip" was an annual event. Paul remembered when he was about six and his brother John was not quite four. Dad set up their old tent in the backyard of their home in Sierra Glen, a small community nestled in the high foothills of the mid-Sierras. The town, located just off the highway that meandered up toward Yosemite and Sonora Pass, was at an elevation where leafy oaks and poplars were giving way to the piney forest.

The Garretts' backyard was woodsy and natural, perfect for a first camping experience. Every year since then, the two boys and their father spent a weekend together. The first few years were in the backyard, but gradually they ventured farther and farther into the forest. Paul smiled when he thought of his mom and his twin sisters. Beginning that very first year, Dad made a big deal about kissing the "womenfolk" good-bye. The twins, Emma and Lucy, were only about ten months old. Now the women of the family enjoyed a shopping weekend while the menfolk were gone.

This year, Daniel decided to schedule their trip midweek. He knew there would be very few other hikers at the higher elevations during the week, especially so early in the season. Paul would not have to shoot his pictures around the crowds that would be sure to come up on the weekend to see the waterfalls.

Paul was depending on the late afternoon sun and especially the early morning sun to produce some interesting shadows and textures in his photos. He was impressed with the natural beauty all around him; he felt sure that he would get some remarkable shots. Here in National Forest land, there was little evidence of human interference. The tent cabin concept was a tentative experiment in careful land usage with minimal ecological impact.

The structures provided shelter, sleeping cots for four, a small camping stove, a pump-up lantern, and a secure bear-proof metal locker for food storage. Campers were expected to provide for every other possible camping need including fresh water and fuel. When the campers left the site, it was expected that no evidence of their visit would be left behind. TVs, radios, and other electronic noisemakers were not welcome.

The very spartan tent cabins were for campers who sought minimal distance from raw nature and great distance from the RV campsites that were scattered all through the forest. Made of wood and canvas, the cabin had two large screen windows on each wall for ventilation.

Daniel Garrett dropped his pack and took out the food packet that was on the very top of his kit. He had learned from previous years that he and the boys would want to eat almost immediately after arriving on site. He prepared some hot soup and sandwiches. The three were quiet until every bite was gone. Although the fare was simple, the Garrett men agreed as always that the food was the best they ever tasted.

"I'm going to relax and read my book for a little while, boys." Daniel was already eyeing a shady spot near the tent where he could drag one of the cots. When the boys started to laugh,

Daniel smiled in return. "I know. You think I might fall asleep. No way. We can have a giant card game in a little while if you want." He checked his watch. It was nearly three. "How about at three-thirty we play a game of hand and foot?"

The boys thought that sounded fun. Daniel reminded them not to wander too far and to stay back from the water until they all had a chance to look it over together.

"Come on, Johnny! Let's see if there are any critters living in that broken tree." Paul was already heading toward the tree they noticed back at the bend where they had turned to reach their tent cabin. The massive trunk had broken off in a jagged mess. It resembled a fist holding a sword pointed toward heaven. The rest of the tree had crashed across shrubs, rocks, and a stand of smaller trees. Dad had remarked that the tree had probably been hit by lightning.

It was apparent by the grass and foliage that grew all around the broken tree that whatever caused it to fall happened long ago. When Paul reached the edge of the narrow clearing that had been formed in one violent moment by the crash of the falling tree, he stopped. Overcome by the magnitude of the damage created by just one tree, he felt a wave of anxiety wash over him, and he shivered slightly. Growing up at the base of the mighty Sierras, Paul had a healthy respect for the mountains.

He knew the forces of nature were more powerful than any human, but he had also been taught well about how to survive in the mountainous forests where he grew up. Paul stood still and stared at the fallen tree for a few moments. He took a big breath, then he slowly exhaled. The anxious sensation gave way to a mixed sense of awe and exhilaration. Behind him, he could hear John galloping up the narrow path.

"Sorry! I had to pee!" John was out of breath. "Did you find anything yet?"

"I haven't looked. I was waiting for you. Come on, let's walk around it first. I want to pace off how tall it was." As he talked, he began to walk with big strides. John followed behind. Frequently, they had to skirt large branches and little stands of saplings that were competing with one another for space and light. At one spot, the tree had broken completely through as it hit an outcropping of granite rocks.

The boys scrambled over them and continued pacing. Near the topmost branches of the fallen tree, the boys found a large boulder that was gently sloped and perfect for climbing. Soon they were both perched on top of the rock. The afternoon sun felt good on their shoulders. Paul was doing some figuring in his head to determine the height of the tree.

"How tall do you think the tree trunk was that was still standing back there? Maybe ten feet?" Paul knew his little brother was really good at figuring out spatial and perceptual problems. Their mom said that John observed everything with an artist's eye and a mathematician's brain.

"You know, I think it was way taller than ten feet. You could have stood with Dad on your shoulders and still not be tall enough to touch the top where it broke off." John did some quick figuring. "I'd say it's more like fifteen or sixteen feet. How many steps did you take from where we started?"

"I think it was about eighty strides. I had to just guess when we climbed over those rocks and branches."

"That's probably about right, eighty strides. I think I took just a little less than a hundred steps, but they were just regular steps. You were trying to keep yours like deliberate strides, you know, the same length. I think you were going about two and a half feet per step, maybe a little less sometimes. So let's say two feet for now. That would be one hundred sixty feet tall, plus the trunk that's still standing." John hesitated, then he spoke quickly, "So it would figure about one hundred eighty to two hundred feet, depending on how much longer your stride was than two feet." John looked up at the tall trees around them. "Hey, I didn't know these got that tall. These are sugar pines, aren't they? I thought they were lots shorter than the sequoias."

"Yeah, but the sequoia gets to be three hundred feet. Remember how Dad said they were as tall as a football field is long?" Paul looked up to see if there were any sequoias nearby, but he didn't spot any. It looked to him that they were in a huge grove of sugar pines with a few random cedar trees growing here and there.

"It's really neat up here. I'm glad we came up to this campsite. It's so quiet and noisy at the same time. You know what I mean. No people noise."

John spoke reverently about his natural surroundings. He liked the annual camping trip for many reasons. Paul and John always had fun with their father. The three of them laughed a lot and played card games that they never seemed to have time for at home. Best of all, at least in John's opinion, was the way Paul treated him when there were no other people around. On these trips, John felt that Paul was his friend. And together, John felt he and Paul were a team. When one spoke, the other listened. When they laughed, they laughed together. The constant teasing that John had to endure at home stopped abruptly as soon as they reached their campsite.

"Remember a couple of years ago when we went to that campground at Pinecrest?" Paul had picked up two sticks and was beating out a rhythm on the big rock while he spoke. "I hope we never go to a place like that again. What about those kids in the RV next to us? They played video games all night."

"Oh yeah!" John's voice got a little louder as he reached into his memory. "They only came out of their RV to get their food from the barbecue."

"Hot dogs and beans!" Paul said with derision. "Dad was just finishing up making our barbecued shish-kabob with fresh pineapple. It was so good! Those guys were so jealous. I wonder what Dad has planned for tonight?"

"The shish kebab was really good, but my favorite was when Dad made barbecued chicken and corn on the cob. Remember that apple salad? That was awesome." John was starting to feel hungry even though they had soup and sandwiches about an hour ago. Traditionally, their father fixed the first night meal. He didn't tell the boys what was planned. Every year they were surprised and pleased with the food choices. It was the only time when John and Paul were not expected to help with preparations. They were expected, however, to clean up afterward.

"We should get back pretty soon." Paul continued to sit on the rock and soak up the warmth of the sun. "After all, Dad wanted to play cards at three thirty." Both boys started to laugh.

"Yeah, right," John said. "He was going to shut his eyes for just a few minutes." They knew from past experience that their father would sleep at least an hour. They didn't have to hurry back at all. Paul started to sing an old Harry Belafonte song as he beat a rhythm on the rock. He sang loud and almost in key. "Day-o! Da-a-ay-o! Daylight come an' I wanna go home!"

Suddenly, there was a clear whistle followed by some chattering. Both boys froze and sat quietly, listening for more of the curious sounds. The chattering faded, but there was another loud whistle. It seemed to come from somewhere under the fallen tree. Paul jumped down from the rock and hurried toward the sound. John was close behind. He shouted to his brother.

"Hey, wait up! Be careful! It might be something dangerous!" Just as John spoke, Paul stopped and pointed. There, under the outcropping of rocks they had climbed over a few minutes before, was the partially hidden burrow entrance. It had been completely hidden by the fallen tree branches when the boys had come from the other direction. Just outside the burrow, a huge yellow-chested marmot stood up on his hind legs. He looked like a chubby soldier standing at attention. He was as big a marmot as either boy had ever seen. Apparently, the critter was not too concerned about the presence of two humans.

He continued to whistle, and before long, some of his family came out from the burrow. They also stood at attention and listened to the whistling. John and Paul backed slowly away down toward the base of the fallen tree. They knew a marmot would probably not harm them, but if there were babies close by, the marmot became a very protective parent. As soon as Paul and John reached the bend in the path, they turned toward the camp site and started to run.

Both boys were laughing. Their father was still sleeping when the boys came toward the tent cabin. Hearing the laughter, Daniel opened his eyes and smiled, and then he asked what was so funny. With that, the boys looked at each other and started laughing harder. John went to get the cards and score-pad. Paul moved the cots together so they would have a surface for playing cards. Soon the three of them were deeply involved in a competitive game of hand and foot. On the final round, Paul was first to go out. After tallying the total score for all four rounds, John announced the winner. Paul beat John by eight hundred points, and he beat his father by 2,300. When Paul heard the final results, he jumped up and stood at attention, stuck out his chin, and began to whistle.

Almost immediately, John stood next to him and whistled. Daniel just shook his head, puzzled. Then John told his father about fallen tree and the family of marmots. They all decided it would be fun to visit the burrow tomorrow to watch the marmots together. Once again, all three were reminded how they derived such pleasure from observing the small, mostly inconsequential happenings in nature. These camping trips not only bonded the three of them together as family, but the trips also helped to remind them how their family fit into the natural world.

"Well, boys, dinner will take about forty-five minutes. Maybe you can decide how you want to set up the cots in the tent, then you can unpack your bags and stow the food in the bear locker. I'll call you when dinner is ready."

By the time John and Paul got everything in place, the sun had just dropped below the horizon. There were a few mosquitos scouting out potential victims, so it was unanimous that Daniel, Paul, and John would eat in the tent cabin. The bugs were thwarted from feasting on human blood, but they could be heard clearly through the netting as they flew from one screened window to the next. Soon their father was calling them to eat.

Something smelled wonderful. Daniel served out three helpings of homemade beef stew. He had prepared the stew at home then froze it in a foil form that would fit into the camp cooking pot. It had already thawed out a little on their afternoon hike into the campsite. He used the camp stove to thaw it thoroughly, then he cooked it over a low flame. After a while, it was simmering. It filled the air with an inviting aroma. After passing out the deep bowls of stew, he sliced thick wedges of warm corn bread and served it with butter and honey.

"That was a perfect meal, Dad," Paul said when they had finished. "I really mean it." He and John wiped down the plates and the pot, then they used some of their precious fresh water to rinse and wash the dishes quickly. The water jugs were the heaviest items in their packs. It was understood that nobody would bathe this trip. Neither Paul nor Daniel even brought a razor. John was past exhausted. He kept falling asleep when Paul or Daniel tried to talk with him.

"Hey, sport." Daniel looked over toward John. "Why don't you hit the sack? In fact, maybe we should all go to sleep. We'll be getting up with the sun pretty early, so we might as well go to bed with the sun tonight. Tomorrow night we can crank up the lantern, but tonight I think we're all pretty beat."

Paul and John agreed, and within fifteen minutes, all three were fast asleep.

Chapter Twenty-One

The next morning, John woke up a few minutes before the sun. There was a colorless glow in the eastern sky, and the dawn air was cold as it blew through the screens in the tent cabin. John took a deep breath. The air was fresh and scented lightly with the sweet pine sap from the surrounding trees. John's father was snoring very softly. The sound Daniel made was whisper quiet with a steady, even rhythm; John found the sound restful and soothing. He always felt safe and secure when he heard his father snore like that. Turning to his side, John looked over toward Paul's cot. It was nestled in the shadows across the small room.

John squinted his eyes and stared at the cot. He couldn't exactly see Paul, although there was something on the cot. Last night, Paul had used the extra blanket over his sleeping bag. Of the three, Paul was most affected by the cold air. Even when he was small, Paul needed to be plenty warm before he could sleep. John was just the opposite. When he was younger, he would kick off the covers as soon as he climbed in bed. By morning, he had usually stripped off his pajama top. Except in the coldest weather, John liked to sleep in his underwear with only his favorite featherweight quilt over him. John kept his eyes on the cot across the room. As it got lighter outside, it became clear to John that Paul was not in the cabin at all.

He's probably outside peeing, John thought to himself. But after several more minutes passed without any sign of Paul, John began to worry. He got out of his sleeping bag and went over to Paul's pack. John could not find Paul's camera anywhere. His jacket was nowhere in sight, and his shoes were missing from under his cot. John dressed quietly and headed for the door. He thought about waking his father, but decided to let him sleep. After all, Daniel had just finished his biggest tax season ever. As one of only three CPAs in Sierra Glen, he kept a busy practice.

John unlatched the wooden door of the tent cabin and opened it slowly to avoid scraping the floor. He slipped out and shut the door gently. The sun was not visible over the eastern range, but its stark yellow rays were brilliant against the blue dawn. John had to stop and draw his breath in at the beauty of the morning.

God has been busy with his paintbrush again. John automatically thought the words that his mother always said out loud when she saw this kind of morning sky. The sun was just beginning to light the tops of the tallest trees. John wondered which direction Paul would have headed to catch the most spectacular views. He turned slowly in place all the way around, and suddenly he knew just where to go. He hurried back up to the bend in the path and then toward the rock where he and Paul had been yesterday.

The view to the east had been completely clear from the vantage point of the boulder top. It would be a perfect place to catch the wide sky, the shadowed forest, and the fallen tree. John suspected the marmot family was out and about this morning. By now, Paul had probably captured some great shots of them as well. John reached the tall broken stump just as Paul was coming to it from the other direction.

"Hey, g'morning. Is Dad up yet?" Paul called when they were about twenty feet apart. He had his camera case slung over his shoulder, and he had his stocking cap pulled over his ears. He wore a jumble of yesterday's hiking clothes, with the addition of their father's slipover sweater that Paul had borrowed to wear under his jacket. John thought his brother looked like one of those war correspondents from Iraq or Afghanistan. Paul moved with the easy grace of a natural athlete and with the poise of someone who was confident in life and comfortable with himself. John wondered if he himself would ever achieve the kind of easy manner that his brother seemed to have naturally.

"No, he was snoring when I slipped out. I knew you'd be here. Did the marmots come out?" John was eager to see the morning through Paul's good photographic eye. "I'm glad you have a digital camera. Can I see what you have? Are there any really good shots?"

"Yeah, I think so. Let's get back to the cabin, and we can look at them together. I was so busy watching and shooting, I didn't take the time to edit anything yet." Paul's excitement over the possibilities of the morning shoot infected John with a vicarious eagerness of his own. When they reached the bend and turned up toward the cabin, they saw their father wandering down the path toward them. He was wearing his jacket over his boxers and his shoes without socks. He waved, and they waved back. Paul and John tried not to laugh.

Paul spoke quietly to John as they continued to walk up the path. "Honestly, if any of Dad's clients saw him out walking in the woods dressed like that, they'd think he was crazy."

Paul tried to keep his facial expression neutral as they drew closer to their father.

"Heck," John said, "if Mom saw him looking like that, she'd be wondering about him too. I'm glad we're up here where nobody can see us. I wonder how long he's been wandering around?"

He stopped talking when they were within earshot of their father.

"Hi, boys. I just got up to go to the bathroom when I heard your voices down here. How long have you been awake?"

"I got up when it was still twilight," Paul answered. "It was such a great morning with a sky that was unreal. If my new lens and the filter are up to doing the job I think they will, then I got some spectacular sunrise shots." Paul paused to see if John wanted to say anything, but John was quiet. Paul continued, "Johnny came up just when I was finishing. He's going to help me choose the best pictures."

"Sounds good. I'm going to get dressed, then let's think about breakfast." Daniel turned back toward the tent, and the boys followed. John took out an apple, two oranges, and two bananas from their pack in the food locker. Paul searched through the sealed plastic bag that said Cereal Bars. He took out six and placed two on each of the three small metal trays that had held their stew bowls and their corn bread last night. John distributed the fruit so that each tray had equal servings. By the time they had finished preparing breakfast, Daniel was dressed and putting on water to heat on the camp stove. Before long, the water began to boil. Daniel poured the steaming water into their mugs that already contained powdered milk and Ovaltine.

They ate everything, even the crumbs that fell into their laps as they took bites of the nutritious bars. They understood from previous years that their menu was necessarily spartan for they had to carry in every ounce of food they planned to eat, all in addition to their camping and sleeping equipment. Over the years, they learned which recipes were most satisfying, which meals travelled well, and which menu items could be completely or partially prepared at home. The goal was to keep the preparation easy while ensuring that every calorie they consumed came from a nutritious source.

When they finished eating, they cleaned up their eating utensils and spent a few minutes tidying up their gear. While John swept the wooden floor of the tent, Paul collected trash left from the meals they had eaten so far. He reused the foil and plastic baggies to seal everything securely. Tomorrow after breakfast, the three of them would leave the tent cabin and begin their hike back to civilization. In addition to their personal gear, they would carry out their waste materials so they could dispose of it properly at home.

"As soon as you're ready, we can take a walk toward the river." Daniel was preparing water bottles for each of them as he spoke. "I'd like to see where we are in relation to the Spires."

Daniel turned to Paul. "You may not remember, but we crossed the Hikers' Bridge somewhere near this section of river when you were about three years old. Your mom had baby Johnny in a tummy pack. I remember how she took one look at the bridge and refused to cross it.

"She said she was unbalanced enough already with John stuck on the outside of her stomach instead of inside. Then she told me that she'd become completely unbalanced if she had to cross that bridge for any reason. I admit it is a pretty exciting section of wild river. The river narrows about a quarter mile upriver above the Spires."

When John looked confused, Daniel smiled at him and continued talking. "The Spires is what they call a natural rock formation upriver. It really does give the impression of several church steeples crowded together, maybe more than a dozen in all. I know we are downriver from the Spires and the waterfalls, but with all the echoing sounds from the river water, it's hard to tell just how far downstream we are. Hopefully we'll be able to see at least the tops of the Spires when we get clear of this stand of sugar pines we're in now."

Daniel decided that should be enough talk about what to expect. Each boy would appreciate the magnificent terrain in his own way. They certainly didn't have to have a travelogue description from their father before they even had a chance to see things for themselves.

"The light is so good now. Let's hurry and get on the trail." Paul was eager to see the wild water. He turned to John and reassured him. "Don't worry, sport, we'll go through all of the shots later." John smiled and nodded in agreement.

Soon, their chores were done and their gear was stowed away. They were ready to go. Each carried a small day pack with snacks, water, Kleenex, and a few other miscellaneous items. Paul had his camera, John had a tablet and pencil for writing random thoughts and perhaps an idea for a poem, and Daniel had his wallet, car keys, and his inhaler on the rare chance that he would have a difficult asthma attack.

The boys followed their father. As they drew closer to the river, they could feel the power of the pounding water. The sound of the crashing falls seemed to mesh with their hearts; each could feel the relentless sound deep in their chests, and it left them breathless. Daniel was beginning to feel relieved that his inhaler was nestled safely in his pack.

The path they followed was gradually gaining altitude. After only ten minutes of walking, the trees thinned as the forest gave way to a small expanse of meadowland. All three of them gasped at the beauty that spread before them. Thick clumps of long, green grass shared the rich soil with a wide variety of wildflowers—pastel pinks and white, rich red and hues of brilliant orange, purple, and yellow blossoms grew everywhere. Daniel surmised that this meadowland that ran along the riverbeds on both banks served as a periodic mini floodplain for the snow-swollen river.

Moving closer to the river and farther from the trees, they could see the towering tops of the Spires upriver. The river above them curved from the east, obscuring from view the series of waterfalls that cascaded from the narrow gorge through the Spires. The sounds coming from upstream, however, could not be ignored. Competing with thousands of tons of water crashing down the falls, Daniel and the boys had to shout at one another to be heard. Daniel took off his pack and sat on a rock in the meadow. The boys did the same. They took small sips from their water bottles and shed their jackets.

"We should be able to follow the path of the river from here all the way upstream to the bridge." Daniel unfolded his trail map and studied it for a moment. "From the maps, it looks like about an hour hike or maybe a little more before we reach the first waterfall. It's up to you two. Shall we go upriver now, or wait until this afternoon when the light will be different? I'm not sure what you want to capture on film, Paul. What do you think?"

"Hmm, I'm not sure." Paul was looking around the meadow as he spoke. Then he seemed to regain his normal sense of confidence. "You know, this area with the flowers is really neat, and the light is perfect here right now. How about if we stay here for a little while, and I'll take some shots. Then we can go back to the tent and go through what we have on film so far. Then a little later this afternoon, we can hike upstream. I think the long shadows and the western sun will give the best results on the waterfalls. What do you think?"

"That sounds like a good plan," Daniel replied. "How about you, Johnny, does that sound okay?" John was sitting on a rock about twenty feet away. He had his tablet and pencil out and was writing furiously. When he didn't respond, Daniel raised his voice and shouted, "Earth to John, do you agree with the plan?"

"Plan?" John looked up from his tablet and glanced over to his father. He answered tentatively, "Uh, sure, Dad, that sounds fine. Whatever you guys decide is fine with me." With a goofy smile that said clearly John had no idea what the plan was, he looked back at his tablet and began to write again. Daniel and Paul exchanged glances. Daniel rolled his eyes, and Paul smiled. Both Paul and his father were decisive and confident extroverts, and as such, neither really understood John.

After a few moments, Paul began to walk around the meadow looking for good photo opportunities. Daniel leaned back on his rock perch and rested on his forearms. He was happy. The path of his life was filled with joyful events and many successes. He had a wonderful family: his wife, Christina, whom he adored; his four children; and his in-laws Fred and Mariel. Daniel loved them all. He had a distant but cordial relationship with his own mother, who had been barely eighteen and unmarried when Daniel was born. Daniel was raised in a loving and happy home by his maternal grandmother, Eleanor, who cherished Daniel as if he were her own son.

If Daniel had been a poet or philosopher, he might have wondered at the balance in his life. Does one need to experience sorrow or misfortune to recognize and appreciate good fortune? Does one need to meet tragedy firsthand in order to experience and savor great joy? Daniel did not think of these things for he was a realist and a doer of deeds. He understood Paul because the same traits lay within father and oldest son. He loved both his sons, but Johnny confused him.

Johnny was a dreamer and a thinker of thoughts. How could someone who kept dreams from interfering with life understand a dreamer? Daniel, who had found and followed one clear path through the infinite possibilities of life choices, decided that life had rules. He learned the rules early and found success in life by following the rules without question: live a good life, do your best, try your hardest, be fair to others, respect authority, appreciate the earth around you, and then know you have done all you could to deserve the good life. In fact, you can bank on it. Expect it; it is yours.

Chapter Twenty-Two

Daniel woke with a start. He was lying flat on his back on the rock where he had been resting on his elbows just a few moments before. Hs jacket was folded neatly under his head. *The boys!* he thought suddenly, a wave of irrational fear washing over him. Where were the boys? He felt a shiver cross the back of his neck although the sun was warm on his body. He sat up abruptly and scanned the meadow. There was Johnny writing something in his tablet. And over there was Paul taking pictures. Daniel relaxed and put the fleeting sense of fear far away from his consciousness. Yes, life was good, and he was happy.

Before long, Paul started packing up his equipment. John looked up and saw that Paul was finished, at least for now. John closed his tablet and put it in his day pack. He searched for a few carrot sticks and another handful of raw almonds from the bottom of his pack but found there was no food left. He smiled to himself when he realized that during the whole time he wrote, he had been grazing on the food he brought in his bag. And now, he could hardly remember taking one bite. Paul and John wandered over to the rock that their father had claimed.

As they drew near, Paul called out in a loud voice so as to be heard over the racket of the roaring water, "We're done for now, Dad. Are you ready to go back to the camp? We can look over the pictures I have so far, then maybe we can play games for a little while, then later we can take the path up to the Spires."

It was typical for Paul to outline a course of action then to assume that everyone else would fall in line with his suggestions. As they followed the path back to camp, both Daniel and John thought Paul's plan was a good one, and they agreed to follow along.

Back at camp, they found sixteen pictures that were worth saving. Of these, Paul felt there were seven remarkable shots that made him very proud and excited. These few shots out of nearly two hundred that he had taken during the past few days showed artistic merit, technical perfection, and also presented a strong point of view or an implied back story. Both Daniel and John were impressed with the quality and depth of the chosen proofs.

There was one picture that Paul and Daniel overlooked, but John chose it immediately as his favorite. It was of the marmots. It showed a large male standing upright by the fallen log with some younger ones emerging from the burrow beneath. The large one faced east, and the early morning rays of the sun ignited his thick scruffy brown fur with a magnificent golden glint. The animal had tilted his head slightly up and to the side just as the picture was snapped. John thought the marmot looked like Don Quixote dressed in a golden breastplate and helmet. John saw a poignant wistfulness in the animal's expression. He tried to explain to the others just what he believed the picture captured.

"Remember when Don Quixote confronted the windmill? You know, where he's trying to reconcile in his mind the conflicts that he feels? He wants to slay the terrible beast, yet he is afraid he will not be successful. He sees the windmill as a foe, yet he understands it is not evil or bad. I guess he knows the windmill is neutral in its response to him and his efforts to destroy it."

John was beginning to wish he hadn't started to explain his thoughts. He looked at his father, who gave him an unexpected smile and nod. John was encouraged as he tried to clarify his ideas. "Well, the marmot in this picture reminds me of Don Quixote. I know the marmot isn't tilting at windmills, but he could be looking at an enemy of his own. It could be he sees a wolf or coyote, I guess, or even a huge storm brewing, but I'm just using the analogy of Don Quixote because they both have that wistful look."

John swallowed audibly and felt himself blushing. Still, he continued. "What I'm saying is the windmill doesn't much care about what the little warrior guy thinks or plans. And if you look at the true function of a windmill, it would probably weigh in as a powerful tool for the good side Quixote knows deep down that his efforts will probably fail to make a difference and will go unrecognized and unappreciated. But mainly, he is compelled to act on his convictions no matter what the consequence. I guess that's the point of what I'm trying to say, that when you look at the total picture, there really is no point at all."

John stopped talking and took a quick breath. His ears started to redden again as he thought back on what he had just said. He felt foolish and young, and he wished he could fade from sight. He thought to himself, *If only my words were like a kite in the wind, then I'd pull hard on that string to bring them back in.* When John realized that this last thought had formed itself into a rhyming couplet, he was completely mortified. His breath came in painful gasps as he sank into his cot with his back toward the others. He sealed his lips together tightly to prevent any other words from escaping as he thought to himself, *Thank you, God, for not letting me say that stupid rhyme out loud.*

Neither Paul nor Daniel responded to John's description of the marmot photo. How did John garner that whole fanciful tale from looking at a tiny picture of an animal standing in the sun? Daniel and Paul were aware of John's intellect. Though they felt proud of John's rare and wonderful mind, they often did not know how to react when John's train of thought would seem to jump synapses and end up in another dimension.

When John made an effort to explain to his family what he was thinking and then received no reaction except silence and blank stares, he felt silly, like the butt of some big joke. This time, John turned away as he retreated into his own thoughts. An electric field of nothingness seemed to encompass him. Not for the first time, he vowed to himself that he would never, ever share his personal thoughts with anyone again.

To break the silence that was beginning to feel uncomfortable, Paul jumped up, grabbed the cards, and began to shuffle them.

He said it was time to give Dad a chance to redeem himself and his score. Soon the awkwardness that all three felt just moments ago faded away as they became more involved in the cards. In this round, the scores were almost even, although Paul was the winner once again.

A little after 3:30 p.m., they each filled water bottles and grabbed some nuts, fruit, and chunks of cheese with a few crackers to carry with them on the hike up to the Spires. They also packed their flashlights just in case it took longer than they expected to reach their destination, take pictures, and then return to camp. Paul double-checked his camera and attachments then packed them carefully in his day pack. Once again they set out on the path toward the river, and soon they were following the river path upstream toward the falls and the Spires.

It was a rougher terrain as they moved higher up the mountain past the meadowland where they had stopped before. Several times the path veered far away from the river's edge because there was no clearance for walking next to the swift-moving water. Paul was worried about missing some good white water shots, but Daniel reassured him there would be plenty to see in just a little while. Soon, the path turned back toward the river, and the sound of the rushing water filled their ears.

They knew they were close to something big and powerful, but when the path turned and suddenly emerged from behind a big boulder, they could only stare in awe at the sight before them. They were about forty feet above the gorge with a panoramic view of a magnificent waterfall that spewed giant spouts of frothy, aerated water high into the air. A gusting wind caught the spray and sprinkled the three hikers with a welcome shower of icy mist. The waterfall was actually made up of several successive cascading falls formed by gigantic granite boulders that seemed to be placed neatly in a tidy pattern down the river canyon.

John imagined there was a family of giants who lived here long ago, and the youngest boy giant found this little trickle of water and decided to make it more interesting. He found the perfect pebbles then placed each one so that it would throw water back upstream to join the new water that was coming down the canyon. John was deep in his fantasy about the giants and their life here long ago when he realized his father was telling them something. Paul was already leaning close to his father's face, and John hurried close to join them.

"This waterfall is called a waterwheel because of how it throws the water back onto itself upstream. In nature, this type of waterfall helps purify the water because it exposes the water to vast amounts of air and sunlight. Our California state water engineers used the same concept on the California Aqueduct. Remember how it passes from the north into Southern California over the Tehachapi Mountains? It looks like a giant ladder with the water splashing all the way down from top to bottom."

Daniel paused for a moment to wipe some of the mist from his face. Then he turned toward Paul.

"Paul, I believe that you'll find opportunities for some brilliant shots as we move upstream. There isn't much room for you to work here. There is better access to another even larger waterwheel if I remember correctly. Shall we go up farther up and check it out?"

The boys picked up their packs and followed their father on the path leading upstream. It was much steeper in this section, and the three of them actually had to use their hands to keep steady in a few places where the outcropping of rocks obscured the trail. After almost forty minutes of steep hiking and climbing, they came upon another huge set of boulders. At the base there was a forest service notice that announced "Hikers' Bridge, 400 yards" with an arrow pointing straight up the rock face.

"Some ranger had fun making that sign, I guess. You know, if we're that close to the Hikers' Bridge, then the waterfalls must be just past these boulders." Daniel had to shout because the roaring water was louder here than anywhere they had been so far. He hollered, "Come on!" as he gestured with his hand.

They climbed up the steep path, dodging between and over the boulders. Daniel estimated they had to climb over one hundred vertical feet to reach the topmost point of the trail. This was an unfamiliar route to him, and he was beginning to worry about the trek back to camp.

The only time he had visited these falls was nearly fifteen years before, and then he had approached from the upstream trail on the other side of the river. He was anxious to actually see the falls so he could get his bearings once again. The river was still hidden by the huge rocks, but the noise was deafening. They reached the top of the last boulder and stood up. Nobody said a word. They stood in silence and marveled at what lay before them. They were looking down at the riverbed. It was close enough that the spray immediately soaked their shirts. There was a short safety fence that was placed between them and the river. It was marked with danger signs.

A steep series of waterwheel falls cascaded ferociously down from a deep pool that was about two hundred yards upstream. A wide ribbon-style waterfall fell into the pool from a cliff behind that was over one hundred feet high. The water twisted and turned as it fell against various rock formations on either side of the waterway. The sun gleamed on the face of the waterfall, and in several places, the reflected rays bounced from the back wall of the cliff face and then shone through the quick-moving sheet of rushing water as it poured down the ribbon fall. There were rainbows everywhere. Paul was already taking pictures, anxious to catch the elusive colors of the rainbows.

The Hikers' Bridge spanned the pool about twenty feet back from the first drop in the waterwheel series. From their vantage point, the three of them could see how fast the water was rushing under the bridge. The afternoon sun was hitting the water from an angle, causing an eerie glow in the air directly over the river. The translucent surface of the water sparkled with colors ranging from light icy sky blue to deep teal. As Paul watched the water assume different shades, he sensed that the most brilliant moment was yet to be. He gestured that he was going to go down to the Hikers' Bridge and get shots of the tall falls and the beginning of the waterwheel as the sun dropped lower in the sky. Daniel and John followed behind on the riverside path that led to the bridge. The descent on this side of the boulders was much more gentle and only dropped down about twenty vertical feet.

Paul had reached the Hikers' Bridge and was about to step onto it when Daniel had a quick flashback. He remembered how Christina refused to cross the narrow span years ago, and that had been in late summer when the spring torrents had faded into a languid summer docility. Daniel shook his head and looked at the bridge. Certainly it was safe. There was no posted warning, and the sides seemed high enough to keep a hiker from an accidental fall. The water below the bridge, however, was anything but docile now. The raging torrent bounced on the base of the bridge and over the walking surface. The spray had completely soaked every part of the bridge, even the stanchions that reached high above in support of the suspended structure.

Daniel watched Paul step onto the bridge, moving carefully with his back toward the ribbon fall and his arms protecting the camera from spray. Daniel hesitated at the edge of the bridge. He shouted back to John and told him to stay back on the trail. Daniel caught the look of fear in John's face and hoped that his own face did not reveal the terror that was brewing deep in his own gut. Daniel reached inside himself to regain his rational outlook. Surely, everything was safe enough. The bridge had withstood several years of weather and it seemed to be rock solid. Paul was showing a fine respect for the elements as he moved cautiously along the railing. Daniel saw that Paul was busy taking picture after picture. His face was streaked with water, and the reflected rays from the late afternoon sun created streaks of rainbow colors on Paul's face just as clearly as if he were a part of the wildness that swirled around him.

Daniel watched in fascination. Surely his firstborn son was at one with the beauty and mystique of the river. Daniel rarely thought in metaphors, nor did he hear the music of life or know the poetry of the ages. But at this moment, he saw the world through Johnny's eyes, and it terrified him. When the bridge piling groaned the first time, just as Daniel knew it would, he did nothing. Somewhere from far away, he heard a voice screaming out to him. What was that? What did it say? Daniel heard the words but could not fathom what the words meant.

"Dad, Paul! Come back! The bridge is breaking up! Hurry, come back! Dad! Paul! Come now! Dad, Daddy!" The voice faded from his awareness. Daniel stared at Paul as the bridge stanchion by the far bank began to buckle and torque. Paul turned in time to see the far end of the bridge begin to drop plank by plank into the raging river. The destruction gained momentum as the weight of each section slammed into the powerful torrent. When Paul turned back toward his father, his face was a mask of uncertainty and fear. In an instant, Paul began to run toward his father. He could hear the bridge collapsing behind him.

The wrenching scream of screws and bolts being pulled from their places added a macabre element to the river's cacophony of sound. Daniel tried to call out, but there was no air in his lungs to support any sound at all. It was then that Daniel realized he could not breathe. Asthma had accepted Daniel's adrenaline rush for what it was—food! The asthma had a life of its own; since Daniel had arrived at high altitude yesterday, the disease had been laying a foundation to wreak havoc in Daniel's life as soon as it found an opening.

The terror inside Daniel now was the catalyst that boosted asthma into the driver's seat. In complete control now of Daniel's well-being, asthma gripped the soft lung tissue and held tight. Daniel lurched, moving forward on the bridge in a desperate attempt to reach Paul. Unable to absorb sufficient oxygen into his bloodstream, Daniel was nearly overcome with weakness. His vision narrowed as he fought the overwhelming urge to lie down and rest. Paul was only two steps away. Daniel's plan was simple: they would clasp hands and run back to safety. They nearly did just that. But as Daniel's hand reached to grasp Paul, the bridge under their feet gave way, and Daniel suddenly found himself clinging to the strap of Paul's camera.

Paul was screaming in pain and fear as the freezing water engulfed his body. Daniel himself was knee deep in a freezing stream of water that was rushing from the ribbon falls to the deadly waterwheel below. The stanchion on this side of the bridge seemed to be holding for now. Daniel locked his legs around the support post and hoped it would not give way. He pulled gently on the strap, thinking he could reel Paul in like a giant fish, but his strength had faded away to nothing.

He watched as his dear son Paul quietly slipped away into the current. Paul, who hated to be cold, would never feel the warmth of the sun or a campfire again. Paul, so full of life and good cheer, would never warm their family with his presence. Paul was gone. Daniel felt a hand grasping his arm. Someone was pulling him back toward the safety of the riverbank.

Wait! We can't leave Paul! Come on, grab Paul! Come on, we can get him out, we can make him warm, please. Please! These and other words formed in his mind and etched into his heart, but only the sound of urgent gasping came from his lips.

Daniel was lying on his back on the shore. Johnny was crying as he dug through his father's saturated day pack. Finding the inhaler, he extracted it from the sodden box and put it up to his father's mouth.

"Take a breath, Dad. Come on, take a breath!" John continued to cry quietly as he helped his father regain some minimal control of his body. Daniel was still too weak to stand up, but John helped prop him into a sitting position. Daniel leaned against a slanted portion of the granite outcropping. He tried to talk but could not form the words that he needed to say. John knew exactly what

Daniel wanted. John swallowed, took a deep breath, and began to talk.

"No, Dad, he's gone. I saw him floating facedown in the water as he slipped over the top of the waterwheels. Daddy, I know he's already safe with God in heaven." John started to cry again softly.

It took John over two hours to climb back down the river path and find their tent. After grabbing the cell phone from the main pack, he had to hike another hour to get out of the wilderness area and into a place with phone reception. When he called the ranger station number to report the accident, they were expecting his call. Two hours before John's call, big sections of the broken bridge began to float by the ranger station four miles downstream.

The rangers took their helicopter up to the site in order to assess the damage. They found Daniel who was lucid but distraught and unable to explain exactly what had happened. Daniel was airlifted to the emergency clinic where, in his confused state, he waited for his sons who would surely meet up with him soon. He was certain they were both climbing down to their campsite. When the rangers learned from John about the tragic fate of Paul, a search was launched for his remains. A week later in a meadow about five miles downstream, some backpackers found Paul's body caught up in the reeds next to the river. Daniel and John never returned to the river, nor did they ever talk about those final hours at the bridge. There was a pictorial record of Paul's last visions, however, for when John pulled his father back from the bridge to safety, Paul's camera was still attached to the strap wrapped so tightly around Daniel's hand.

Chapter Twenty-Three

On Thursday, the morning sun streamed through John's window and nudged him awake from a deep sleep. The night had passed without a single dream and without the restlessness that John had recently learned to accept as normal. He rolled over onto his back and stretched his arms up toward the ceiling. He felt good. No, he felt better than good. Certainly, he felt eager to face the challenges that he knew lay before him this very day. Rising quickly, he showered and dressed. Then he pulled the chair from his desk over to the bank of cabinets that covered the wall across from his bed.

Stepping solidly on the middle of the seat, he reached up to the highest cabinet door and pulled it open. Steadying himself with one hand, he reached inside the cupboard with the other. He was barely able to brush the item he sought with his fingertips. It was lodged firmly in the deepest recess of the space. No matter how much he stretched, John could not quite grasp it. He thought for a moment, then he climbed down to get his old bamboo back scratcher from the desk drawer.

Standing on the chair once again, John was able to reach the straps of the heavy backpack. John had thrown it into the cupboard the first night he arrived to live at Eagle Cove. Pulling the backpack close with the back scratcher, he was able to get a good hold of the strap to drag it out. He set the blue pack on the floor in the middle of his room.

Seeing it there, John was momentarily transported to an earlier time back in Sierra Glen. He and Paul were standing in their shared room, and they were staring at this same backpack. It was almost new then, and all of the zippers worked, even the big one that was ripped now and only opened halfway.

"Really? I can have it? Wow! It's really awesome." John couldn't believe his good fortune. His big brother was not usually inclined to be generous with his belongings, so John was surprised and pleased at the unexpected gift. John had wanted a backpack like this ever since he had started junior high school.

"Sure, kiddo, I got my new one this morning. The UPS guy finally delivered it." Paul had opened his package but had not yet shown John its contents. Now, Paul reached in the box and extracted a brand-new USC crimson and gold backpack. Paul was looking forward to attending the university where his parents had met and where he could pursue his serious and long-standing interests in still photography and filmmaking.

Shaking his head, John was transported back to the present. He coughed back a choking sob that threatened to overtake him and weaken his resolve. Without hesitation, he picked up the pack and set it on the bed. In one motion, he reached over and unzipped the big zipper as far as it would go, then he stretched the opening as wide as possible so that he could extract the metal box that was inside. John remembered back to the very day he had shoved the box in through the small opening. It was the last of Paul's belongings that John had stored in the old blue pack. When John finally had pulled the old zipper shut, it was as if he had packed Paul away as well.

John forced himself to think back to the last week in April, a little over one year ago, when he had last closed up the backpack. The remaining members of the family—Daniel, Christina, John, Emma, and Lucy—had just finished dinner. It had been another awkward meal in a long series of family suppers where everyone was careful not to say anything that would elicit any thought at all of Paul. But Emma, so noisy and demanding as a baby and so outspoken as a child, said aloud what each of the others had been thinking.

"Tomorrow is Paul's birthday."

The simple declaration hung in the air over the table. The electrified field that held the family captive in their seats at the table was almost visible; so strong was the emotion that caused it.

All at once, the room was filled with shouting, crying, blaming, hating—all these on account of loving and losing so much. The painful and unending anguish was silent no longer.

But when Christina shouted, "You should have kept him safe! You should have saved him! He was our firstborn, our golden child, the special one, and you let him die a horrible, awful death! Your stupid weakness killed him, my precious Paul, my best creation, you killed him!"

And John remembered how his father sat with his elbows bent on the table, head resting in his hands, moaning and crying, never denying a single word that Christina was hurling toward him. Each word cut like a dagger, yet he never moved. The twins and John sat motionless. All three had heard that Paul was golden, special, and yes, in his mother's estimation, her best creation.

Each of the remaining three were assured of something they had only suspected before. All of them were, at best, second best. For how could they compete now with the memory of Paul? Paul would surely become more golden, more special year after year, for any smudges on his character would be polished away from their mother's memory by the passage of time.

"Well, I guess it's now or never," John, willing himself to stay focused on the present, spoke aloud. Suddenly he felt foolish and inadequate. Not only was he talking to himself, but he was using trite and tired phrases. Then when the old Elvis tune of "It's Now or Never" invaded his mind, causing him to hum the tune a few moments later, he had to laugh at himself. The backpack and the metal box were still on his bed. After staring at the items for a few moments, John turned to leave the room. Just as he was about to cross the threshold into the hall, something made him turn back and stare at the metal box.

"Oh, all right!" John spoke aloud to whatever it was that had called him back. He grabbed the box, then he went to search for his family.

When he knocked on the twins' door, Lucy opened it immediately. She was already dressed and seemed ready to face the day. Emma was still in bed.

"Hi, Lucy. Say, how long would it take for Emma to get dressed and ready to meet in the dining room?" John had to smile when Emma groaned and pulled the covers up over her head.

"Well, it depends on why she has to meet in the dining room. Does it have to do with food?" Lucy dropped her voice to a whisper. "Because if you promise something good like pastries or doughnuts, she'll be there in ten minutes."

"I'm calling a family meeting, like we used to have when we were little, when Paul was still alive, remember?" John decided he should stick with the truth rather than bribery to get Emma going. Both girls cringed when they heard John say Paul's name. It made John feel sad that his family was so fragmented and cautious around one another. How could they be honest and authentic in their feelings if they couldn't even acknowledge that Paul had once lived in their home and had been a part of them?

"Yes, and we are going to talk a lot about Paul, so start thinking about him, okay?"

John was getting anxious to find his parents before they got involved in some projects with Nana Mariel and Grandpa Fred. Still unsure about whether or not to include Nana and Grandpa, John just decided to wait and play it by ear. "So I guess I'll see you in the dining room at eight thirty?" John waited for some answer, but neither girl would promise to come.

"Maybe," Lucy said. Then she amended it to, "Well, probably."

"Wait, now. You guys remember the rules of calling a family meeting. Everyone has to come." John couldn't believe his sisters would ignore this fundamental rule, even if there had been no meeting called for almost three years.

"Yeah, we know. We'll be there, don't worry, but you better make it at nine because Emma is kind of slow in the morning."

Lucy smiled at John. Then she added, "You know, as far as the meeting you are calling, all I can say is it's about time."

Chapter Twenty-Four

John found his mother and father in the kitchen sitting at the big table with Nana Mariel. His father was drinking coffee, and the women were drinking tea. John approached them, deciding at that moment to include his grandparents in the meeting if they wanted to come. The rule of compulsory attendance only affected the immediate family. The three of them smiled as John took a seat across from his father.

"Good morning, Johnny." His mother stood up to get him a glass of orange juice. "You're up and about kind of early. Do you have plans?" As she spoke, she set the glass in front of him and went back to her chair next to her own mother.

"Well, actually, I do have a plan, and I'm glad that you are all here so I can tell you about it. I am calling a family meeting. Since the girls are going to be arriving in the dining room at nine this morning fully expecting our first family meeting in nearly three years, I really hope you two can be there. Nana, you and Grandpa Fred are welcome to come too."

John hesitated before he continued. He felt that a storm was brewing, and he had to pass through it with his family in tow before any of them could arrive home safely. John was silent for another moment, then he said quietly, "It's about Paul. We need to talk about Paul." The name fell upon their ears like a thunderclap. His father started to stand up, but Mariel put her hand gently on his arm.

"Please, Daniel. I think Johnny is right. And I think I know why he is bringing this up now. In fact, I think you know too." Mariel kept her hand on his arm as she looked in his eyes. "Please, for your sake and for Johnny's, please stay with the group for the meeting."

Daniel said nothing, but his face looked gray and drawn. His shoulders sagged so severely that John thought he might fold into himself and disappear. Meanwhile, Christina gazed down at the table in front of her, effectively closing out everyone from her vision. John could sense that her uneven breaths were the precursor of an attack of tears, tears she was working hard to keep at bay.

"So I guess I'll meet you all in the dining room at nine o'clock." John finished his juice in one gulp then stood and left the room, still clutching the metal box.

By nine o'clock, the whole family sat at one of the round tables in the dining room. The room was bright and cheery, filled with beautiful morning sun yet protected from the gusty winds that were shaking the trees outside and rattling the north-facing windows. The center of the table was filled with a variety of edibles that Mariel had hastily prepared: a platter of sliced fruit, a plate of scones, and a selection of Danishes were all proving to be popular with the three teenagers. Christina poured ice water from a large pitcher for her parents and her husband, but they all declined any food.

John sat between his parents and across the table from the twins. Mariel sat between Christina and Lucy, and Grandpa Fred, looking rather out of place, sat between Daniel and Emma. Emma sensed his discomfort and reached over to take his hand. She squeezed it gently and whispered to him, leaning close to his ear so that nobody else could hear.

"Don't worry, Grandpa Fred. Family meetings are fun. The rules are pretty simple. Anyone in the family can call a meeting, and everyone has to come. Everyone has to say the truth, but Mom always reminds us to say the truth gently."

"That sounds like a good idea. Do you have these very often?" Grandpa Fred was enjoying his conversation with Emma. Ever since she fell off the horse in the corral, she was less boisterous and self-centered. Fred was relieved that she wasn't hurt seriously, but he secretly felt the injury to her pride was a blessing in disguise.

"We haven't had one in almost three years, or maybe more." Emma was thoughtful for a moment, then she added, "I know we haven't had one since Paul, uh, you know, when Paul died." When she stumbled over Paul's name, Grandpa Fred squeezed her hand gently.

She smiled up at him then added, "Oh, and the last thing about the meetings is you don't have to talk at all."

After a few minutes of serving and eating food, the family grew quiet. They looked toward John, for the one who called the meeting was always the first to speak. John sensed that it was time to start. Suddenly, a wave of nauseating anxiety gripped him. He felt like he was suffering from a terrible case of stage fright. Why had he called this meeting? Why did it fall upon his shoulders to do this? He was the one who needed help and nurturing, he was one of the kids, he saw his father try to save Paul, and he was the last person to see Paul before he perished. Then the mind-numbing fear gave way to a righteous anger that strengthened and sustained him as he stood to start the meeting.

"Today we are going to face up to some pretty sad things that have happened to our family. I know you are expecting to talk about Paul, and we will. But what I want to start with is Papa Jacob. Ever since the sea camp dance a couple of weeks ago, I've been thinking about him. We kids never really knew Sofia, but we know some of the wonderful family stories about Jacob and Sofia when they were young. We know the exciting tales, the funny stories, the happy memories. We've seen the scrapbooks and the photos.

"Our lodge has a rich, wonderful history. But there is a whole wealth of family lore that we don't know. For example, I imagine that even my father doesn't know what happened to Grandpa Fred's sister. Or that he had a sister at all. And then there is the feud between the sea camp and the lodge. Everyone knows about the long-standing feud, but does anyone really know what caused it? Or why it seemed to get worse as time passed? But mostly, I'd like everyone to think about Papa Jacob. I remember him from when I was really little. He was a gruff old man, and the truth is I was a little afraid of him."

"I was, too," Lucy said, "and I think Emma was kind of scared too, but she wouldn't ever admit it." Lucy and Emma looked at each other and giggled. John was thrown off his train of thought for a moment. He and the family had just witnessed Lucy behaving as the alpha twin. What a dramatic change had occurred in their relationship since arriving at Eagle Cove. John took a big breath and sighed in an effort to clear his head. He needed to stay on track if anything was to become of this meeting.

"You—Mom and Dad and Nana and Grandpa—all knew Papa Jacob when he was more like the man who is described in the scrapbook stories and news clippings. Maybe you didn't notice how he changed as he grew older. The girls and I met him when he was in his seventies. Truly, I cannot remember hearing him laugh, and I don't remember seeing more than a fleeting smile on his face. In fact, the only time I can picture him smiling at all was when he was sitting in the church courtyard after Mass."

Everyone looked at the twins and noted that they were nodding in agreement. John waited for a moment; then he continued speaking. "Now I'd like you to think about Papa Jacob's last couple of days." John stopped talking and looked over at his grandfather. John reached across the table and grasped the big man's hand. "Grandpa, I'm sorry to talk so frankly now when it's so soon after losing Papa Jacob, but I think as a family we have to do this. Please forgive me, I'm sorry—"

"No, Johnny, I know what you are getting at, and I agree with you. I miss my pop more than I ever could have imagined, but I love the rest of you, my remaining family, too much to pass up this chance today for, well, you know, Johnny is getting to what we really need to understand. I'm just glad he's talking and not me."

Fred stammered and coughed through his declaration, then he grabbed one of the cloth napkins and blew his nose loudly. The girls giggled, and Mariel started to say something, but Daniel touched her arm gently and reminded her that it was better than a sleeve. Mariel laughed along with the rest of the family, then she relaxed back into her chair.

"Now think what Papa Jacob faced in his last two days. I think he knew that he didn't have much time left, and I think he finally realized how much of his life he had wasted harboring anger and hatred inside his heart. With ugly thoughts of blame and retribution for all the very real tragedies that had happened in his family, he never had a chance to put the bad events behind him and begin living, really living, for the remaining time he had. Instead, it was as if he died a little each day he had lived because the anger, guilt, remorse, blame, or whatever emotion he was stuck on feeling robbed time from his days, day after day. Oh, it would only be a minute here, a few minutes there, and maybe five minutes of ranting about the sea camp, or ten minutes of angry thoughts about the tragic loss of Anne Marie and Kara Cecile, but year after year, he paid dearly with his precious life's time, time that is irrevocable, time that is ours to use or squander."

"What happened to Anne whoever, and who is that Kara person?" Emma spoke up clearly. Apparently she was back in assertive mode, and she wanted to know the details of everything. Lucy was nodding in agreement.

"I was hoping you would be curious about that, Emma. I knew I could count on you. This is where I'm hoping Nana will agree to tell a short version of our family history that includes all the important facts, not just the ones that sound good on an advertising brochure or in the scrapbook."

John looked at Mariel, hoping she would agree. Otherwise, he would have to reconstruct the events on the spot. Would he be able to make a smooth description of everything that had happened and keep it all in chronological order? Probably not, since he had learned bits and pieces from many sources. Luckily, Mariel pushed her chair back and stood up slowly. John sat down, relieved to hand the lead over to his grandmother.

"I will do the best I can, Johnny. Would you mind, though, if I sat down while I speak?" Mariel smiled as John nodded. "Now, Fred dear, I'll trust that you jump in whenever I get confused or stuck."

She waited for Fred to agree with her. He was quiet. The silence in the room lasted a few more seconds before Fred suddenly sat up straight and looked around the table.

"Oh, were you waiting for me to say something? Oh, of course, sugar beet, I'll be glad to help you out, though I've not known you to get confused about much of anything. I'm sure your description of events will be just fine." Fred leaned back again in his chair and put his hands behind his neck with elbows stretched out to each side.

"Thanks, dear, and remember, it's sugar*plum*. Just think of when I showed you one of those ugly looking sugar beets on the Internet? You might as well call me warthog or slug."

Mariel quickly held up her finger to keep the room silent as she added, "Now don't get any ideas." She sat down, put her palms on the table, and sighed. "I'm not sure exactly how to proceed. I'll try to keep things in order, but I may have to backtrack a few times." She gathered herself and took a big breath. She let it out slowly then took a normal breath as she started to speak. "Well, as you know, it all started with a poker game."

Mariel spoke for almost half an hour. From the poker game, she took the group back in time to Minnesota where Peter Sorenson and Jacob Engstrom first met. She told of how the Sorenson Sea Camp came to be, and how Harriet Sorenson had had the brilliant idea to affiliate with the schools. She told of the misunderstanding over the fire ring hill. She stopped for a moment and asked John to describe his impression of the fire ring area since he had visited there within the past couple of weeks. John was enthusiastic about the beauty and the potential of the site. Somehow, in his mind there was no taint of sadness nor any lingering sign of the rancor the fire ring had created between the families. The hill and the lush foliage combined to form a beautiful and unique place that could be an asset to the lodge.

It was as if a spell had been broken. Even when Mariel talked of Anne Marie and how she had fallen from the cliff, the family shed tears for the loss of one of their own, but no anger was directed at the place where Anne Marie had perished. And when Fred described the stone walls that Jacob had designed and built to prevent any similar accidents from happening, the family was glad that Jacob had made it safe. Nobody cursed the mountain for its potential for danger.

A few minutes later, Mariel reached the part in the family history where Carolyn Peterson and Kara Cecile had gone to Surfside Beach with the large group of young campers from the sea camp. When she told of the daring rescue, everyone clapped and cheered. Meanwhile, Emma and Fred each told of several accidents they heard had occurred at that same beach. Everyone knew it could be very dangerous.

Then the twins were very interested in how much Carolyn and Kara Cecile looked alike. As identical twins, Emma and Lucy were intrigued with other matched pairs. John hurried back to his room to retrieve the big shoe box from his shelf that had all the old pictures from the lodge past. When he returned, he set the box on the table and made a grand gesture as he opened the top.

"I should have organized this for today. There are lots of pictures and things that are not in the scrapbooks." As he spoke, he searched for the news article that showed the girls dressed like twins. He found it under the stack of newspapers. "Here it is! Even

Carolyn's sons Ian and Mark think Kara Cecile and their mom looked exactly alike, even though they only had seen pictures of Kara Cecile. It is kind of bizarre when you think about it."

"Maybe they had the same ancestors back in Minnesota," Lucy offered. "After all, they were all a bunch of Swedes."

"Hey, that's right. What if Papa Jacob and Old Mr. Sorenson were long-lost cousins or something? Wouldn't that be weird?" Emma laughed at the thought even as she spoke. After the group looked at a few of the pictures, John asked Nana Mariel to finish the story.

As she told of the birthday trip to San Francisco and the flight home in the seaplane, she had to stop several times. Somehow, losing Anne Marie and then Kara Cecile was just too much to bear. Everyone at the table felt the tragic loss as a blow to the family. But for the first time, it was clear to Fred and Mariel that here was the catalyst for Jacob's complete disassembling. No wonder, they said to one another. It was too much for him. Now they understood Jacob's dark moods and anger. The family all agreed that poor Papa Jacob had too many awful events thrown at him in quick succession. How could anyone pass through such pain unscathed? They all recognized why hate and resentment lived and thrived inside him. It was clear to all why Papa Jacob had become so sad and bitter.

John watched the group and listened to the statements and discussions concerning a newfound understanding of Jacob. There was a renewed sense of compassion for the poor old man, and a genuine empathic mood swirled in and around each in the family. John felt it too and was heartened by all he saw and heard. But he also sensed the presence of a less noble emotion—a collective smugness that seemed to hold them all above the pain that felled Jacob. It was as if they were safe from suffering because Jacob had absorbed all the sadness and held it close, leaving nothing in the form of enduring pain for the rest of his family to experience. Yet there was no sense of gratitude offered for his sacrifices in carrying the burden of tragedy for nobody except John even realized how they had been spared.

Wake up and smell the coffee! Connect the dots! Better watch out! John's mind was a thick soup of clichés and stupid euphemisms. Oh no! He shook his head to clear it enough so that he could assume leadership of the family meeting. But by then, the flow of old adages had risen in quality to become song titles. "Help!," "Straighten Up and Fly Right," "Wake Up, Little Susie," until finally, a vintage Broadway tune from *Brigadoon* flowed into his psyche and lodged in his mind's ear: "There But For You Go I," the song he had always thought should win an award for the most awkward title.

Now there it was, and before he knew it, the song overpowered him and seeped out through his pursed lips in the form of an eerie, breathy whistle. Suddenly, Daniel and Christina froze and listened. Within a few seconds, the whole family sat as still as statues while John finished a few phrases of the song. When he stopped, no one moved.

Slowly, John stood. He said a silent prayer to God, begging for help. He tagged on a little message for Jacob and Paul as well. Somehow he felt their presence, and he was fortified by it. John scanned the faces of his family. They were all staring at him, waiting for him to act. Just as he straightened his shoulders and prepared to speak, Emma raised her hand. The gesture was unexpected and seemed out of place, and Lucy started to giggle. John smiled and called on Emma, just as if they were in school.

"How did you make that whistling exactly like Paul's whistling when he used to do it on family music nights?" Emma expressed the same question that had formed in the minds of Lucy and Christina and Daniel. John did not realize until his sister spoke that the sound emanating from his mouth did have an uncanny resemblance to Paul's whistling.

"Honestly, I really don't know, Emma," John answered slowly. "Since I have never been much of a whistler, I have no idea where it came from. I guess I got a little help from someone, so I figure this must be the time where I lead the meeting. It could be that Paul himself called us to order. So the least we can do is get on with things." John took a deep breath and prepared to start once again. This time, the others were silent. They all looked at John with anticipation.

"I guess the first thing I want to say is to Dad and Mom." John looked at his mom then his dad. "I just want to thank you both for deciding to come to the island. Until this week, I couldn't figure out why it was so important that our family ended up here. After all, we had a nice home and a pretty good life up in Sierra Glen. But I think in a little while, it will be clear why our family needed to move here to survive."

When Emma gasped at John's words, Grandpa Fred reached over and squeezed her hand. John waited for a moment, then he continued. "I know how serious that sounds, but when you stop and think about our family history, everything we've heard today from Nana Mariel, isn't it full of serious events? Well, getting back to our meeting, there's one other thing I need to say to Mom and Dad. I already said thanks to you both. Now I need to apologize to you both, and to the rest of the family too. Mom, you always remind us that we must tell the truth gently. I'm going to try, but I really believe we need to all promise to tell the truth during this meeting—"

"The whole truth and nothing but the truth, so help me God!" blurted Emma, who, as usual, could not contain herself. She felt silly until John spoke once again.

"Actually, Emma, that's a good slogan for us to adopt today. The point I'm trying make here is that the truth we must speak today isn't gentle. It isn't tidy, and it isn't really clear-cut or safe from interpretation or spin. Now, I'm going to tell you what caused me to start thinking about all of this. As you know, the Baldwin family arrived not long after we moved here. I first met the Baldwin kids in the kitchen. They were making sandwiches and offered me one. We were just talking about nothing in particular. They introduced themselves and asked about my family.

"I told June about the twins, and JP said something about how when his family came last summer, Papa Jacob had mentioned to JP that our family might be moving to the island. Well, then out of nowhere, JP asked me where Paul was. He remembered our names because his name is really John Paul, you know, JP. I guess Papa Jacob was a little confused because he had neglected to mention that Paul had died. Well, here is the crazy thing. I couldn't talk about Paul. I couldn't even say his name. All I wanted to do was run away to my room and hide.

"When I finally got away from everyone and reached my room, I sat on my bed and tried, really tried, to make myself think about Paul. I couldn't do it! I tried to remember those last two days in the mountains. I could not concentrate at all. It was like my brain had a roadblock up that said *Danger, No Trespassing*. It wasn't until I forced myself to think that everything had happened to someone else. If I pretended to be observing other people instead of Dad and Paul and me, then I could trace the course of those last two days.

"Even so, by the time I waded through my memories of the whole hiking trip from the time we left home until the day that the rangers recovered Paul, I was a wreck, sweaty, crying, angry, sad, and I still couldn't make myself think of the experience again without switching to third person. The whole experience was not a breakthrough at all. It wasn't until Papa Jacob was so ill that I could see how our contribution to the list of family tragedies, the one that took Paul from us, was poisoning each of us just as surely as if we were taking tiny grains of arsenic each day.

"The earlier tragedies had poisoned Papa Jacob. Do we want to become bitter and sad? Do we want to be filled with anger and hate when we get to be in our eighties or nineties? Well, I saw how unhappy Papa Jacob was, and I don't want to end up the same way. So maybe the first thing we must do is break the wall of silence we've built around our memories of Paul."

John stopped talking and looked around the table. Everyone seemed to be listening, and Fred and Mariel were nodding with encouragement.

"We need to talk about Paul," John continued. "We need to have him in our family once again. I had a brother, and we shared a room. He teased me and drove me crazy, but I'd gladly take five hours every day of teasing if I could bring him back to life. Of course I can't … we can't bring him back, but we can remember him and talk about him. We need to laugh about the funny memories we all carry within us.

"We need to remember how Paul was at his best when he had a cause to champion or a race to win. But we never talk about any of these or any other family stories because we are afraid to conjure up a memory that might include Paul. So why don't we think of a couple of old family experiences right now that have Paul right smack in the middle?"

John stopped talking. He waited for a few seconds, but nobody spoke. He forced himself to remain silent. He knew from his English teacher last year that you can't have a discussion if the leader keeps talking. If you want others to talk, sit down and be quiet. So John sat. Before long, Lucy started to giggle, and soon Emma joined her.

"Do you remember the time that Paul got locked out of the front door in his ratty old pajamas? You know, the pajamas with connected feet and that flap in the back?" Lucy said.

"I remember, it was when he went to get the paper and the door blew shut!" Emma added. "And then Samantha jogged by with her dog, and her dog ran up the walk to see Paul … " By then the adults were laughing with the twins. Who could forget how angry and embarrassed Paul was when he finally got someone to open the door. Luckily, Samantha hadn't told anyone in school about catching the seventh grade class president outside in his yard banging frantically on his front door dressed in his old Spiderman flannels with the flap hanging open in the back.

The girls and John were full of stories that involved Paul. Most had Paul as the hero of the day, for truly that was his role in the family, at least in the eyes of the other children. Christina and Daniel did not offer any memories, but as the children spoke and reminisced, their parents were drawn more and more into the dialogue. Soon they were listening and laughing along with Fred and Mariel. John had opened the metal case with Paul's collection of special photographs. At first, nobody wanted to touch them, but soon Emma leaned over and grabbed a few. She shuffled through the stack, and suddenly she stood and stepped over toward Lucy.

"Hey, Lucy, remember this? I forgot all about that day. We never got to see the finished picture. This is so neat!" Emma held a five-by-seven print of the two girls sitting on the floor, each in front of a large framed mirror. Paul had arranged the mirrors so that they reflected each other again and again, creating an infinite path deep into the mirror world that obviously existed behind the glass fronts. Each girl was reflected doubly through the depth of each mirror path, resulting in a visual rendition of the title Paul had written on the back: *Infinitwins.*

John was glad that he had listened to the little voice inside him that had urged him to bring the metal box to the family meeting. Soon they were all passing the various prints around the table, in awe once again of Paul's critical eye and sharp wit. After a while, John sensed that enough had been said to break the stranglehold of silence concerning Paul. Perhaps now, the family might be able to include Paul in their lives—as a memory, as an inspiration, as a guardian angel?

Chapter Twenty-Five

John stood. The group gradually quieted down. When everyone seemed to be finished and their attention was again focused on him, John began to speak. "This is where it gets hard," he said softly. Suddenly, the atmosphere in the room changed. Just as the sky was darkening outside as a result of the brewing storm, a sinister cloud of foreboding seemed to seep in through the walls of the dining room, extinguishing the last bit of merriment from the group. John knew there was no stopping now. He turned to face his father.

"Dad, when the family was keeping vigil in Papa Jacob's room during those last hours, there was a span of time when, for one reason or another, everyone else had stepped out of the room and just you and I sat alone with Papa. We didn't speak, and we didn't even acknowledge one another, but I knew you were just as aware of me there as I was of you. I kept thinking about the tableau I saw in front of me—you and Papa Jacob in the dim light, and how something was there I should notice. I stared at you sitting across the bed from me.

"Papa Jacob kind of floated between us in my peripheral vision. Then by adjusting my sight lines just a little, my eyes refocused so that Papa Jacob was in sharp focus. As I stared at Papa, the clear sight of you faded into the background. Then a strange thing happened. I kept looking from you to him, back and forth. Changing perspectives so much in a short span of time felt odd, but even weirder was how the separate images of each of you began to fuse together. Somehow I saw you and Papa Jacob as two facets of the same person, and I could not break free from that perception.

"Then it hit me. The two of you had been forged by your personal tragedies into the same kind of bitter, angry, and defeated person. The only difference between the two of you was that Papa Jacob had no time left to escape the miserable path he chose to follow so many years ago, but you still have plenty of time to embrace life if you choose to do it. I wanted to scream at you, and I wish now I had. I wanted to beg you to choose life, I ached to tell you to choose hope and happiness, but I was afraid to do anything, so I just stayed quiet. It's a lot like I had always felt afraid of Papa Jacob.

"Since Paul died and you absorbed full responsibility for his death, I have been just as afraid of you. I don't mean that I thought you would hit me or anything like that, but since Paul died, nothing I do seems to please you. One month last year, I kept a journal of every single thing you said to me for the whole month. Do you know that for the thirty days of April, every word you spoke to me or yelled at me was to tell me how bad or lazy or selfish or messy or dirty or inconsiderate or whatever other undesirable word I was? Every single time you spoke to me! So, yes, I've been afraid, Dad. I've been scared every day for the past two years that you'd never love me the way you used to love me."

John heard the twins whimpering softly, each being consoled by a grandparent. He felt warm tears on his own cheeks, tears that were beginning to wash the anger from his soul. His father sat quietly, staring at his hands that he held clenched together on the table. John wasn't sure what to do. His mother still sat in the chair to his left. She was staring out the window. The storm that up to that moment had only consisted of howling wind, lightning, and thunder finally released a deluge on the island. It was as if the sky wept along with the family. Suddenly, a bright flash of lightning illuminated the sky. Almost immediately, a booming crash of thunder shook the dining room windows. Christina started to stand, but John had one other important piece of business. He had been delaying this moment, not sure how to say the words that must be spoken. The truth that he was about to speak was not gentle. He touched his mother's arm. She pulled away quickly.

"Johnny, I know you think this is helpful, and goodness knows it might be, but your father needs to take a break. You can see he is distraught. Let's stop now and perhaps we can pick this up another time."

Christina had used her "Mother knows best" voice and so assumed that the rest of them would fall into line and do as she suggested. After all, that was the pattern in the family, at least lately. But John did not move. He stood still and shook his head in disagreement.

"No, Mom. I'm not done. Dad can't feel any worse now than he has felt every minute since Paul slipped from his grasp in the river. But I have one more important thing to say. I owe it to the girls and to myself also to finish this."

Christina looked around the room to find a comrade who would join her in her plea to stop. Finding no sympathetic face, she sat down. John began speaking slowly. He addressed his words to the whole group.

"After Paul died, our family lost its way. We used to be the family that everyone wanted to be. We had fun, we took care of each other, and we loved each other lots, and we let each other know it too. But after the accident, it was painful to sit at dinner or even at breakfast before school. We tried to act normal, but I felt like I had a hole in my heart, and I'll bet you all felt the same. Well, the day before Paul's birthday last year, everything erupted. You must remember that night. We were yelling and crying and carrying on. But then something was said, something was revealed, something told in anger or rage, but all who heard it knew it was the truth … And it was not gentle."

John stopped and looked at the girls. Their faces, mirror images of each other, were white and drawn, but they were both nodding at John, encouraging him to continue. Christina tried to stand once again, but John looked at her and spoke to her in a clear voice.

"Mom, we heard you, and we remember what you said." John wanted to speak softly, but the storm was raging outside, and the wind howled with noisy abandon all around the lodge, so John needed to raise his voice to be heard.

"This is enough now, John. I'm going to take your father, and we're going to rest for a while." Christina moved to pass John, but he stood his ground.

"We all heard you, Mom. And we know you spoke from your heart. It was the not-so-gentle truth that came crashing out from deep inside you, and we heard every word. First you blamed Dad, you still blame Dad for what happened, but you weren't even there. How can you be so mad at Dad? I'm the one you should hate! I knew that Paul was already lost, and I made Dad come back off the bridge. He was ready to dive in after Paul, but I was afraid. I knew they would both be gone, and I was afraid. He hates me now because I wouldn't let him die trying to save Paul!

"I dragged him back off the bridge. And you've been hating him all this time because somehow you think he killed your precious, favorite, best creation! Paul was your firstborn, that's true. But mothers aren't supposed to have favorites. You always told us when we were small that you had plenty of love to go around because each of us came with a lifetime supply of special unconditional love that God had packed inside, ready to infuse our family with all the love we could ever need. But something happened. When you lost Paul, the love seemed to be sucked right out of our family, at least out of you!" John's voice cracked with emotion.

"You know, Mom, you have three kids now. Us! And we all know what you think of us. We know because we heard you say it! We know the best we can ever be will never be anything more than second best to the memory you worship, the memory of Paul!"

Christina turned away from John and rushed to the kitchen. Mariel saw that pain and anger had etched the contours of

Christina's face into a mask of sharp angles and deep creases. Mariel had a swarm of disjointed thoughts buzz through her mind. *Oh, Christina, how I ache for you! How has it come to this? How could this day that was beautiful and normal, a typical morning, turn into such a relentless storm of accusation and hurt feelings? Couldn't we just keep the demons at bay? Is this confrontational approach even safe? Poor Christina!*

In Mariel's eyes, Christina was an enigma. Mariel saw her daughter both as the woman she had become and the young girl she used to be; Mariel ached for both images. The mother title was written indelibly on Mariel's psyche, and she understood that their mother-daughter bond would always be solid. Mariel knew that whether a daughter was six or sixty, she would always be capable of playing a melody on Mom's heartstrings. A profound need to comfort her daughter washed over Mariel. She knew that right now, her daughter needed some unconditional motherly love. It took a few moments to shift Lucy back onto her own chair for as John spoke, Lucy had moved closer and closer to her grandmother, finally ending up cuddled on her lap like a small child.

Fred stood and intercepted Mariel. He too wanted to console their daughter, but he spoke to Mariel from his own unique perspective. After all, he was the child of Papa Jacob, the man who sacrificed his entire life to the three-stage illness of anger, guilt, and blame. Fred knew firsthand how his father had been unable to deal with the emotional needs of his own son, and Fred certainly didn't want these three grandchildren of his to suffer the same fate. Fred worried that Christina was reading from the same script that his father had used. Jacob had perfected his interpretation of the starring role—bitter victim. Christina might have difficulty assuming the role at first.

But if she took the best years of her life to hone each nuanced inflection of speech and each nonverbal mannerism, she would be a star in her own right someday. Who knows? She may even eclipse Jacob when she performed her final show from her own deathbed. So caught up in her own unresolved issues surrounding the loss of Paul, she was neglecting the needs of her three children. Fred wanted to scream at her. But he was wise enough to realize the limitations of lecturing or warning. Some things had to be discovered from within.

"Let her be, Mariel. She needs to think about what she heard. Let her have the chance to be the adult in the room. These kids deserve at least that from their mother."

Fred sounded frustrated. During the past few weeks that the family was together on the island, he had seen firsthand how Daniel was suffering from his own internal monsters. On many occasions, Fred had also witnessed the way Christina snapped at Daniel and belittled him. She had never been cruel as a child. What caused it now?

Fred had never heard anything about the details of Paul's death, and he was anxious for John to give him a full account someday of that fateful camping trip. But for now, Fred silently willed his daughter to heed the pleas of her children. John had certainly expressed how all three felt; that was clear. If only Christina could step up in her responsibilities as a parent. She had been such a good mother when the children were younger. But the accident changed everything. Couldn't she see that time continued to pass and the family continued to live and grow? Didn't she notice that they all were having difficulties since Paul's death?

Fred and Mariel had learned long ago that those who choose to be parents must relinquish certain freedoms. A parent cannot be self-absorbed. A parent cannot control the minutes and the hours of the day. And a parent must be sure to follow the cardinal rule: no playing favorites. How bold of Johnny to challenge his parents to grow up, and how selfish of Christina to ignore the suffering of others under her own roof.

Fred stepped into the kitchen. The light was off, and the door from the kitchen to the back porch was open. He could hear the rain pounding outside. Hurrying through the kitchen, he felt a wave of foreboding. *No wonder the rain is so loud, the outside porch door is wide open!* Fred thought to himself as he pushed the door shut. Then he grabbed some towels from the laundry basket to sop up the floor. He knew that Christina was out there somewhere, and he had a good idea where to find her.

When she was small, she would rush to the animals in the barns for solace. Somehow, the horses and even that silly mule would soothe her angry outbursts. But just as he finished drying the floor, he heard the engine of the Ford pickup roar to life. He hurried out to the yard in time to see Christina driving up toward the Island Summit Road.

He hurried back into the house. By now, the whole family was in the kitchen. All the lights were on, and Fred could see the concern on each face. Mariel cocked her head slightly, silently asking what had happened. Daniel looked pale and ill. Fred worried that Christina might have finally overstepped in her need to punish her husband for his perceived failures. How much more could Daniel endure? Would Daniel and Christina ever reach the level of intimacy they took for granted until the accident? Now Fred observed them and saw how cordial Christina and Daniel were in public, but Fred knew from Daniel that Christina avoided being alone with him, and when they did talk, it was basic communication regarding topics of family management.

Fred was chagrined to think how clear everything seemed during the past few weeks. He was sure things were almost back to normal. There had been laughter, lively conversation, and a strong shared work ethic in preparing for guests. Were all families like his? Were there terrible problems and unresolved issues below the surface in every American home? Life in its ordinary way just goes on. Problems are put aside, not forgotten but ignored until something causes an eruption. *Well*, he thought, *we have a major eruption in our family today. God help us get through this without any further problems*. Fred finished his thought aloud. "And, God, if you would, I'd be grateful if you could please watch out for my little girl." Fred spoke quietly to a father that he rarely addressed yet trusted at this moment with all his heart.

Chapter Twenty-Six

Holding two yellow slickers and a couple of sweatshirts, Daniel grabbed Fred's arm. "Here, Fred. Put these on! I'll get the van and meet you by the barn." Daniel finished putting on his slicker and dashed out the door. Fred called back to Mariel to take care of things with the children and maybe get some sandwiches together for when he and Daniel brought Christina home. He tried to sound optimistic for her sake, but he was shaking with fear. He finished getting his gear on then grabbed some boots from the shoe rack on the back porch. By the time he reached the driveway, Daniel was waiting for him in the van. Fred was surprised to see John already dressed in a slicker and sitting behind the driver's seat. Fred made a quick decision and went around to the driver's side.

"Slide over, Daniel. I'll drive." Fred spoke with the conviction of a man who was a superior driver and had no time to mince words or soothe Daniel's ego. Everyone knew that Daniel was a terrible driver. Daniel climbed over the gear console and slipped into the passenger seat. He fastened his seat belt as Fred started up the hill past the orchard toward the ISR. Luckily, he had observed Christina turning left toward Mirabella on the ISR. The van did not have four-wheel drive, but Fred used the gears effectively, downshifting instead of braking on the steep hills.

Although last week Fred had cursed the poor condition of the road, he was glad now that the new coat of slurry had not yet been applied because he was able to follow the tracks of the pickup. As he passed the turnout for the fire ring, something caught his eye. Backing up carefully, he looked down on the ground at the junction. Yes! There it was! He was sure that there was a smeared fresh tire track that looked like the ones he had been following.

For some reason, Christina had decided to go to the old fire ring, probably because John had spoken of it just a short while ago. Fred turned down the narrow track and immediately started to slide. It was all he could do to stop the van from careening sideways down the steep slope. As it was, it took almost forty feet to stop.

They came to rest with both passenger side tires mired deep in the thick mud. They all let their breath out audibly, thankful that they were safe for the moment. As they climbed out of the driver's side of the van, a flash of lightning ignited the sky with a fiery white light. In that moment, John saw the light reflected in something down farther toward the fire ring.

"Look! Down there! I think it's the pickup! See? There, on the left!" John had to shout to be heard. Immediately, Daniel started off toward the ring. He slipped on a slick section of mud, but he caught himself, and soon he was adjacent to the outer row of logs. The pickup was lodged in between two stumps. The driver's side door was open, and the rain was pelting the steering wheel and running freely onto the seat. Fred and John caught up with Daniel, and together they tried to shut the door, but it was caught on a sturdy bush that grew out from one of the stumps. They had to leave it ajar.

"Where do you think she is? Why would she come here?" Fred was worried and afraid. He could not make any sense of his daughter's actions. He began to wonder if he knew her at all.

"I don't know, but she can't be far." Daniel began to walk toward the center of the ring, calling Christina's name as he went. Fred climbed over the outer row of the logs and joined Daniel. Together they shouted, "Christina, Christina!" They heard nothing but the wild storm, and they saw nothing beyond the storm pelting the fire ring with its fury. John, who had circled from the opposite direction, met up with the others in the center of the ring. Another flash of lightning illuminated the sky and the ground around them. They saw a figure outlined in the light.

There on the nearest of the two stone walls Jacob had built to protect them all from the dangerous mud slick sat Christina. She was as still as the stones beneath her. She did not react to the shouts from her father, her son, or her husband. She sat and faced the sea, a sad figure that projected an aura of aloof detachment. Here was a soul who had no anchor in the present, who found no pleasure in the promise of a future, and who had forgotten how to love anyone except the child who, forevermore, could only be a memory from the past.

Suddenly, a violent bolt of lightning burst from the heavens, followed immediately by a crashing roll of thunder. John had a fleeting thought of how dangerous it was for them to be out and exposed in a lightning storm. How close was that last burst? He thought about counting *one one thousand, two one thousand*, but there was no time between the light and the sound. As he mulled over the dilemma of their danger, he sensed that Grandpa Fred had come up and was standing beside him. They both gasped as they caught a flicker of motion. Christina was beginning to stand up on the wall. What was she doing? In an instant, Daniel was dashing down the hill on the low wall.

"No!" he screamed as he saw his beloved wife lose her footing then disappear behind the wall.

Oh no! Fred thought. *She'll slide down over the cliff!* He rushed toward the wall. John followed close behind. Real time seemed to slow down as John and Fred reached the edge of the wall. They looked down toward Misty Falls. Christina was careening down the slippery grass toward the edge, and Daniel was sprinting on the wall itself in a desperate effort to reach her. Even over the howling wind, Fred could hear Daniel gasping for breath. Daniel moved faster and faster, defying the power that his disease tried to wield over him. Faster he moved toward his wife, faster still toward redemption. He could not fail, he would not fail. He grew closer, so close that he could almost brush her shoulder with his fingertips.

Stretching his arm out as he ran, he screamed to Christina, "Take my hand, Christina, I'm here! Grab my hand!" At the sound of Daniel's voice, Christina turned and stretched her arm toward him. Another few inches, and there! Just when Fred thought all was lost, he saw Daniel's hand close firmly around Christina's outstretched hand.

"Yes!" Fred yelled as he saw Daniel's hand clutching Christina's. "Hold on! Hold on! Daniel, we're coming! Oh, dear God, hold on, Son! Just a few more seconds!" Somehow, Fred lurched forward, using the last dregs of energy reserves that he found deep within himself. John rushed past Fred. They had intercepted the exhausted couple less than twenty feet from the cliff. John grabbed Daniel while Fred reached for Christina's other hand. John's hand felt a jolt as his father's free hand grabbed his with a vise-like grip. This time, the message was clear. There was no power on earth that could keep Daniel from protecting his own. Bring on the wind, the rain, the blowing branches, mud, a raging river: Daniel was mightier than all. Daniel turned to look into Fred's face. He nodded once. Then, in unison, Daniel and Fred hoisted Christina up onto the safety of the wall. Gasping for breath, Fred was laughing and sobbing all at once.

"From the bottom of my heart, thank you. Oh, thank you, Daniel!" Fred knew that only Daniel had been able to reach Christina in time. Daniel had anticipated the danger and rushed to prevent his precious Christina from succumbing to a terrible fate.

"Bless you, Daniel," he said. Then turning to Christina, who was shaking violently either from the cold or from her inconsolable sobs, Fred spoke softly. "He saved you. Daniel caught you and saved you, oh sweet child! Daniel followed you and searched for you and found you, and now he saved you." Fred was weeping from exhaustion and with relief. "Johnny and I are holding you both, and we never want to let you go. But you don't need us now because you've discovered each other again. The connection between you must be healing. Look how strong your hands are bonded. Nothing is going to tear you apart again. Come on, let's go home. Come, let's go home."

John helped his mother down from the rock wall. Daniel, who was weak from his asthma episode, could barely stand. Fred knew that what he had wished for was sure to become reality when he heard his daughter speak to her husband.

Her voice was gentle and her concern was genuine when she said, "Come on, Danny, lean on my shoulder. You can do it. That's right. Easy now. Just a little farther."

John and Christina nearly carried Daniel up the hill. The rain was falling steadily, but the violent wind and lightning had subsided during the past few minutes. The four of them were cold, and Christina was sopping wet. She had run from the house without thought of jacket or slicker. It took nearly ten minutes to reach the pick-up. Fred knew that if they had any chance of driving home tonight, it would be in the pick-up, since the van was hopelessly mired in at least a foot of mud. John and Daniel kept Christina close between them, trying to transfer some body heat as they waited to see if Fred could start the engine.

Fred was heartened to see that the keys were in the ignition. It was a glorious sound that filled his ears as the engine turned over on the second try. He maneuvered the vehicle back and forth patiently, working carefully to extricate it from between the logs of the fire ring. Finally, he had a clear path up toward the summit road. John helped his father climb into the passenger seat; then he helped his mother get settled on Daniel's lap. Daniel opened his slicker and took Christina's arms inside the jacket. He told her to hold tight as he wrapped his own arms firmly around her. Christina snuggled her head down into Daniel's neck. John squeezed into the jump seat behind his grandfather. Fred drove slowly up the dirt road, and by the time he turned onto the ISR back toward the lodge, Christina was sound asleep.

Chapter Twenty-Seven

John and Rocky walked down to the beach as the sun was heading toward the western horizon. It was only the middle of May, but it had been unseasonably warm and balmy all day long. The guest season had arrived in full force at the lodge a few weeks ago around Easter, and almost every Wednesday through Sunday span was booked to capacity up through Thanksgiving. John had adapted to the ebb and flow of the lodge duties. No matter how busy he was, John always found a few moments to walk down to the beach and feel the sand under his feet. Today, he decided to sit on the warm sand about thirty feet away from the water's edge. The sun felt good on his back.

Rocky ran toward a flock of seagulls that were gathered on the wet sand down near the water. The birds scattered in a noisy cloud of complaining. John laughed out loud as Rocky barked and chased the birds all the way to the boat house. Satisfied that the beach was cleared of nuisances, the black dog returned and plopped down next to his master.

"Good dog, Rocky. You showed those noisy seagulls a thing or two." John stroked the old dog's head and scratched behind his ears. Rocky rolled over onto his back with his feet up in the air as if to ask for a massage. John rubbed and patted Rocky's tummy, and soon the dog was snoring contentedly. John sat with his knees up and his arms wrapped around them. The sun made the sand shimmer with heat; John knew that later in the year it would be too hot to sit on the beach without a towel spread out under him. By late August, the sand would be so hot that ghostly mirages would shimmer daily on the beach, eerie visions that looked remarkably real in the white-hot heat.

His thoughts drifted back to the weeks after Papa Jacob's death and the fateful family meeting. As he always did, he felt a little guilty about how his decision to call the meeting almost brought more tragedy upon his family. John could not help but wonder how his family would be faring now if his mother had slipped all the way down the hill and over Misty Falls. Would his father have survived another traumatic incident where he could not save one of his own? First his son Paul, and then his wife, Christina—both lost forever because Daniel could not protect either one from harm. John felt a shudder as he contemplated that scenario.

But Christina was saved by the very hand that had failed Paul. The growth and healing that was happening every day in John's family might not have ever been possible without such a dramatic incident to get things started. Ironically, it was Casey's father, Keith Sorenson, who helped John see how all of the parts in his family drama fit together. Somehow, Paul's senseless and tragic death derailed the family from the track of real living and onto a spur that seemed to travel into a surreal parallel universe.

It was a place where time passed in normal fashion and all the family members were cast as themselves, but the script they read from was a poor imitation of life. In that altered world, Daniel was unable to grow beyond guilt just as Christina was stuck in a quagmire of blame. John couldn't move beyond his feelings of rejection, and the girls were adrift as they felt confused over their own places in the family.

But now, the family was healing slowly. With the help of a family counselor recommended by Dr. Sorenson, each family member recognized how important it was to have a single common goal: strengthening the family. Christina was ashamed and embarrassed over her behavior at the sea camp dance when she poured out her miseries to Keith. When she begged him to provide her with prescriptions for medication to make her feel as if life was worth living again, Keith recognized immediately how fragile and broken she was. He tried to help her see that drugs would not repair the wounds deep within her, but she was unable to hear of anything beyond her pain. Daniel, who saw but did not hear the exchange between his wife and Dr. Sorenson, was convinced that Christina was trying to establish or reestablish a relationship with Keith. Finally, when John saw his mother with Keith and combined that with the recollection of her inconsolable sobbing, he reached the same conclusion as his father. John often thought how much pain could have been avoided if his family had been more open with one another.

Though Keith refused to give Christina what she asked for that night, he did not ignore her plea for help. After the frightening events that occurred as a result of the family meeting, Keith, Anita, and Casey spent many hours at the lodge lending support and encouragement. When the Sorensons returned to San Francisco, the two families stayed in touch with one another.

Through all the turmoil, one thing was clear: The Lodge, Jacob's dream, would endure. Hadn't the family pulled together on the weekend after Jacob died? They all worked hard to create an atmosphere of normalcy as a group of men, all new guests, arrived on Friday afternoon for a weekend of fishing. A little before dawn on Saturday, Fred skippered the big sport fishing rig out into the channel and around to the windward side of the island. John helped the men with their gear, and Daniel made sure that everyone had plenty to eat and drink. While the men were gone, Christina and Mariel planned Jacob's funeral, and the twins took care of all the animals. After Sunday brunch, Fred prepared to take the fishermen to Mirabella in the LaZboat. With their catch carefully packed in ice and their stomachs filled with good food, the men asked Fred to book another visit sometime in the next few months.

Even the emotional fallout from the family meeting did not disrupt the habits and traditions of the Lodge. Daniel and Christina were unavailable to help much in the day-to-day operations, for they needed to focus on recovering from their ordeal. The home-schooling program started a few weeks late, but Nana Mariel stepped in to organize and run the lessons. She proved to be a demanding teacher, and the three teenagers thrived under her tutelage. As Fred, Mariel, John, and the twins assumed full responsibility for running the lodge, they found it was not hard to insulate visitors from any residual unpleasantness, for the lodge itself seemed to have a goal of its own: to please the guests.

Months passed. Then one solemn evening in February, after the whole Engstrom family had pledged to put family before friends, school, work, clubs, or anything else that might vie for attention and time, Christina and Daniel renewed their wedding vows. It was a good decision, and the family seemed to be thriving.

The girls were growing up and learning everything they could about the horses and stable operations. Daniel had taken over the financial business of the lodge—cash management, purchasing, salaries, investments, capital improvements, and long-range planning. Mariel started working seriously in marketing and advertising, all resulting in the record number of reservations they had on the books, and Christina was becoming the official hostess for the lodge. John had been Grandpa Fred's right-hand man all year. The two were nearly fifty years apart in age, but they were fast friends who shared a love of corny puns and silliness just as surely as they loved the natural beauty of the island.

John had applied to several universities and conservatories and was accepted to all but one. He was pleased to learn that his first-choice school not only accepted him but offered him a very generous scholarship package to help with expenses. Last year, he could hardly wait to go away somewhere to escape the swirling undercurrent of unrest in his home. But now, he was not so sure he wanted to leave at all. Further, he knew now how much more time was needed for healing; encounters with real life had produced deep scars on the psyche of each family member.

John believed it was important for the family to stay physically close to one another so the new bonds they were creating could have time enough to become strong and resilient. He sighed and wondered if his family would eventually be so bound by love and loyalty, so committed to one another, that nothing could harm them again.

Rocky woke up and raised his head from the sand. He sniffed the air, then jumped up and stared down the beach. Then in his best form, he stretched his snout to the east, his tail to the west, and he raised his foreleg in a graceful imitation of an authentic pointer. John stood to see who it was that Rocky saw. In the distance, John saw the lone silhouette of a person walking toward him along the waterline.

"Come on, Rocky," John called. "Let's go down and see who it is." John thought he knew, but he couldn't be sure. He walked faster. Sure enough, it was Casey. Rocky, sensing John's excitement, began to bark. He rushed back and forth between the two teenagers who, by now, were grinning at each other. When they were about fifty feet apart, Casey shouted to Rocky, "Race you back to John!" And they ran fast as they could along the damp sand. When they were within ten feet of the spot where John stood, Rocky cut in front of Casey, causing an awkward mishap. Dog, girl, and boy ended up in a heap on the ground. Rocky was busy slurping big dog kisses on Casey's face and neck while John stood and reached down to assist her in getting to her feet.

"Here, use my sleeve if you want to get that slobber off." John offered his arm to Casey. As she laughed, she grabbed the back of John's T-shirt and wiped her face and hands.

"Thanks! The sleeve didn't look big enough for the job." Casey looked directly at John. "You look good, John. It's really wonderful to be back here on the island. I've missed you. Say, is this a good time to talk? My family just came down a couple of days ago. Dad is meeting with Grandpa Peter and the rest of the family at the sea camp to decide how to continue running the place when Grandpa Peter retires next month." Casey stopped and waited for an answer.

"Yeah, this is a good time," John said. "I'm done with all my little projects for today. So let's go and sit up on the veranda. This is a perfect time of day to watch the sky. The sun will be dropping behind the west end in just a few minutes. Come on." He took her hand and turned to walk up the path toward the lodge.

"You know, all those years of feuding made for some tough times." Casey kept hold of John's hand as they climbed the wide steps to the lawn. "But now, every time I come along the beach toward your property, I feel like I'm walking from the shadows into the sun. Can you sense how different the atmosphere around this part of the island feels now? It's like the lodge is smiling at me and saying 'Welcome, neighbor!'"

They reached the veranda and pivoted two of the chairs so that they were facing west. The sun was only halfway visible. It was sinking behind the summit that overlooked Three Ships. The sky had pink and red streaks through the high clouds and the contrails from planes on their way to Los Angeles.

John and Casey sat without speaking for a few minutes, each soothed by the beauty of the late afternoon, and each warmed by the hand of the other clasped firmly between them. When the sun had set completely and the sky had faded to a dark blue gray, Casey turned toward John. He was still staring at the sky, but when he felt her eyes on him, he smiled.

"How long will you be here?" he asked. "If you're still here tomorrow, how about if we take a boat out for a few hours?"

"Tomorrow probably won't work, but maybe we can make it another day this week?" Casey said hopefully.

John was disappointed that she was busy tomorrow. That meant the two of them probably wouldn't be able to see each other this visit. Beginning the day after tomorrow, John was committed to helping his father and Grandpa Fred dig a new sewer line behind the service porch. It was going to be at least a three-day project. When he told Casey about his schedule, she just shrugged.

"Well I guess we'll just have to wait for another time to get together. I suppose you're busy with guests on the weekend, and Dad has to be back in San Francisco for meetings on Monday morning—"

"Darn!" John interrupted. "It seems we never have a chance to spend much time together. So when are you coming back down to visit?"

" That's why I wanted to talk to you. You know how I've been having a hard time making a choice about where to go to school or if I should even go to school. Plus, I still don't know what major I would choose."

Casey groaned as she enumerated all the difficulties that had plagued her since last fall. Then she sighed and added, "After thinking everything over and then making lists, then modifying the lists, I finally decided the best thing for me. I'm going take next year off and work down here at the sea camp. They need another staff counselor for girls, and I asked if they would consider me for the job."

Casey laughed out loud, then she added, "So I'm not going anywhere! As of yesterday morning, Santa Teresa Island is my home for the next year! That means this summer we can see each other lots and lots, at least until you have to go back east for school. When do you have to leave?"

John smiled and took a letter from the pocket of his cutoffs. He had read it so often that he nearly had it memorized. Still, as he unfolded it, he recalled the rush of pleasure he had experienced when he opened it for the first time. He handed it to Casey. She looked confused, but John asked her to read it out loud. She did.

May 15, 2012

Mr. John Garrett
Eagle Cove Lodge
Santa Teresa Island, CA 90704

Dear Mr. Garrett,

We are pleased to inform you that your request for delayed admission has been granted. We understand that sometimes there are circumstances that require some flexibility on our part to meet the needs of our students. We are pleased that you felt comfortable in presenting

> your proposal to us. The selection committee was most impressed with your entrance exam scores and your audition. You will be a valuable member of our academic artist community. And in turn, we are certain that you will find our program satisfying and challenging. We look forward to your enrollment in the fall class of 2013.
>
> We have enclosed a schedule of dates for you and your parents so that enrollment procedures will proceed smoothly next year. Your scholarships and prizes are being held in an escrow account for you to draw upon when enrollment time comes around. Please contact us anytime if you have questions or concerns.
>
> I hope your year is productive and that your family will begin to experience the peace that comes from healing and acceptance. And please, John, say hello to your grandmother from her old friend and ensemble partner. Perhaps someday soon I will take you up on your offer to see sunny California and your beautiful island.
>
> Sincerely,
> Dr. Patrick G. Fontaine
> Dean of Students
> Delaware Conservatory
> Dover, DE 19900

John took the letter from Casey, folded it carefully, and put it back in his pocket. He grinned. "Well, I guess we're stuck with each other for the next year. Maybe there's time after all to go sailing together, or maybe horseback riding, or dancing, or—"

"Or hiking, or cooking and eating," Casey added.

Then she was quiet for a moment. The sky was dark enough to expose the brightest stars of the May sky. Casey and John gazed up in time to see a vivid shooting star streak in a high arc across the night. Casey gasped at the unexpected gift she had been given from the heavens. John turned slightly so that he could see Casey's face. Although from this angle he could only see her in profile, he was heartened to see that she still wore an expression of wonder. He hoped she would always see the world as she did tonight: a place fresh and exciting, full of possibilities.

Little tendrils of blonde hair blew gently in the light breeze of the evening. She reached up to brush the strands from her eyes. The gesture caught John unaware, and he was swept back to their initial encounter eight months before. It was a time when John had first fallen in love with an exquisite musical composition—the elusive Rachmaninoff prelude—and then had fallen in love with the personification of the same work: a musical portrait named Casey Sorenson.

Yes, he admitted to himself. He cherished Casey, and for all the right reasons. She was good and kind and thoroughly unselfish. Looking back, John could now see why she had become such an important part of his life. It was simple. In the most fundamental way, she made him become a better person. She helped him to stretch and grow beyond the limits he once set for himself. She gave him courage to challenge the family. In the most loving manner, she helped Jacob finally face his own mortality with serenity and grace. She was the spark that brought forgiveness and redemption to all of John's family, and he was grateful.

Once an enigma, a spirit, a dream, the Casey he sat with today was none of those. His Casey was flesh and bone, as real as he. John smiled. With a sudden flash of insight, he knew that this girl who had first emerged from the shadows of his past, who was a constant in his life today, and who promised to be an essential part of his future was the friend he had been seeking as long as he could remember. He was no longer alone. With a clear understanding and acceptance of his family history and with a blueprint in hand outlining tomorrow's opportunities, John felt comfortably settled in the present. Today was a gift to savor and enjoy—all the better to share with his best friend.

Afterword

The Channel Islands, an archipelago just off the coast of Southern California, consist of eight islands: Anacapa, San Miguel, Santa Barbara, Santa Cruz, Santa Rosa, San Nicolas, San Clementi, and Santa Catalina. Several of the islands are part of the National Park System; and one, San Clementi, is under the governance of the US Military. Only one, Santa Catalina Island, has a substantial permanent population. Close to 4,000 people live on Catalina Island. About 3,500 of these live in the tiny resort town of Avalon. My folks lived in Avalon for many decades, and my husband and I retired to Avalon several years ago.

Santa Teresa Island is fashioned after Catalina Island, and its corresponding town of Mirabella resembles Avalon. The people in *Shadows in the Past* are fictional. The coves and island topography, though similar to Catalina, are all products of my imagination. Most of the customs, travel practices, and attitudes of the characters reflect real life on the island.

My father was a Seabee stationed in the Aleutians during the war. He really did win (then subsequently lose) a plot of land in a poker game. He also won a bearskin rug that lay in front of our fireplace at home for years. Sadly, it gradually disintegrated, and we had to dispose of it.

The excerpt "A Canaanite Hunger" is from a collection of poems, *The Dearest Freshness Deep Down Things, An Album of Poetry* by my good friend and poetry buddy, Bishop Sylvester D. Ryan. Bishop Ryan, who served as the bishop of Monterey, California, until his retirement in 2007, is a very gifted fellow who inspires us all to be the best we can be.

I must take a moment to thank some special friends and family members who read and reread this book as it grew and developed. Matt, Kit, Ruth, Sue, Debbie, Maureen, Keith, Linda, and dear Marie, how I treasure each of you! A special thanks is in order to Susie, who went through one of the final drafts and found a gazillion mistakes: typos, syntax errors, continuity issues. Susie, you are a marvel! And of course, I never could have finished even one chapter without the love and support of my husband, Dave, who listened as I read and reread sections aloud. His suggestions were spot on, and his good sense was and is invaluable. I am thankful that early in our marriage we learned to tell the truth gently.

Shadows in the Past